From the videotaped last will and testament of Max McKendrick

To my youngest and orneriest nephew Cody I bequeath my Silver Spur Ranch cattle operation and grazing range. A quarter million acres and 10,000 head of cattle are all yours—except for a bull's-eye parcel of land, which will go to Callie Sheridan.

'Course I know how stubborn you are so I put a few conditions on this here inheritance. Should you refuse, the stipulation will reverse. Now I reckon that won't sit well with you so I advise you to forget the past and get on with the courtship and weddin'. 'Cause either way Callie is going to inherit some of my land, and one way or another the two of you are going to be stuck together for all eternity.

Dear Reader,

The Silver Spur Ranch has a quarter million acres, but even it isn't big enough for the three McKendrick siblings and the intended spouses their Uncle Max has bequeathed them. No place really is!

Once Max gives them the ultimatum—marry the mate he's chosen for them within forty-eight hours or lose their inheritance—it's a virtual stampede!

Join Cathy Gillen Thacker as she brings you all the sexy cowboys and wacky weddings you'd expect from WILD WEST WEDDINGS!

Don't miss any of the three WILD WEST WEDDINGS titles. The West was never like this!

Regards,

Debra Matteucci
Senior Editor & Editorial Coordinator
Harlequin Books
300 E. 42nd St.
New York, NY 10017

Cathy Gillen Thacker

THE COWBOY'S BRIDE

Harlequin Books

TORONTO • NEW YORK • LONDON
AMSTERDAM • PARIS • SYDNEY • HAMBURG
STOCKHOLM • ATHENS • TOKYO • MILAN
MADRID • WARSAW • BUDAPEST • AUCKLAND

ISBN 0-373-16625-7

THE COWBOY'S BRIDE

Prologue

Montana attorney Cisco Kidd greeted the three Mc-Kendrick heirs as they somberly filtered into the private sitting room at the Fort Benton Gentlemen's Club. Crumpled tissue in her hand, thirty-six-year-old Patience sank into one of the thick leather armchairs gracing the masculinely decorated room. Wordlessly, she blotted at the tears continually appearing in her eyes. Her older brother, Trace, stood nearby, a comforting hand placed on her shoulder. Cody, the youngest, stalked morosely to the window facing out at the Old Fort Park and the adjacent Lewis and Clark Memorial, his collar turned up and both hands shoved deep in the pockets of his denim jacket.

"I'm glad you all could be here," Cisco Kidd began as gently as possible, knowing he had his work cut out for him if he wanted to see that his mentor's fondest wishes became reality. "Max wanted you to be together when you found out what he'd left you."

"Enough with the flowery speeches. Let's just get on with it," Cody interrupted bad-temperedly, pulling the brim of his battered Stetson even lower across his brow.

Cisco Kidd nodded. He knew Max McKendrick's sudden departure from this world had been hard on all three heirs, but in many ways the reclusive Cody seemed to be taking it the hardest, just as the wily Max had predicted.

"If that's what you want," Cisco allowed gravely. One hand pushing back the edge of his western-cut suit coat, he leaned over to switch on the television set, then stepped back to watch.

The videotaped will began with the flourish all three McKendrick heirs seemed to expect. Their Uncle Max, clad in his trademark fringed buckskin jacket, mustard yellow chaps and silver spurs, appeared on the screen. His skin was a deep, leathery tan, in contrast to his white, shoulder-length hair and long, Lone Star mustache. Nearly as old as the hills and as energetic as the day was long, Max had seemed immortal. It was impossible for any of the McKendrick heirs to believe their uncle was dead, his ashes scattered on the rugged Montana earth long before they'd all arrived at his sprawling Silver Spur Ranch to pay their respects.

"I know what you're thinking," Uncle Max began in his deep, raspy voice as the three heirs—the two men surreptitiously—wiped their eyes and gathered round. "You miss me. You wish we'd all settled our quarrels and got a better handle on things before I bit the bullet. Well, I wish that, too. I promised my only sibling, my beloved brother Wyatt, that I would take care of his family should anything ever happen to him—none of us ever dreaming that we would lose his dear wife, Annie, too, in the same cruel blow. But we did. And you all know I did my best to do right by all three of you since your mammy and pappy died." Briefly, sadness glimmered in Max's eyes. "But wanting something to work out right doesn't always mean it will," he continued a little thickly. "And sometimes when you fail, you gotta pick yourself up, dust yourself off and get back in that saddle again."

"I'd say that would depend on what you fell off of," Cody interjected. He looked at his brother, Trace, meaningfully. "Some wild broncs aren't worth trying to saddle up again, especially after they pitch you."

Looking every bit the wildly successful CEO he was, with his short haircut and tailored business suit, Trace nodded. "I agree," he said firmly.

"Shh!" Patience admonished, her fingers nervously pleating the circle skirt of her long denim dress. "I want to hear this!"

"No one knows better than this old coot right here," Uncle Max pointed a thumb at his chest "that I more than anyone was responsible for the messes you've all made of your love lives. And don't argue with me. They are a mess, every one of 'em. And that makes me feel sad as a hound dog whose family moved away and left him behind. But not to worry." Max shook a lecturing finger at them. "Just 'cause I'm not around no more doesn't mean your lives are over, no sirree. Which is why I've taken it upon myself to fix things for you now, the best way I know how. Starting with Cody. I know we haven't been on good terms since you got back from Mexico seven years ago, on account of you blaming me for your fiasco of a marriage with Callie."

Briefly, Cody looked both guilty and uncomfortable. Seeing this, Patience stood and crossed to his side.

"But I aim to fix all that," Max continued affably.

"How?" Cody spit out at the screen, as if Max could still hear him.

Max grinned triumphantly, announcing, "I not only willed you my cattle operation and the grazing range that goes with it, I've ordered you a wife from my Western Ranch Wives video matchmaking service. And if Cisco's carried out my orders, as I expect he has, she's ready for pickup in one of the private reading rooms upstairs. Cisco Kidd, my attorney, will let you know which one."

Cody swore as he yanked off his Stetson and slapped it against one rock-hard thigh. "I don't believe this!" he muttered, and swept both hands through the wheat-colored hair that fell past his shoulders. "What in blazes gave Uncle Max the idea he could just order me up a wife? Like I'd even want one."

"Or one would want you," Trace added, feeling free to tease and making obvious note of the uncivilized way Cody had been living.

"Watch it, big brother." Cody narrowed his eyes at Trace. "I have a feeling you're going to get yours, too."

"I have a feeling we all are," Patience murmured, joining in the conversation and taking Cody's hand in an attempt to calm him down.

Max continued with his will, speaking genially from the screen. "Patience, my sweet girl, I know how badly you want a child but I still don't want to see you go to no clinic. Therefore, I have left you a state-of-the-art writing studio along with the substantial parcel of land the horse-breeding and cutting business is situated on. Naturally, you'll need a vet to help you run things, and that being the case, you might as well marry him and bring more than baby horses and brand-new stories to life, if you catch my meaning. You'll find him in the barns. He's handsome and smart and willing and his name is Josh Colter."

"Good grief, Uncle Max, the last thing I need is a ranch stud." Patience blew out an exasperated breath and threw up her hands. "Never mind one you've brought in to service me!"

Cisco hadn't been surprised by Max's gift to his only niece or her less-than-pleased reaction to it. The truth was, Max had always coddled Patience after she'd been jilted at the tender age of nineteen, even though he knew her being left at the altar was for the best. And though she had been mad at her uncle at first for his attitude, she had kept in touch with Max after she had cooled off and gotten settled in Denver.

"Furthermore, I don't care what he looks like or does for a living! If I wanted a man to give me a baby, I could find him on my own!" Patience continued, pacing the floor.

"Amen to that," Cody remarked, still looking steamed at how he had been set up.

"I expect you could, little sis," Trace said, edging closer to both Patience and Cody. "Not that that would be the right way to go, either. Making babies is serious business. Bringing them up right is even harder. Parenting is a full-time job on its own and should not be entered into solo if there's another way. As the single father of two, who's lost many a night's sleep worrying over the general inadequacies of a one-parent home, I can attest to that."

Cody turned to his older brother. "I'll bet you can," he drawled, looking glad that was Trace's problem and not his own. All Cody cared about these days was the Silver Spur Ranch and the cattle he raised....

"And, Trace," Max continued on-screen, "I'm giving you two things of utmost importance, the lumber business I should have given you years ago, and a second chance with the love of your life. No need for me to mention names because we all know who she is. You'll find her in the lumber camp kitchen."

While Cisco watched, Trace, ever the cool one, merely crossed his arms in front of him and quirked a discerning brow. "I have no idea who Uncle Max's talking about," Trace said.

"Yeah, right," Cody drawled, rolling his eyes as he turned to square off with his older brother.

"Like we don't all know you've never gotten over Susannah," Patience teased with a shake of her head. "At least you'll be getting hooked up with someone you really want to be hooked up with, unlike Cody and I." She gave him a sisterly punch in the gut.

Trace stiffened self-righteously and worked at containing a self-conscious flush. As they all watched Trace fight his embarrassment, Cisco was pleased to see that even the ever surly Cody cracked what looked like a quarter grin. Maybe this crazy plan of Max's, to see that each and every member of his family lived happily ever after, would work after all....

Patience's facetious remark about Susannah earned her a glare from Trace, even as Uncle Max continued gleefully from the screen.

"Naturally, I put a few strings on these gifts of mine."

Long accustomed to their uncle's eccentric behavior, Cody, Patience and Trace lifted their glances heavenward and groaned in unison, expecting the worst.

As Max's attorney, Cisco had been instrumental in writing the contracts that would govern the McKendrick heirs' behavior over the next several days. Knowing the reactions were bound to be potent, he braced himself for the outcry sure to come.

On-screen, Max continued to spell out his stipulations sternly. "One, you all must seek and find your intended bride or groom, such as the case may be, within the next thirty minutes. Two, you must all attach yourself like glue to your affianced's side for the next forty-eight hours. And three, you all must marry in a joint wedding ceremony at the end of the forty-eight hours. I've already taken care of the details there, too," Uncle Max assured. "So not to worry. None of you have to plan a wedding. I've already done that, down to sending out invitations before you all were even assembled at the club."

"Which means a hundred to one the whole damn state has been invited," Cody muttered cantankerously.

"Including, no doubt, every damn one of my business associates. I'll never live this down," Trace agreed.

"None of us will," Patience moaned. "Which was, no doubt, part of Uncle Max's plan. He wanted to force us to live up to our responsibilities, romantic and otherwise."

"Not that any of this will be easy for y'all," Max continued. "But it is do-able, if you all are committed to making a fresh start for yourselves. All you gotta do is listen to your hearts. If you do, you'll know what to do." Max tipped his hat at them. "Adios," he said softly. "And remember, I love you."

The screen went blank.

The room vibrated with a poignant silence. Patience wiped her eyes. Cody scowled, but there was a lonesome look in his blue eyes, a sad set to Trace's shoulders.

Only Cisco, Max's thirty-year-old protégé and attorney, had control of his emotions, and that was because he'd known beforehand that this was coming and had had time to prepare himself for the inevitable.

"Well," Cisco said finally, working hard to inject a little lightness into the somber room, just as Max would've wanted. "You three bronco busters have your orders from Max. What do you think? Are you going to be able to carry 'em out?" If so, it would make his job a lot easier, Cisco thought.

Patience was the first to pull herself together. She faced her brothers, her pretty chin set determinedly, and gave the kind of advice one would expect from a western-based advice columnist to the lovelorn. "Under the circumstances, I guess we should at least try to grant Uncle Max's wishes."

"Or at least follow through with meeting our intendeds," Trace suggested grudgingly, though it was clear he wasn't promising anything more. Not right off the bat.

Cody merely scowled, his every instinct obviously telling him to resist.

"I know this is a little crazy, but we all owe Max a helluva lot," Cisco reminded. And that included himself. If Max hadn't rescued him from the streets years ago and seen to it he had a place to live and an education, who knew what would've happened to him? And the same could be said, he thought passionately, for the true McKendrick heirs, who would have ended up in an orphanage if not for the eccentric but bighearted Max.

Max had earned his final request.

Granting his last wish was not too much to ask.

"Cody?" Patience looked at her baby brother expectantly. "You intend to go along with this, too, don't you?"

Cody merely shrugged. And they all waited with bated breath for his reply.

Chapter One

48:00 hours and counting...

Cody stomped upstairs to the private reading room where his mail-order bride was waiting. Uncle Max had always been unconventional to the extreme. But this time he had outdone himself, linking Cody to a woman he'd never even met, never mind wanted to marry. Well, he'd get things straightened out quick enough, Cody thought with a determined scowl as he strode hell-bent for leather toward the Louis L'Amour room. He'd explain the situation to the desperate woman, pay her if he had to and send her on her way, and that would be that. Then he'd go out and get a loan, buy the land he should have inherited and continue on as he had been. Alone. Temper still simmering, mind made up, he pulled his Stetson low over his brow and knocked on the door.

The door opened a crack. Cody stared into a pair of familiar emerald green eyes and felt as if every bit of wind had been blown right out of him.

"Hi, there." The woman Max had designated as his bride-to-be smiled up at him officiously, even as she stepped back and away. "I knew you were going to be here this afternoon," she said as she set her book aside. "But I wasn't sure exactly when you'd arrive, or even what your name was, so I..." She glanced at the way he was gripping the doorjamb on either side of him, paused and wet her lips. "Is something the matter?"

I'll say, Cody thought, still feeling shaken to the core.

Cautiously, she edged toward him. Looking a tad nervous at the way he was bracing his weight against the door, she said, "Look. I know this is awkward—"

"Awkward?" Cody gasped. *Try insane!*

Continuing with her innocent act, she wet her lips and tried again. "I don't know what you were expecting, but—"

"Not this," Cody growled, inclining his head toward her smaller, trimmer form, with the soft, delectable curves. A man would have to be a saint not to desire her, and he was no saint. Damn it all to hell anyway, Cody thought. If this was what Max had had up his sleeve, why hadn't he forewarned him, like he had Trace?

"Well, if you want to be blunt, you are not exactly what I had in mind, either," she retorted hotly, self-conscious color sweeping into her pretty cheeks. "I definitely asked for someone clean-shaven. But here we are anyway. So..." she clasped her hands in front of her. "Would you like to come in?"

Unable to believe she didn't recognize him—surely he hadn't changed that much, had he?—Cody continued gripping the doorjamb and staring at her.

Evidently realizing something was very wrong, she cautiously moved closer, not stopping until she was right under him. And it was then, as she tipped her head back to look directly up into his face, that the significance of the moment hit her, too. Just that quickly the color left her face. She began to tremble from head to toe.

"Cody?" she choked out in her deep, throaty voice, looking as if she couldn't believe it, either.

The loathing, shock and fear she was doing little to hide had a galvanizing impact on him.

"Callie Sheridan." Cody finally recovered enough to spit out the words. There was no welcome in his low voice. "I should have known." She always had been full of unpleasant surprises.

"Well, I didn't!" The color came back into her cheeks with a vengeance, and Callie started to slam the door in his face. Cody caught it in midslam and held it firmly open. "I wanted to be set up with a prospective husband!" she cried, upset.

"Not," Cody said as he let go of the door and shouldered his way into the room, "a husband you'd already dumped!"

Callie tossed the sexily cut layers of her shoulder-length sunflower blond hair and squared off with him, looking prettier and more enraged than he had ever seen her. "Let's get something straight here, cowboy. I did not dump you."

"What do you call running away on our wedding night, then?" Cody demanded as he let his gaze drift over her sensual curves in a manner meant to incense her.

Callie might be something of a tomboy at heart—as was indicated by the dark blue blazer, plain white T-shirt, snug-fitting jeans and red cowgirl boots she wore—but there was nothing the least bit unfeminine about her. She was slender in all the right places, curved just so in all the others. Looking at her made his mouth water and his heart race. He remembered all too well what it had been like to kiss her and hold her in his arms, as well as the crushing guilt that had followed. Seven years his junior, Callie was too young for him and always had been. It was just too bad he hadn't known that when he was twenty-four and she was seventeen. Instead, he'd let the fact she was somehow older than her years fool him into thinking they could make their relationship work. What a damn fool he had been!

For a long moment, Callie looked as if she wanted to confess something to him. Then she shook her head. "I call my leaving you coming to my senses," she retorted. Looking more agitated than ever, she roamed the small, wood-paneled room and came to a halt beside the high-backed leather reading chair and matching footstool.

"Or bringing me to mine," Cody muttered, stepping even closer and dwarfing her by a good ten inches. "That was one expensive expedition for a honeymoon that never happened."

Cody noted he'd struck gold again with his insult.

"What's that supposed to mean?" Callie planted her hands on her slender hips and tilted her head back to better see into his face. Her green eyes sparkled indignantly. "You didn't spend any money on me."

"Just the entire trust fund my parents had left me upon their death," Cody corrected. Which had amounted to a cool twenty-five thousand dollars.

Callie's thick-lashed eyes widened. "What are you talking about?" she demanded warily.

Finding the floral-and-spice scent of her perfume a bit too distracting, Cody swung away from her. Shoving his hands in the pockets of his denim jacket, he focused on a Remington painting of a cowboy and his cutting horse, hard at work herding cattle across a dusty plain. "Never mind. I am not getting into all that again," he replied. The fiasco had already turned his heart to stone.

Balling his hands into fists, Cody paced back and forth. Before anything worse happened, they needed to get to the bottom of this to discover if they had any more surprises waiting for them. Cody was betting they did, unfortunately. "How did Uncle Max find you?" he demanded irritably.

Callie regarded Cody with a surly impatience of her own. She did not look of a mind to cooperate with him in his quest for answers.

"What does your Uncle Max have to do with anything?" When he didn't answer right away, she jammed an interrogating finger at his chest. "And what are *you* doing here anyway?"

Cody caught her wrist before she could jab that finger at him again and held it tight, wishing all the while he was not so aware of the warmth and softness of her skin, or the sweet innocence of her kisses. "You might as well know. I didn't come to see you of my own accord."

She arched a brow. Outside in the corridor voices rose and fell, and footsteps neared and receded. "I'm supposed to believe that?" she challenged, looking as if there weren't a chance in the West she would. "When I knew you, you were such an independent hellion no one got you to do anything you didn't want to do."

"Well, this time it's different," Cody said gruffly. "Max sent me here. The circumstances being what they were— are, I couldn't refuse."

"What are you talking about?" Wrenching her wrist from his staying grip, Callie stepped back a pace. "Max sent you here, to see me?"

"Yes." With effort, Cody quelled the urge to grab her again and, this time, pull her close.

"Why?" Callie demanded suspiciously.

"Because he was a hopeless romantic and a fool that didn't know any better, that's why!" Cody retorted, completely exasperated with the situation he found himself in and his own unexpectedly emotional reaction to it. First he had to deal with his grief at losing Max. And now this on top of it? Uncle Max had really laid one on him this time.

Feeling he was going to explode if he didn't do *something* physical to abate the powerful emotions erupting within him, Cody wheeled away from Callie. It was either grab her and kiss that disbelieving smirk off her face or— *What was he thinking?*

More irritated with himself than ever, Cody yanked off his hat, threw it against the wall, picked it up and threw it again. Unhappily, the violence did little to curb the storm of emotions roiling around inside him. It did, however, bend the brim of his hat at an untoward angle.

"Well, that'll fix that," Callie said dryly as Cody picked up his hat, bent it back and swung around to face her.

Realizing she had recovered from the shock of seeing each other again, much more swiftly than he had, Cody glared at her.

She mimicked his look facetiously.

Much more, Cody thought, and he really would kiss her. But for now . . .

Steadfastly ignoring her reaction to what he already knew had been a childish display of temper, he watched her breeze past him toward the built-in bookcases filled with western novels, classic literature and how-to ranch books. For a moment, she stared down at the portable TV and VCR that had been wheeled into the room and set in a corner. Whirling back to him, she asked with provoking foolishness, "So, if we're all through with the hat bashing, how did Max know I was here?"

Cody continued working on the brim of his hat. Giving up, he slapped it on his head and sat on the arm of the chair. He was curious to see her reaction to this. "Apparently, one of the agents at the company recognized your name and alerted Max to the fact you had filled out an application and were looking for a husband."

Callie looked as if she wanted to find an escape hatch and fall through it. "Then you knew he had ties to the WRW videomatchmaking service?" She bit the words out, dragging a distracting hand through the soft, silky layers of her hair.

"No," Cody replied shortly, exasperated by that turn of events, too. "Finding out he owned it was news to me, too. Apparently, Max has been up to a lot my siblings and I knew nothing about."

But she had no pity for him, then or now, Cody noticed unhappily. "How sad for you," Callie remarked.

That said, she marched past him toward the door. Hand on the doorknob, she yanked it open. "Now. If you'll excuse me. I think you should get out of here, pronto, Cody. Max's plan to reconcile us has failed," she continued loftily. "And seeing as how I'm still expecting my prospective husband to appear at any moment, I—"

Effectively cutting her off in midsentence, Cody reached over and slammed the door shut with the flat of his hand. This was nobody's business but their own. "You don't get it, do you?" Cody towered over her. "There is no other man. There's only a will with some mighty peculiar instructions that Max left upon his death a few days ago. I'm your prospective husband, Callie."

A heartrending silence fell between them. Had Cody not already known what a little con artist Callie was at heart, he would've been convinced she hadn't known anything about Max's demise. The will, either.

Finally Callie put a hand to her throat. Her green eyes gleaming moistly, she gasped, "Max is—"

"Yes," Cody answered harshly.

Callie drew in another breath. Her eyes glimmered even more. "So you're not—"

"No."

"And the rest—"

"Is true, too," Cody admitted, fighting the debilitating sadness that threatened to overtake him any second.

Callie regarded him like the straight man in a comedy act. Not tearing her eyes from his, she blew out a long, exasperated breath and appeared not to believe a single word he said. "I don't know what kind of game you are playing with me, Cody, but this is not funny."

His own gaze grew colder. "Notice I'm not laughing, either," he replied hoarsely.

His blunt statement, coupled with the simmering intensity in his gaze, captured her attention. They stared at each other in a silence that seemed to go on forever and made Cody all the more aware of her.

"I'm sorry, about Max," Callie said finally.

Cody nodded.

"But that doesn't... When was the last time you had a shave and a haircut?" Callie demanded, as if seeing him for the first time.

Cody touched his beard self-consciously, wondering if he really looked as bad as she, and Max, had seemed to think. Not that it mattered to him one darn bit, anyway. "Don't know and don't care," he spit out laconically. What in blue blazes did that have to do with anything?

Callie turned up her pert little nose at him and made a provoking face. "No wonder your uncle had to advertise for a wife for you, then."

Cody lifted a dissenting brow. His pulse racing, he leaned treacherously close. "Let's get something straight, Callie. I didn't ask for this. Max arranged this little tête-à-tête of ours all on his own. I had nothing to do with it!"

"Ha! Like I'm supposed to believe that," Callie countered as a knock sounded on the other side of the door. Her temper still flaring, she shouldered past him and yanked it open once again.

Cody was not surprised to see Max's attorney, Cisco Kidd, standing on the other side. He gave them both a long look, as if he were wondering how they were doing, then handed over a duffel bag to Callie. "This is for you. It's got a change of clothes or two, and a toothbrush, your basic toiletries." Cisco gave Cody a videotape marked Last Will and Testament of Max McKendrick, Part Two. "You'll want to listen to this right away," Cisco said. Not waiting for a reply, Cisco tipped his hat at them and quietly took his leave.

"I wondered why there was a VCR and television in here," Callie murmured. Looking more ready for the next surprising turn of events than he was, she sank down on the edge of the leather chair.

Cody shut the door, closeting them in together once again. "Knowing Max, it's only the first of many surprises," Cody grumbled recalcitrantly, as he started the tape and then pulling the footstool as far away from Callie as possible, sat down beside her to view it.

As they stared at the TV with trepidation, Uncle Max appeared on the screen. "Hello, Callie and Cody. Guess you had your reunion, bittersweet as it may have been. And you're probably anxious for me to quit jawin' and cut to the chase, so here's the deal. Cody, I am leaving you the entire Silver Spur cattle ranching operation—all quarter million acres and ten thousand head of cattle. Except for one bull's-eye parcel of land, twenty head of cattle and the original homestead—all of which are to go to Callie."

"I don't believe this," Cody muttered.

"Yeah, well, if your ego can stand the news, you are not currently on my dance card, either, Cody McKendrick," Callie muttered beneath her breath.

"I suppose you're both wondering why I am willing the land to Callie," Max said.

Cody glared at Callie. "No doubt another scheme."

"I checked with the agency, which, by the way, I own and operate, and the only reason Callie signed up with the video matchmaking service was to find a hubby to go in on a little homestead with her. I don't imagine this news will sit with you too well, Cody, but you bear in mind that she's been working hard just like you have. And since you've been outta touch some with polite society, don't forget your manners." Max added sternly.

"Amen to that," Callie agreed wholeheartedly.

A muscle working in his jaw, Cody glared at her. Again, Callie glared right back. Only she looked a little more exasperated.

"'Course, I know how stubborn you are, Cody," Uncle Max continued from the screen as, outside in the corridor, voices rose and fell again. Not wanting to miss a word of his late uncle's message, Cody leaned forward, elbows on his knees.

"So I put a few conditions on this inheritance of yours. Should you refuse to marry Callie, the situation will reverse, and you will inherit the bull's-eye parcel of land and she will inherit the entire two hundred and fifty thousand acre cattle operation. Now, I imagine that wouldn't sit well with you, her being the primary landowner, so I'd advise you to forget the heartache of the past—''

"Not very damn likely," Cody muttered.

"And get on with the courtship and wedding. 'Cause either way, Callie is going to inherit some land of mine, and one way or another, the two of you are going to be stuck together for all eternity.

"Unless of course," Uncle Max continued, "Callie refuses to marry you, Cody. In that case, she gets nothing from my estate. I don't think that will happen, either. Callie's a smart girl. She knows if she just sticks with my plan, she'll be set for life. And what are forty-eight hours and a wedding, after all?"

"Plenty," Callie muttered beneath her breath as she glared at Cody.

"My feelings exactly," Cody retorted as the videotape continued.

"I'll see you at the wedding forty-eight hours from now. Meantime, although the two of you are free to roam wherever you want or need to go, I expect the two of you to stay together under the same roof twenty-four hours a day, with no more than three thirty-minute breaks apart. You break the rules and the deal is off. I don't imagine you'll like that much, either."

"An understatement if I ever heard one," Cody muttered.

"Ditto for me," Callie snapped right back.

"But I want you two young'uns to listen up and listen good anyway. In my rodeo days, when I took to riding buckin' horses and bulls, I was given a bit of priceless advice by an old hand. He told me, 'You got eight seconds to ride, and a lifetime to think about it.'" Max smiled his encouragement. "So make the most of your eight seconds, kids. You already blew it once. You don't want to do it again." Max gave them a two-fingered salute. "Happy trails," he said huskily. "And know I'll always be thinking of you."

There was a lump in Cody's throat the size of a walnut and an ache in his heart just as bad as Uncle Max's picture faded to a endless vista of blue Montana sky, then to black.

Fighting another onslaught of tears, Cody switched off the VCR. It took every bit of fortitude he had, but finally he regained control of his emotions, and with that control came a very bad mood.

Anxious to get out of there before that self-imposed control, already stretched hopelessly thin, snapped, he let his glance flicker to the duffel bag on the floor next to Callie. Figuring he'd already done enough for Callie in years past, he made no move to pick it up for her. "Get your gear," he said gruffly, already striding to the door. "We're getting out of here."

"I'M SORRY ABOUT MAX, really I am. I'll miss him, too. But don't think this will of his means you can boss me around," Callie warned Cody.

Still working to put her grief over Max's death aside, she climbed unassisted into the passenger side of the battered Silver Spur Ranch pickup truck. Prior to her meeting with Cody, she'd had no idea Max was gone, and in fact was still reeling inwardly from the unexpected news of his death, but she'd be damned if she would look to Cody McKendrick for comfort. Not that he was likely to give her any, after the way she had run out on him in Acapulco seven years ago, leaving only a note full of lies behind. She'd meant to protect him in doing what she had. Obviously, he didn't see it that way. She wondered if he ever would.

"You can save the sad-eyed look for someone who cares." Cody leaned in the cab, planted a hand on either side of her and caged her against the seat. "You may have fooled my uncle into thinking you were a helpless waif in need of protection. When it came to women and kids, Max always was too softhearted for his own good. But you damn well won't fool me.''

Not about to be outdone in the physical intimidation department, Callie grabbed Cody by the shirtfront and tugged him even nearer, though they were already nose to nose. "To borrow a phrase from your Uncle Max, Cody, you listen up and listen good. Your Uncle Max was one of the kindest, most understanding men I have ever met. Just because you don't have a heart gives you no right to bad-mouth him, Cody.''

Cody grabbed her wrist and pried her fingers from his shirtfront. "Perhaps we better get something straight," he retorted, holding her right hand aloft. "I don't want or need you in my life. Nor do I want to listen to any hypocritical speeches a heartless woman like you might be moved to give. Got it?" Not waiting for her reply, he shoved her hand away and stepped back against the open truck door.

Callie shot one long leg out to bar his way. "There's something you should understand, Cody." She kept the sole of her cowboy boot flat against the door. "I am no longer the shrinking violet you ran away with. When I feel the urge to speak my mind, I do. Got that, cowboy?" These days she fought her own battles. And even stood up to an injustice or two....

He leaned over her, staring down at her with glittering eyes. "Just as long as you understand you do it at your own risk," he warned softly as he ran a hand contemplatively down her thigh.

Ignoring the tingles of awareness his touch generated, Callie smiled at him sweetly. "As do you." She brought her leg back in the cab. Bent it at the knee. Squared her shoulders stubbornly, even as she continued to go head to head with him. "And I meant what I said earlier. Our being thrown together now does not give you the right to boss me around.''

He shot her an angry stare as he circled around the front of the truck and climbed behind the wheel. He slapped the key in the ignition. ''Darlin', that is exactly what this means!''

''And don't call me darlin'.'' Callie had to shout to be heard above the roar of the engine.

Cody paused and slid his hand along the back of the seat behind her. He looked her up and down. ''You used to like it, as I recall.''

Callie reminded herself how she had hurt him, years past. She could see he wanted to hurt her in return. And there was no point to that. Just as there was no point to this. She didn't care what Max had planned. ''I'm different now, Cody,'' Callie told him quietly. Different in some ways. More vulnerable in others, especially where he was concerned.

''And yet you signed up for this lunacy,'' Cody allowed as he thrust the truck roughly in gear and backed out of the parking space. ''I didn't.''

Callie was slammed forward and then back as he stomped on the brakes. Recovering her balance, she sent him a withering glare to let him know she was neither impressed nor frightened by his incredibly bad driving. ''I was looking for a rancher to go in on a homestead with, not you.''

Assuming he would continue to drive as poorly as possible simply in order to irk her, she held on to the door with her right hand, the seat with her left.

Cody shifted the truck back into drive and spun out onto the road. ''A rancher to con, you mean,'' he corrected, as they headed out of town. ''Or more specifically, someone who wasn't on to your tricks.''

Callie stared at Cody, unable to believe the change in him. When she had known him seven years ago, he had been a clean-cut twenty-four-year-old cattleman. Gentle and gallant to the core. Now, seven years later, he looked dark and dangerous. His wheat blond hair, though sparkling clean and tied back with a rawhide strip, was shoulder-length. A sexy brown beard, a shade or two darker than his hair, lined the handsome suntanned contours of his face. But it was his eyes that registered the most change. Oh, they were still the same wild blue of the ocean on a sunny day, rimmed with a wealth of short, thick lashes. But there was a cynical guardedness in his gaze. And a rough economy to his actions that had not been there before. "What happened to you?"

Cody's eyes glimmered with unchecked hurt as he confided hoarsely, "You. You happened to me, Callie. And you taught me a lesson I'm never gonna forget."

Then she would just have to undo it. And the only way to handle Cody was to stand up to him completely. Callie set her chin. "That, wild man, goes both ways."

His interest was caught, as she knew it would be, by her made-up term, and she watched as he cocked a brow. "Wild man?" he echoed.

She gave him another dramatic once-over, this one more disapproving than her last. "You want the truth, Cody McKendrick? Well, here it is. You look like Robert Redford in that *Jeremiah Johnson* movie. Minus the buffalo coat."

To her irritation, Cody looked pleased—not insulted, as she had intended—with the comparison. "I'll get a buffalo coat if it'd make you happy."

Callie sighed, rolled her eyes and settled back into her seat as he turned the truck onto McKendrick land. The only thing to do with an outdoorsy hellion like Cody was ignore him, and considering the dazzling scenery, that was pretty easy to do. She'd forgotten how beautiful Montana was in early June. The vast grassland rolled out on either side of them like a rich green carpet. Mountains were visible in the distance beneath the beautiful blue of the sky. Stands of trees—ash and box elder here—rimmed the edge of every fenced pasture, while bands of white-faced Herefords grazed.

"Perhaps I could wear it to the public wedding ceremony Max has planned for us," Cody continued in an obvious effort to recapture her attention and increase her irritation. Which was also, she hated to admit, pretty darn easy for him to do.

But the wedding ceremony Max had more or less ordered them to attend was not something Callie wanted to think about. Or even actually do. It had been hard enough leaving Cody once, just hours after their wedding ceremony in Acapulco. Never mind the idea of marrying him again....

Aware Cody was waiting for her answer, Callie advised dryly, "Forget the buffalo coat, Cody. I'd settle for a haircut," Callie murmured. Anything to make Cody into the man he had been, and not the man he apparently was now. Anything so she wouldn't have to look at him and feel so damn guilty, when she knew deep inside she'd only had his best interests at heart. "Or maybe just a shave..."

Oblivious to the depth of her private regrets, Cody hit the brakes and brought them to a skidding halt. With his hand behind her seat, he came right up in her face. "You want to try shaving me?"

"No," Callie admitted truthfully. The whole idea of it was too sensual to be borne. "But I will if it will keep Max from being humiliated posthumously," she qualified frankly. "Obviously, you have taken this rough-hewn attitude of yours too far. Although I suppose there's some comfort to be found in the fact you apparently bathe," she continued with a bluntness meant to shame him into behaving in a more gentlemanly manner.

Although she was fudging a bit there, too.

The fact of the matter was he smelled almost too good, like pine and winter and sunshine all rolled into one. As for the way he dressed... The soft cotton of his western shirt gleamed snowy white against the suntanned hue of his skin, the worn Levi's gloved his long legs and lean hips with distracting snugness, just as the taupe suede vest he'd left open drew her eyes to his broad shoulders and the muscled contours of his chest. His boots were made of handcrafted, dark brown leather. So was the belt, with the rodeo buckle, at his waist. A creased, bone-colored Stetson was on the bench seat between them.

Cody slanted her an unrepentant smile and continued to drive like a maniac. "That, too, could be remedied. I don't have to bathe prior to the wedding. After, either."

Callie hadn't had much time to think about Max's proposition, but she had already decided she wanted the independence that the bull's-eye property and small herd of cattle would afford her. She wasn't going to let Cody get in the way of her building a new life for herself, even if she had to marry him to come into her unexpected inheritance from his Uncle Max. Nor was she planning to put up with any untoward behavior on his part. She was not the helpless teenager he'd run off to Mexico with seven years ago. If he was fool enough to challenge her, he was going to get a taste of his own medicine. Max probably had known that would be the case, too. He'd treated her like one of his own kids and had been more of a father to her than her own. No doubt Max was counting on her to recivilize his nephew. And perhaps after all the grief and heartache she had reluctantly caused Cody, she even owed him that, Callie thought.

Holding on to the dash and door to keep from being rocked about the cab, she drew a deep breath. "Cody, I'm warning you. Slow down. Straighten up. Or suffer the consequence."

He shot her a cockeyed grin and recklessly turned to face her, veering off the road and hitting a rock in the process before he recovered his grip on the wheel and swung them back onto the road again. "Is that a threat I hear from you, Callie dear?"

"No, it's a promise." Callie accented her words with a long, level look. "Thanks to the terms of Max's will, we're going to be sharing quarters for the next two days and two nights. And I am not—I repeat, not—going to spend the whole time either correcting you or holding my nose." He may have started this tough-guy stuff to keep others at bay and ease his suffering, but it wasn't working. It was time the wall he'd built around himself came down. And Callie knew exactly where to start. "So bathe or I'll do it for you."

Her warning only served to make Cody step on the accelerator even harder. "Try and I won't be the only one getting naked and wet," he warned.

Callie couldn't help it; losing her composure, she flushed at the mental image his words evoked. Nevertheless, she stubbornly held her ground as she folded her arms in front of her. "You're not only rude, you're incorrigible," she scolded.

Cody's grin grew smugger while the look in his blue eyes grew darker. "Well, don't worry. You only have to put up with me for the next two days. Then you can go your way and I can go mine. 'Cause Uncle Max's will didn't say anything about us staying under the same roof once the vows were said, only until then."

He spoke with grim confidence, as if in the short time that had transpired since the will had been read, he already had their course charted out. The only problem was, he hadn't bothered to take her feelings into consideration. Unable to help herself, Callie decided to put him in his place. "Of course, I could opt out now," she threatened softly, watching his face.

"But you won't," Cody shot back intrepidly, recklessly guiding the truck through another stand of trees—pines this time—and off the road, across an unfenced pasture.

As she bounced around, Callie held even more tightly on to the seat. "What makes you so sure?"

"The loot at the end of the rainbow." Cody flashed her another insufferable smirk. "The day you pass up money you didn't have to work for is the day the world comes to an end."

Little did he know... Callie shook her head.

Cody guided the truck into another clearing and parked on the other side of what looked like a small, very weathered barn.

"You think you know me so well," she remarked as he cut the motor and they were left with the silence of the Montana countryside on a warm June day.

Cody pocketed the keys and avoided her eyes altogether. "I learned the hard way," he announced cavalierly.

From what Callie had seen thus far, he hadn't learned anything about her at all. Their honeymoon had been a disaster, with—unbeknownst to him—her family showing up almost from the get-go.

Furthermore, she had been suffering, too, since the demise of their very short-lived marriage, and she didn't have to bulldoze everyone in her path because life had been unfair to her.

"What?" Cody prodded when she continued staring straight at the barn in front of them. "No smart remark?" He grabbed his Stetson and jumped out of the truck.

Callie hopped out on her own side, watching as he settled the Stetson squarely on his head. "I don't have the audience for it."

He folded his arms in front of him and squinted over at her. "You're right. I stopped appreciating your sense of humor in Acapulco."

Their abruptly-cut-short honeymoon again. Pushing her own heartbreak and sense of loss aside—there was so much they hadn't had a chance to experience!—Callie lifted her chin. "I don't want to talk about that," she replied, forcing the words through clenched teeth. She had tried to do what was best and let Cody down easily in the note she'd left him. Obviously, it hadn't worked.

"I'll just bet you don't," Cody shot right back. He grabbed her arm and whirled her around. For a tantalizingly brief second, he looked as if he didn't know whether to scream at her or kiss her. "But we will get around to it, when the time is right."

Callie could not imagine that. Not now, not ever. Hadn't they both suffered enough? Did he have to rub her nose in it? She had no control over who she was related to! That was pure biology!

She yanked loose of him. "As far as I'm concerned," Callie predicted tightly, backing up until she hit the tailgate, "the time will never be right."

He stepped around in front of her and boxed her in. "I got that message, too," he drawled in a low, sexy voice, "loud and clear."

Callie blinked, confused, then realized he was talking about their honeymoon again. About what should have happened but hadn't. But not because she hadn't wanted to make their marriage a real and lasting one. Pressing her lips together, she tilted her head back and looked up into his face. And that was when she saw it. The determination, and the desire. To set things to right between them? Or simply to even the score? Cody obviously thought he owed her something in way of revenge for running out on him. If only he knew, Callie thought, how much she had wanted to stay. But she hadn't been able to then, and she wouldn't be able to now, since he wasn't about to forgive her, so there was no use thinking about it, Callie thought morosely as she sidestepped stiffly past him. Even worse, in their anger and disillusionment, they could end up hurting each other even more than they already had. And that she didn't want for either of them. And neither would Max, she knew. "Cody... maybe this is a mistake."

"Try telling me something I don't know." Cody strode past her, knocking into her a little as he paused to study a small weathered barn and a corral that contained several horses before he pivoted abruptly back to face her. "But Uncle Max's will is ironclad," Cody reminded her grimly. "I marry you in two days or I don't inherit." They faced off, glowering at each other, like two fighters about to enter the ring. "So for the next forty-eight hours, Callie," Cody decreed as he grabbed her arm and propelled her toward a lone cabin at the end of the gravel path, "we stick to each other like glue."

CALLIE LET CODY GUIDE HER as far as the front door of the small log cabin with the haphazardly patched roof before she finally dug in her heels and refused to go any farther. She was tired of playing games with him, she thought as she pried her arm from his resolute grip. "What's this?"

Cody stepped back and, looking as if he expected her to bolt in either terror or disgust at any moment, announced smugly, "It's home sweet home, for the moment."

Callie blinked in surprise, not sure what she thought. Did she feel sorry for him? Or just disgusted? And annoyed. Greatly annoyed that he would even think of bringing her here. "You live here?" Callie gasped. No wonder his uncle was so concerned! The turn-of-the-century cabin was a disgrace. The floorboards on the front porch were uneven and rotting. Cobwebs hung from the roof to the door. The single window to the left of the front door was grimy and uncurtained.

Cody gave her a curt nod. "And so will you for the next two days," he predicted, tucking his thumbs into the belt loops on either side of his fly. He regarded her with a challenging air that quickly let her know he intended to make her as miserable as possible for ever running out on him. "Got a problem with that?"

Callie had never considered herself a snob. But the cabin couldn't have been more than twelve by eighteen feet in its entirety. That would not give them much room to maneuver within.

Cody rocked back on his heels and continued to look at her. "You're not afraid to be alone with me, are you?"

Callie tossed her head. Her hair flew in every direction. "Should I be?"

Cody leaned toward her until she could feel the warmth of his breath on her face. "Depends," he taunted brusquely.

"On what?" Callie asked.

Cody sensually traced the curve of her cheekbone with the back of his hand, the hurt and bitter disillusionment he still felt reflected in his eyes. "How you feel about giving me that wedding night you owe me."

The next thing Callie knew she was swept into the warm cage of his arms, every soft inch of her slender body firmly aligned against every hard, muscular inch of him. The heat of him was every bit as electrifying as his sheer physical strength. But even that was nothing compared to his lips. Soft, sensual, seductive, they wrenched a response from her that had her trembling. She wrapped her arms about his neck and kissed him back. Kissed him until the years they'd spent apart faded to a distant, inconsequential memory. She kissed him until she felt him tremble, too. Until her hands were in his hair... until she was caught against his hard chest... until the world was tilting on its axis and to continue would be very, very dangerous indeed....

Realizing what she was allowing to happen, Callie moaned, low in her throat. "Damn you, Cody," she whispered shakily, gathering her resolve and pushing him away. He obviously felt nothing but loathing for her now. His kiss, however seductively delivered, was nothing but a punishment.

Determined not to let him make something meaningful of something that wasn't, Callie remained motionless in his arms. "Get this straight, Cody McKendrick—I do not owe you a wedding night," she said, enunciating her words clearly. Even if, his hostility aside, she still wanted very much to give him one.

"So you once indicated by running away, but I beg to differ with you there, darlin'. 'Cause you very much owe me a wedding night," he finished in a soft, deadly voice that let her know he would not be satisfied until he had thoroughly and completely wreaked his revenge in the most sensual, devastating way possible.

Callie leaned forward, stepping on his toe with all her might. "Hold your horses there, cowboy. We aren't married yet!"

He winced, grew very still and just as stubbornly refused to release her. The silence between them stretched out dangerously. Callie wondered what he was thinking. "You're telling me you got an annulment?" he asked finally.

Callie tilted her head back. The tense look on his face told her the idea of that was as loathsome to him as it was to her. Trying hard to ignore the warmth of his hands on her, she volleyed back her reply as cavalierly as possible. "You're the one with the rich uncle. I always just assumed you got one."

"Nope."

"You don't mean—" Hope rose in Callie. Was it possible Cody hadn't given up on them entirely after all?

"Yep. I do." Never taking his eyes from her face, he released a long, slow breath and kept the rest of his emotions on the subject, whatever they were, strictly unreadable. "We're still married." And at the moment, Callie thought, it appeared to her that he wasn't regretting the overlooked technicality all that much.

Nor, to her growing dissatisfaction, was she. If she wasn't careful, if she let Cody move too fast or for all the wrong reasons, she might get her heart broken again, too.

Callie swallowed and flattened her hands over the hardness of his chest. "Maybe we are still technically married, but since that marriage was never consummated, it can't possibly be valid." Could it? And how could he be affecting her this way, after all this time, when she knew he didn't want her here? He hadn't kissed her because he loved her and wanted her back. He had kissed her to put her in her place.

Cody's hand slid down her spine, eliciting tingles of awareness wherever he touched. Lower still, there was a peculiar weakness in her knees, a melting ache.

"Fortunately for us that's something that's easy enough to remedy," Cody drawled.

Like heck it was. If he thought she was going to sleep with him and consummate their marriage now, after the way he had just treated her, and thereby forever ruin any slim chance they had of ever getting back together, he had another thing coming. "Dream on." Her pulse skittering with reaction, Callie pushed him aside. If and when Cody ever made love to her, it was going to be because he loved her and wanted her back in his life, from this day forward. It would not be to collect on his inheritance.

Deciding the best thing to do was to stay busy, she did an about-face and marched back toward the pickup truck.

"You can't run away from me forever," Cody predicted, dogging her every step of the way. "Sooner or later we're going to have to settle the score, Callie."

She regarded his he-man expression with a defiant one of her own. "Now you are really deluding yourself." Callie yanked open the door on the passenger side, reached behind the seat and brought out her duffel bag.

"I'm not going to be used again, Callie. If I put myself on the line for you again, I expect to get something out of it this time. Something I want."

CALLIE STARED AT CODY, her heart pounding. "Which is?" she taunted.

"For starters, our marriage certificate," Cody plainly specified.

She stared at him. "I don't have it!"

His shock turned to dismay. He leaned forward urgently. "You must have it."

Callie shook her head. Suddenly, she didn't like the way he was looking at her. As if he didn't believe her. Didn't want to believe her.

"If you're playing a game with me," Cody growled, "hoping to get even more out of this than Max offered—by holding that over my head—"

"Oh, stop," Callie cut him off, completely exasperated by his continuing and utterly groundless, as far as she was concerned, suspicions. "As if I would. And as for you, Cody McKendrick, you stand to get plenty out of this arrangement. You stand to get the ranch, all quarter million acres of it. So don't you stand there and lecture me." Callie slammed the door and tossed the duffel bag over her shoulder in one jaunty motion.

He stepped to block her way, all tough, indomitable male. "I've already earned the ranch." His voice dropped a husky notch that reverberated with sexual undertones. "And as for what I want, aside from the marriage certificate, which should probably be burned or at least somehow nullified so it doesn't show up later and muck up or otherwise complicate our eventual divorce, let's just say I'm thinking about something infinitely more satisfying."

And they both knew what that was. "Trust me." Cutting a wide swath around him, Callie lugged her duffel bag all the way to the front porch. She tossed it down with all the fire of an activist making a hugely political statement. "Making love to me—" *for any reason other than that you love me desperately,* Callie amended silently "—would not fall into that category, Cody."

"I'll be the judge of that." Stepping back, he regarded her with a smug look. Apparently deciding he was doing an excellent job of getting under her skin, he drawled, "Come to think of it, seems like I might enjoy the next two days more than I thought."

Don't count on it, Callie thought. But not wanting to give him the satisfaction of a comeback, she remained silent. "What happens after that?" she asked finally.

Cody shrugged. "We get married, just as Uncle Max willed that we must, we divorce as soon as his will allows, and then we go our separate ways."

Callie tossed her hair. There was no way she was letting him get away with such a lame proposal. "I think I'll pass. Now, if you don't mind I'm tired, and I'd like to go inside." She pushed on the door. It swung open with a creak. "Where's the light?"

Almost as an afterthought, Cody picked up her duffel and tossed it inside. "The *candles* are inside."

Callie took a quick look around. The interior of the cabin appeared to be divided neatly in two, one half acting as a living area and kitchen, the other the bedroom. Unlike the outside, it was clean and neat. But very, very spare.

"You're joking, right?" If he wasn't, he was definitely taking this revenge kick too far. "C'mon, Cody. It's going to be dark soon," Callie pointed out.

He flashed her an unrepentant grin, determined, it seemed, to be as difficult and rascally as possible. "Then we'd better find those candles, hadn't we?"

Callie drew a tranquilizing breath. "Surely you have a flashlight," she persisted.

"Only for emergencies," Cody allowed.

Obviously, to his frame of mind, this wasn't one of them.

She looked around, her displeasure growing. "There's no refrigerator."

Cody nodded, feigning surprise. "So there isn't."

Callie silently counted to ten and back down again. Keeping her eyes locked with his, she inquired, "No bathroom?"

Cody shrugged in a way she was sure he meant to irritate her. "Nature's right outdoors."

She exhaled brusquely. "I am not amused, Cody."

He nodded, not the least surprised. "Then you better use the powder room out back." Jerking a thumb over his shoulder, he pointed to a dilapidated building that most certainly did not come equipped with any plumbing.

"Surely you jest," Callie muttered, as she spun around to see where he was pointing. She hadn't used a latrine since the summer she'd been sent to camp. Never mind one that looked rickety and unkempt.

Cody shrugged his broad shoulders. "Suit yourself, but if you don't use it you might be getting a mite uncomfortable after two days."

CALLIE FOLDED HER ARMS in front of her. "I can't believe Max wanted this for me."

Neither could he, Cody thought.

Only a few hours had passed since they'd met up with each other again, and he'd already done what he'd silently sworn he would not do in the forty-eight hours before their wedding. He'd taken Callie in his arms again and held her and kissed her as if she were, and always would be, the only woman in his life.

He'd tried everything to finally get her out of his system—with little or no success—the past seven years. Which was, no doubt, why Uncle Max had ordered up something this crazy. Max had probably figured that more time together would be the only way they'd ever know in their hearts that this relationship of theirs was not meant to be. Heck, maybe if he made Callie's life miserable enough, Cody thought, she would even let him buy her out. And then she could go and settle elsewhere and he could live his life in peace.

Either that, Cody scoffed inwardly, or they'd find out they were madly in love after all and meant to spend the rest of their days together, just as Max, he and Callie had all once hoped.

Aware Callie was studying him curiously, as if wondering just what he was ruminating on for so long, Cody remained stone-faced as they looked around at the stiff velvet love seat, the shade of canned peas, and the rough-hewn table for two, complete with straight-backed chairs. Aside from a supplies shelf, which contained a bag of self-rising flour, a bottle of real maple syrup, a can of shortening, box of powdered milk, salt, coffee and two tins of canned vegetables, plus a cast-iron skillet, coffeepot and set of tin camp-style dishes and cutlery, there was nothing else in the place. It was spare and efficient to the extreme, just the way he liked it. Seeing Callie's displeasure, Cody asked, "What's the matter? This place not fancy enough for you?"

His temper simmering, he still couldn't get over the way she had run out on him without so much as even a note or a word of goodbye. Cody reminded himself of his promise to proceed with caution where Callie was concerned. "I thought you were dying to be a rancher's wife."

"I am."

"Good." Cody forced a tight smile. He was very interested to see just how far Callie would or would not take her quest for a buck. "Then like a good little ranch wife, you'll be rustling us up some supper."

Callie's chin slid out in an unruly pout. Her green eyes shimmered with temper, too. "Thanks, I'll pass. Besides, we're not completely married yet, Cody. And considering the fact neither of us have the wedding certificate, we may not even have an in-name-only marriage, either. So you have no right to try and act like a husband to me, even an unruly, surly one. So put that in your pipe and smoke it!"

So, Callie was already laying out the con. Giving precious little herself and expecting a lot in return. Cody regarded her steadily. He couldn't believe how easily he had almost been suckered in. Again. Of course, Callie responding so passionately to his kisses and then looking up at him all misty-eyed had been a nice touch. Had he not been at the receiving end of her innocent act before, and landed in a heap of trouble because he'd allowed himself to be taken in by the vulnerability beneath her typically feisty attitude, he might even have believed she had waited all this time for him.

But these days, he was older and wiser and he knew better.

Callie had saved her most convincing display of passion yet for the time when she needed it most. In other words, the big con. The one that would set her up for life. And she was here with him for one reason only, Cody reminded himself sternly. To collect on the land that Uncle Max had left her in his will. Pretending to be falling for him all over again was only a means to distract him, while she and her kin tried to con him out of everything.

Well, it wasn't going to work this time, Cody swore silently to himself. He was going to keep her at arm's length emotionally, even if he had to be mean as a rattlesnake to do so.

"Don't worry," he said dryly. "We can get another copy of the marriage certificate from the judge who married us in Mexico." Which would maybe, if he was lucky, save him from having to marry her again. "In the meantime, consider this a trial run," he advised succinctly, wishing she didn't look so all-fired beautiful or vulnerable in the fading daylight.

"Aren't you forgetting something, Cody?" Callie stepped forward to confront him toe-to-toe, quickly letting him know he wasn't the only one who could dish it out. "If I leave, you lose everything."

So what? Cody thought. Because, unlike Callie, he could not be bought. He was only going through with this lunatic exercise of his dear departed uncle because he wanted to see where all this would lead. As far as the Silver Spur cattle operation went, Cody thought, he had already earned that through seven years of unrelenting hard and devoted labor. This marriage business was merely the paperwork and bureaucracy he had to suffer through to cement the deal.

"If I lose, so do you," Cody pointed out matter-of-factly to Callie. "Is that what you want?" he asked as he towered over her. "To walk away from this windfall empty-handed?"

They stared each other down in an age-old battle of the sexes.

Eventually, Cody won as he knew he would, and Callie gave a resigned sigh. "Fine. Point me to the kitchen, wherever it is."

With a grin, Cody inclined his head to the left. He couldn't wait to see her reaction to that. "You're looking at it," he said.

CALLIE KNEW Cody was giving her a hard time on purpose. No doubt he was angry at his Uncle Max for attaching such a ridiculously provincial stipulation to his inheritance. But that was not her fault and she'd be damned if she'd be the outlet for his frustration. "That's a fireplace, Cody, not a stove."

Cody tugged the brim of the Stetson low across his brow. "A pity," he sighed. "If you can't figure out how to cook on it, you'll probably have to go hungry, then."

Callie edged closer, aware it was getting darker with every second that passed. She knew how to cook over an open fire but saw no reason to tell him that, lest he find yet another way to make her miserable just so she would be hurting as much as he was. "Don't you mean we'll both go hungry?"

"No," Cody announced with complete disregard to her comfort and well-being, " 'cause I know how to cook over an open fire."

Too nervous to eat earlier, Callie had merely picked at her breakfast and had forgone lunch altogether. Now her stomach was growling hungrily. "Meaning what exactly, Cody?" Callie prodded, balling her hands into fists at her side.

"Meaning I can cook for myself."

Callie fought to contain her growing exasperation. "Would you at least carry in some firewood so I can build a fire in here?" she asked with a sweet gentleness that would have done any Southern belle proud.

Cody sprawled on the love seat and stretched his long, jean-clad legs out in front of him. "Nope."

Callie could tell by the gleam in his eyes that he was up to something again. She might as well know what it was. Falling for the bait, she asked politely, "Why not?"

Cody pointed a thumb at his chest. "'Cause I won't be needing a fire in here. I'm sleeping in the bedroom."

Callie glanced at the love seat, which would barely accommodate the two of them sitting down, and then back at him. "Where am I sleeping?" she asked curiously. Was there a loft in the bedroom beyond?

Cody shrugged and glanced around thoughtfully. "On the floor?"

"That's not funny!" Darn his ungallant soul, he was really going to make her sleep on the sofa, while he took the bed!

"Probably won't be, come tomorrow morning," Cody agreed as he pushed lazily to his feet. "By the way, we get up early around here. Ranch life starts at dawn. Perhaps even a little before."

Callie folded her arms in front of her. "Rest assured, cowboy, I have no illusions that you'll do anything but try and make my life hell."

Cody's eyes gleamed with vengeful lights. "Just returning the favor. You made my life miserable the last seven years. It's my turn to do the same for you, for at least the next—" he glanced at his watch "—forty-five hours."

She really had hurt him, Callie thought. "Can you at least loan me a pillow and blanket?" she said.

Again, to her frustration, Cody refused to be even the least bit accommodating. "Sorry, no can do," he allowed calmly as she walked over to the bedroom and peered in. There was a very comfortable-looking double bed, with two pillows and a wealth of blankets, a dresser, and a fireplace, and nothing else. Still, for him not to share...

Doing his best to rile her up, he patted her shoulder condescendingly. "Look at it this way, Callie. At least you've got a piece of furniture to sleep on." He inclined his head toward the love seat. "We ranchers don't always even have that."

He wanted to give her a hard time. He thought she couldn't take it. He was dead wrong about that. She pivoted to face him and regarded him impatiently. "I need matches."

"Let's see." He searched around without any particular energy.

Though the afternoon had been warm, the June evening looked as if it were going to be dipping down into the fifties. There was no way she'd be able to sleep without some source of warmth. "I'll buy them from you," she said desperately.

The mention of money made him frown. "No need for that," Cody said brusquely as he swiftly located a canister on the top of the supply shelf, opened the lid and tossed her a pack. "Have it."

Determined to show him what a trooper she could be, Callie asked, "Where is the water?"

"In the pump out front."

They had to pump their own water, too? Damn. Callie looked around with a sigh. It was going to be a long night.

43:47

No WONDER Max had summoned her via his will, Callie thought long minutes later. She couldn't believe the changes in his nephew Cody, either. Okay, so seven years had passed since she'd seen Cody, she acknowledged as she tossed off her blue blazer and rolled up the sleeves on her long-sleeved white T-shirt and got down to work building a fire. But when she had known him he had been easygoing, generous to a fault and gallant beyond belief. The Cody who'd confronted her at the Fort Benton Gentlemen's Club was tough, suspicious, intense. Not at all like the Cody she had once known and loved with all her heart.

As if on cue, Cody came in with an armload of wood and unceremoniously took it into the bedroom. "Doesn't look like you're doing too good," he drawled as he strode past.

"I'll get it," Callie vowed meditatively as she lit the long twig that was going to serve as kindling. *Just as I'll eventually get you back on track or die trying.*

"Let's hope so," Cody called over his shoulder. "Otherwise you'll be a mite chilly tonight."

Callie sat back on her haunches. Cody always had a touch of hellion in him, just as she did in her, but in the past his disorderly, reckless side of him had always had a playful quality lurking underneath. Always before, she had known if he teased her he would also be sweet and loving. Now as she studied him she wondered if, beneath the bad-boy persona that had always been Cody's best defense, at heart he was still the deeply sensitive, innately gallant man she'd fallen in love with, or if he'd become someone else. Someone she didn't want to know. Not surprisingly, she found herself hoping for the first alternative. If only there was some surefire way to bring the goodness out in him again, she thought. "You could give me a hand with the fire in here, you know," she suggested gently. Maybe simple kindness, in continual doses, and some tender loving care were all Cody really needed to get himself back on track. But to her disappointment, her efforts fell on deaf ears.

Cody tipped the brim of his hat back with the tip of his finger and mocked her with cynical blue eyes. "And deprive you of your chance to show me what a good ranch wife you'd make me?" he retorted softly. "I don't think so. Unless..." Cody gave her a slow, lazy once-over that set her pulse to racing.

Not about to let him intimidate her that way, whether she still loved him or not, and she was beginning to think maybe she did, Callie brushed off her hands and stood. She lifted her brow. "Unless what?" she asked impatiently.

Cody manacled her wrist with his strong fingers and tugged her against his chest. Their bodies collided, head to toe, and suddenly he looked very much willing to barter with her for very high stakes. "You've changed your mind about that wedding night you owe me."

Chapter Two

"Anyone ever tell you that you have a one-track mind?" Callie asked, exasperated. Not that she hadn't been thinking the same things herself. She had been wondering what it would be like to share his bed almost from the first minute she'd laid eyes on him, in Pearl's diner, years ago. Now that they were older, she was finding her imagination more vivid and persistent. But there was no reason he needed to know that in his current frame of mind, she thought. Pushing away from him, she lifted three logs from the wooden bucket next to the fireplace and, after some deliberation, stacked them one on top of another so there was plenty of room for the fire to catch and the air to circulate in between.

"Considering I had to wait seven long years to enjoy the privilege of spending the night under the same roof as my new bride, there are some who might find my preoccupation understandable." He flashed her a bad-boy grin meant, she was sure, to intimidate.

"Well, I'm not one of them," Callie announced dryly as she turned her back on him and stuffed the twigs she had gathered to serve as kindling between the logs, then swiveled around on her haunches and studied him. With his hair tied back with a rawhide strip, in jeans, shirt and a suede vest, he looked as if he had stepped out of a recent movie she'd seen on the Old West. In the movie, the hero was a brooding cowboy who lusted after the woman he wanted but knew he shouldn't pursue. Of course the hero had pursued the heroine, and the movie had ended as their romance had, tragically.

But not, Callie thought with a whimsical smile, before the hero and heroine had enjoyed a wonderfully lusty, romantic time in bed.

Cody was every bit as sexy and attractive as the hero in the movie had been, and she couldn't help but wonder what he would look like with his hair down around his shoulders, his shirt off. Would his wheat blond hair be as soft and silky to the touch as it looked? Would his muscles gleam in the glow of the firelight? Was his chest covered with a mat of crinkly wheat blond hair? Callie didn't know the answers to any of that. Nor, the way things were going, was she ever likely to find out. Still, she couldn't help but wonder how their lives would have been if... But it was too late to go back now and change things. All they could do was go forward. Find a way to make peace now. That being the case, she released a small sigh of resignation and tilted her chin up at him in a way that signaled saucy wench—in the movies, anyway. "Furthermore, there's a lot more to marriage than just what goes on or does not go on in the bedroom. In fact, I'd wager the most critical things," *such as kindness, tenderness and caring,* Callie added to herself "happen outside the marriage bed."

Cody shook his head at her. "Where'd you ever get that notion? For a ranch wife, you have a lot to learn," he said.

Callie refused to back down on either her statement or the position she'd taken. "For a ranch husband, so do you."

His lips curved in a challenging grimace as she dusted off her hands and got to her feet. "Cute."

Moving forward until they stood toe-to-toe, she held his gaze defiantly. "And true. I don't know what you're thinking, Cody McKendrick, but you'll never win my heart—or any other woman's, for that matter—with these macho tactics. So unless you want to spend the rest of your life alone, you'll clean up your act. Pronto.''

For a moment, her blunt assessment of his behavior left him speechless. The moments ticked by, and she could see he was struggling with himself. It was just as she thought. Hoped. Somewhere deep inside, it still went against the grain for him not to rush in to her rescue. Max had brought him and his siblings up to always lend a helping hand, to friend and foe alike. That was why Max and all the McKendricks had had so many friends.

But Cody clearly did not want to remember that, Callie thought. Nor did he seem to want to think about how he'd let Max, and himself, down in his ruthless quest for solitude.

His lips thinning in obvious irritation, Cody held himself aloof and told her gruffly, ''Uncle Max was wrong. You don't belong here, Callie. You never did and you never will.'' Not bothering to even light a candle for her, he turned on his heel and disappeared into the bedroom.

Callie watched him go but made no move to follow him. Seconds later, she heard the shifting of logs into the bedroom fireplace. The strike of a match. She knew she could go after him and at least try one more time this evening to make peace between them, as Max probably would've wanted. Or she could accept that her mission was a lost cause, at least for the moment, and leave him to his solitude, she thought as she continued building her own fire. Finished, she hazarded a glance into the adjacent bedroom.

Cody was down on one knee before the fire, one hand bracing his jaw. He was staring into his fire, looking every bit as lonely as she felt. And yet unapproachable in a way she was not. Callie shook her head and sighed as her spirits plummeted all the more. Somehow, she had the feeling, this was not what Uncle Max had planned for them.

36:00

"RISE AND SHINE, DARLIN'."

"You *must* be kidding." Callie pulled the wadded-up sweatshirt that had been serving as her pillow back over her face. Despite the fire still glowing in the grate, it was achingly cold in the cabin. She was stiff and sore all over and covered with a makeshift blanket of her clothes.

Cody plucked the sweatshirt out of her hands again. "A rancher's life starts at dawn."

Callie propped herself up on her elbows and glared up at him. Bad enough he'd been completely ungentlemanly the night before. Now he was rudely depriving her of her rest, when she wanted nothing more than to sink back into sleep. "So I'll hire cowboys to get up for me," she grumbled back. As uncaringly as he had behaved, what did it matter to him what she did, anyway?

He grinned, apparently pleased he'd managed to start the day off badly for her. "I'm leaving here in ten minutes, Callie," he warned, "which means you are, too."

Ha! Callie pushed herself into a sitting position. She leaned her head on the sweetheart-shaped back of the love seat and barely stifled a huge yawn. "I thought I'd made it clear. As much as you would like to be, you are not the boss of me, Cody McKendrick."

"No," he agreed as he tucked his thumbs into his belt loops and settled into a spread-legged stance that put her at eye level with his rock-hard thighs. "But I am stronger."

His quiet words had an ominous quality that quickly brought her the rest of the way awake. Slowly and deliberately, Callie lifted her eyes to his. "Meaning what, exactly?"

"That I'm quite capable of lifting you up and hog-tying you to the saddle of your horse if that's the only way I can get my work done today."

Callie drew a quick breath. The hellion was back. "You wouldn't."

His eyes full of a mischief she recalled only too well, he merely grinned. "Try me."

Callie swore as she pushed her hands through the length of her hair. The truth was she knew absolutely nothing about ranches. She did want to learn. This was as good an opportunity as any, even if every muscle in her body ached from sleeping on a love seat that was several feet too short and very thinly cushioned.

He tilted his head to the side as she lifted her arms over her head and gingerly worked out the kinks in her shoulders, back and arms. "Sore?"

"You wish," Callie fibbed, dropping her arms and straightening. She stood and started to look for the bathroom before she remembered what she'd managed to avoid dealing with so far. With a disgruntled scowl, she sat back down and reached for her handcrafted, red leather cowboy boots. She knew darn well what he was attempting with this poorly scheduled activity of his, but he was not chasing her off the property this way. She could be a rugged individualist, too, when she wanted to be, and furthermore, she was going to prove it.

"Want the flashlight?"

"Yes. What time is it, anyway?"

Cody consulted his watch and continued surveying her with thinly disguised pleasure. "Four a.m."

With effort, Callie suppressed another long, gusty sigh. Which meant she'd had what? Three, four hours of sleep, if you subtracted the three hours prior to that when she'd tossed and turned while Cody sat staring at the fire in the next room. There were limits, even for rugged individualists. Cody might as well learn right now what those were. She smiled at him cheerfully. "I'll pay you back for this."

"Now, Callie, you're sounding a little cranky," he teased, looking as if he would welcome any and all kinds of tussles with her, so sure was he that he would emerge the victor.

"So sue me," Callie grumbled right back after another deep breath. "I'm not a morning person." Nor was she a patsy he could steamroll right over, potential wife or no.

"I'll be waiting for you. Remember. Ten minutes. Actually—" he consulted his watch again "—about seven now."

Wanting him to know she did not appreciate his attempts at humor, especially so early in the morning, Callie gave him a last debilitating look and slipped out the door. Flashlight in hand, she trudged through the wet grass to the outhouse, muttering about the hour and the condition of the facilities all the while, and yanked open the door. A couple minutes later, she stepped out and was promptly grabbed from behind. A rough hand clamped over her mouth, cutting off her air and stifling her reflexive scream.

Struggling, Callie felt herself being dragged back behind the outhouse, shoved up against the crude wooden building. "Hello, there . . . Callie," a familiar voice said.

She stared into the shadowed face of her older brother and only sibling. As she relaxed, he eased his hand off her mouth. "Buck? What are you doing here?"

He regarded her scornfully. "You aren't the only one who saw the ads for the video matchmaking service and decided that might be a way to hook up with someone wealthy and get rich quick."

Oh, no, Callie thought as dread swept through her. She'd thought—hoped—she'd put this part of her life behind her permanently seven years ago. Apparently not, now that they'd finally caught up with her again. "You signed up with the agency, too?" Even as she asked, she had a sinking feeling she already knew the answer.

"Even better." Buck flashed a malicious smile. He shrugged and lit a cigarette. "I know someone who works there, who is now my girlfriend. She told me Max owned it. Even let me take a peek at the tapes on file. When I saw yours . . . let's just say I couldn't resist finding out what you were up to. Have to hand it to you, Callie. I really admire the way you've come back to take advantage of old Cody's grief. Of course, with Max McKendrick dying, Pa and I figured you couldn't be far behind... especially since, according to our research, there's been no annulment filed in Acapulco, so you're still married to one of the richest men in the West.''

If only she'd taken care of that, Callie thought miserably.

"You leave Cody out of it," Callie whispered fiercely, balling her hands into tight fists at her sides. There was no way she was going to let Buck take advantage of Cody or any of his kin!

"Now, Callie," Buck drawled with an evil smile as he took another drag on his cigarette and blew the smoke right back at her, "you know we can't do that. That lover boy of yours was destined to make us all rich. He's already failed us once, a fact Pa laments over almost daily. We can't let him do it again. 'Cause if we do, Pa'll be swearing more than revenge on your beloved. If it happens again, Pa'll be out for blood. Cody's blood.''

Trembling from head to toe, Callie shoved her brother aside. Although she no longer feared she would turn out like Buck or Pa, it was one of the great miseries of her life that they were related. "Is Pa here with you?" She looked past him fearfully at the darkness of the woods.

Buck tossed his cigarette aside and caught a lock of her hair. Twisting it around his fist, he yanked her back to his side. "What do you think?"

Callie shivered and told herself it was the cool night air making her so cold. "I'm not helping you," she warned fiercely. And she meant it this time.

Buck tightened his grip on her hair and studied her with a knowing smirk. "You talk as if you have a choice." According to him, and Pa, she didn't.

"I'll tell Cody you're here," Callie threatened.

"Do and you'll force me to take care of him, too."

Though Buck and Pa had always been more conniving con artists than violent criminals, Callie had the feeling Buck wouldn't hesitate to harm Cody if it was the only way Buck could protect himself.

"So if you care about your health and Cody's," Buck continued in a low, threatening voice, "you'll keep quiet and do as I say."

"Callie!" Cody called from the door of the cabin. "Time's up!"

"Remember what I said, Callie. I'll be in touch." Buck disappeared into the woods behind the outhouse.

Shaking, Callie leaned against the outhouse. She'd thought that part of her life was over. And maybe it would have been if she hadn't come back to Montana, looking to try to recapture some of the small measure of happiness she'd had here in the past.

She heard Cody's heavy footsteps coming toward her. He couldn't know about Buck or his plans. Cody's opinion of her was low enough as it was. She would just have to get rid of Buck on her own. She stepped out from behind the outhouse.

"What are you doing back there?" Cody asked. "Is that...cigarette smoke?" He leaned closer, taking in a whiff of her hair.

"Of course not." Callie pushed him away. Trying her best to recover from the encounter with her brother, she countered evenly, "You know I don't smoke."

Cody shone the flashlight up into her face and looked her up and down. "Then what are you doing behind the outhouse?" he demanded.

"Getting some air."

Cody studied her some more. Finally, he growled, "Well hurry up."

"Hold your horses," Callie grumbled back, reverting to her former uncooperative attitude as perspiration trickled down her neck. That had been a close call. Too close for comfort.

"So how long since you've been on a horse?" Cody asked.

"Never you mind." Callie finished tightening the cinch. Grabbing the saddle horn, she swung herself up in the saddle, just as Cody had taught her to when she was seventeen. "This is one part of living out west I haven't forgotten. What I want to know is what's in those saddlebags you packed."

"You'll find out soon enough." Cody swung up onto his horse and took off.

Callie caught up so she was riding beside—not behind—him. "Determined to be mysterious?"

"And then some," he admitted, studying the landscape as they rode through the woods and into the wide open spaces of the canyon land.

As they rode, Callie looked around, too. Birds sang intermittently in the trees. The morning air felt refreshingly cold and clear against her face. There was no smog out here, no city noises, no traffic. Only man and horse and the beauty of a Montana sunrise. Dawn was coming soon; she could tell by the ever lightening hue of the blue gray sky, the hint of pale gold just above the horizon in the east. The thick grass beneath them glistened with dew. In the distance, she could see the granite-topped mountains rise.

More potent than all of that were the memories of other times she and Cody had ridden out together. Sometimes during the day, sometimes at night. They hadn't gone to see movies or eat in restaurants on their dates; they'd gone out to ride, and had long, lazy picnics in wildflower-strewn meadows. They'd taken off their socks and shoes and waded barefoot in clear, cold mountain streams. They'd watched the sunrise and the sunset. Until she had only wanted to be with him. Until she had only wanted to run away....

"Where have you been the last seven years?"

Cody's unexpected question brought her out of her reverie. Callie kept her eyes trained on the trail in front of her, hesitating a moment, her teeth worrying her bottom lip. "I think the question is, Where haven't I been?"

"I'm listening."

Callie shrugged, trying hard not to reveal the deep loneliness and uncertainty she'd felt during that time, when she'd left everyone and everything she had ever known far behind her. "I worked as a dishwasher in Laredo, a receptionist in Florida, a lifeguard in California and a retail sales clerk in Martha's Vineyard." And though she had excelled at all her jobs, none had brought her the happiness she sought. Which was why she'd come back, why she'd taken such a chance. . . .

"How'd you hear about the matchmaking service?"

"I saw an ad in the back of *Farms and Ranches* magazine. Who knew Max ran the whole operation?"

He studied her thoroughly. "What were you doing reading that?"

Callie shrugged and shifted her reins to her other hand. "I don't know. I saw an issue on a newsstand in Vermont when I was there one weekend, and I picked up a copy and got a little homesick, and I bought it."

Cody led the way across a shallow mountain stream. When her mount hesitated midstream, he pulled his stallion up beside her mare and reached over and took hold of her reins. "You expect me to buy that?"

Callie stiffened in the saddle. Because her horse was being difficult, she let Cody guide her across the stream. As they crossed to the opposite bank, she turned toward him, looking him straight in the eye. "I don't care what you buy."

Cody leaned over and petted her mare, then handed the reins back to Callie. "So you didn't know Uncle Max owned the WRW video matchmaking service?"

"No." Once again, Callie followed Cody's lead.

Cody tipped the brim of his hat back, off his face. "If you had, would you still have made a tape and sent it in?"

That was not easy to answer. Callie knew, deep down, she had never given up entirely on the idea of the two of them someday being together again. She'd even had fantasies about Cody finding her, telling her nothing had really changed, that he still loved her and always would. "I don't know," Callie said finally as they led their horses through yet another section of woods. "I admit to being curious about what happened to you, Trace and Patience. But I was busy trying to make ends meet. I had no time to follow through." And more to the point...would Cody ever be safe with her as long as Buck and Pa were around? Did she want to subject him to their money-grubbing schemes?

"Well, financial security isn't all it's cracked up to be. We're all three a living testament to the fact that money doesn't buy happiness."

Callie turned in the saddle and gave Cody a sharp glance. "Being poor doesn't automatically guarantee happiness, either." How well she knew that.

He gave her a long, contemplative look. "So what does, then?" he asked after a moment.

"I don't know." Callie shook her head, wishing she knew. She looked at the horizon, focusing on the pale gold of the sun. "I'm still searching for the answer to that."

"OH, CODY, IT'S BEAUTIFUL," Callie said long minutes later as they paused in front of a fenced-in site, complete with private woods, stream and a flower-filled meadow. "This fenced-in area..." Callie began.

"It's the fifteen to twenty acres Uncle Max willed to you," Cody finished. Strong hands encircling her waist, he helped her down from her horse. "I was planning on building a house here one day."

"That's why you fenced it in." Callie briefly rested her hands on his shoulders to steady herself, then, aware of how he was looking at her, half in yearning, half in mistrust, pulled away.

Cody nodded, his expression grim. "It was the first step to my plan. Next, I was gonna have a road built, leading to this section of the property, then the foundation laid, and so on and so on."

"And Max knew that," Callie guessed unhappily, hating to think she'd taken anything else away from him.

"Of course," Cody said furiously. "It's why he willed it to you." He gave her a level look. "To make sure I'd marry you again."

Callie flushed at his bluntness. She had never wanted to be the booby prize in an unwanted game, but here she was anyway. "I'm sorry Max put you in such a predicament. I'm sure he felt he was doing the right thing," Callie continued as she tethered her mare to a tree. "So you shouldn't be angry with him."

Cody merely shrugged and, hands braced loosely on his waist, continued looking out at the neat brown fence. She could tell by the tense set of his shoulders he wasn't going to take her advice on that or anything else.

Callie swallowed, beginning to feel uneasy again. "I thought we were going to do some ranchwork this morning." But there were no cattle in sight.

Cody swung back around to face her, his look a little too easygoing to be trusted. "I've taken pity on you," he said matter-of-factly. "I'm going to cook you breakfast before we get down to business."

Breakfast sounded good. After last night's meager supper of a lone granola bar she'd found in the cabinet, which she had devoured as if it were a three-course meal, and the long ride this morning, Callie was famished. Deciding to meet him halfway on this, she smiled at him gregariously. "Need help?"

"Nope." He shrugged off her offer of help with a broad sweep of his hand. "But feel free to look around."

While he unpacked his saddlebags, Callie decided to do just that. When she came back long minutes later, a bouquet of wildflowers clutched in her hand, he had a campfire going. The rich, aromatic scent of freshly brewed coffee filled the air. Golden brown hotcakes sizzled in the cast-iron skillet.

"Sit down," he said with surprising and suspicious generosity. "Grab a plate."

From the looks of things, Cody was a great cook. Nevertheless, Callie didn't quite trust his abrupt change of mood. Last night he couldn't be bothered to even share a pillow with her. This morning he was waking her at dawn, which was a bad thing, and cooking her a delicious breakfast, which was a good thing. He also seemed awfully cheerful for a man who had lost his dream-home site to her. Unable to help herself, she hesitated briefly, then teased, "This food isn't poisoned, is it?"

He glanced over at her, amusement glimmering in his ocean blue eyes. "Hope not," he drawled with a conciliatory smile, "'cause it's what I'm eating, too." He handed her a stack of fluffy pancakes and a plastic bottle of real maple syrup. Callie drenched her pancakes with the syrup. He drenched his. Together, they began to eat.

Callie wasn't disappointed by his efforts. The pancakes were so light and tender they fairly melted on her tongue. "This really is good."

Cody smiled. "Thanks."

As Callie forked up another bite, she figured they might as well lay it all on the line. "I have to wonder why you're being so nice to me, though." As much as she hated to admit it, it didn't feel quite right. Maybe because she sensed his warm, caring attitude was not genuine. Too late, she saw her instinct about the situation was right on the money.

Cody's expression turned serious. His eyes pinned her. "Maybe because, our parting aside, you always seemed like a practical person at heart."

Practical, Callie thought as his coldly calculated words echoed in her ears. The fluffy pancakes settled like lead in her stomach. Cody was leading up to something. A deal. Something, anything that would get them swiftly out of each other's lives. It was probably what he'd been think-ing about all last evening when he'd been sitting before the fire.

With hands that trembled, she set her nearly empty plate aside. "So in other words, this is a bribe," she said in her coldest tone, trying and failing to conceal her hurt.

"An effort to set the mood," Cody corrected with forced affability, leaning over to pour her more coffee. "For the bargain I'd like to make with you."

Callie swallowed hard and lifted the tin mug to her lips, not sure what was making her the angriest. The knowledge he felt she could be bought? Or the knowledge he thought she could be bought so easily.

She took a sip of the coffee and found it had grown as bitter as her mood. "I see," she said finally, more curious than willing to hear him out. "And that bargain is . . . ?"

Cody set the coffee back on the fire and leaned forward earnestly, one forearm resting on his bent knee. "After we get married as per terms of the will, I want you to sell the land you've inherited back to me. I'll pay a fair market price. All you have to do is agree to leave Montana, di-vorce me and never come back."

Callie set her chin. That was quite a bargain all right. "Suppose I don't want to leave Montana or sell it."

Cody followed his grimace with a deep draft of coffee. "Then we have a problem," he drawled as his superficial cordiality began to dissolve as swiftly as it had appeared. "'Cause I am determined to get this land, one way or an-other."

Callie had the feeling he wouldn't hesitate to do what-ever it took to get rid of her. And while she admired his te-nacity when it came to getting what he wanted, she hated his shortsighted, narrow-minded view. He was basing ev-erything on a past that was no longer valid. Even she could see that. She set her tin cup down with a thud. "Why do you hate me so much?" She had taken great pains writing that note so he wouldn't!

Cody snorted impatiently. "After what happened in Mexico, you even have to ask?" He regarded her incredulously.

"Yes," Callie said flatly. "I do."

Chapter Three

Cody dumped his coffee on the fire and watched it hiss and smoke as it hit the burning coals. His lips thinning grimly, he drawled, "That's quite a gutsy—if unwise—attitude coming from the bride who lured me to Mexico and then pulled the scam of the century."

Callie watched as he emptied the coffeepot over the coals. Hunkering down beside the campfire, he began gathering up their dirty dishes and utensils. "What are you talking about?" she asked warily, helping him carry the dishes down to the stream.

"Like you don't know!" he countered harshly as he rinsed their dishes in the water, item by item, and laid them on the grassy bank to dry.

Because there was nothing more for her to do, Callie stood and began to pace. She wasn't sure how much he knew, although it was clear he had discerned something, so she started at the beginning. "I ran away from you, Cody, because I had no choice."

He nodded, looking as if he didn't believe her for a second. "And the ransom demand?" he countered coolly. "Did you have no choice about that, either?"

Callie blinked. "Wait a red-hot minute. I never asked you for money."

"That's right. You didn't, Callie. Your brother Buck and your pa were the ones who came to me with the news you'd been kidnapped. They were the ones who delivered the ransom note. But I have no doubt you are as familiar with the bottom of the deck as they are.''

"I was never kidnapped! I ran away from you on our wedding night."

Cody's eyes glimmered with suppressed temper. "I eventually figured that out. But not," he emphasized bluntly as he stood and straightened to his full six feet, "before your brother and your pa put me through forty-eight hours of sheer hell."

Callie gulped. "They actually came to you and told you I'd been kidnapped?" she asked apprehensively. She had figured Buck and Pa would back off with their schemes to extort money from Cody when she was no longer around to help. This explained a lot about why he detested her as much as he did! It didn't, however, make it fair.

He glared at her. "Yes, Callie, they did."

Indignant at being unjustly lumped in with her no-account father and brother, Callie squared off with Cody. "What happened to the note I left you?" she demanded, furious he was so quick to judge her. She closed the distance between them. "Or did you completely disregard that?"

Cody regarded her with unbridled skepticism. "What note?"

Callie blew out an impatient breath. "The one I left on the hotel room dresser, the one that said I was leaving you because I loved you too much to subject you to the hell I'd already been through with my kin. The one that said I wanted you to have a happy life and I knew you'd never have it with me. And don't tell me that note blew away. I put a heavy brush on top of it to weigh it down and hold it firmly in place. That note was plainly visible to anyone who walked in the room," Callie continued emotionally before he could interrupt.

For once, Cody was silent. "Your note wasn't there when I got back to the hotel room," he conceded finally, looking for a moment as if he were tempted to believe her—and even more, had his own share of regrets.

His brief show of vulnerability touched her in a way his smug attitude had not. Ruefully, Callie realized she hadn't given him much chance to explain, either. "Is that why you've been so angry with me?" she asked softly. "Because you thought I left you without so much as a note or word of goodbye?"

Cody released a long, ragged breath. "I didn't know why you left me," he confessed huskily. As he looked at her, his blue eyes glimmered with hurt. "I just figured you'd had second thoughts. That you'd decided you were too young to get married or didn't love me after all." Cody tugged the brim of his Stetson a little lower across his brow. "After all, everything had happened pretty quickly once you'd made the decision to run away from your family. I asked you to elope. Max suggested Mexico, because you were underage, and loaned us his Learjet airplane."

Callie shook her head at him, annoyed that Cody—who was incredibly bright about everything else—could be so dense when it came to romance. Stepping closer, she tapped a hand against his chest. "You shortchanged us both by thinking so little of me, Cody McKendrick."

Cody stared down at her, looking as if he wanted so much to believe in her, the way she had once believed in him. But trust no longer came easily to either of them, it seemed. "You're telling me that your walking out that way wasn't a setup all along?" he persisted.

Callie nodded. That was exactly what she was saying. "I'm sorry my brother and Pa tried to run a con on you," she added, wondering if she would ever stop being ashamed of them, of feeling somehow sullied by the illegal, unethical and immoral things they had done, simply by virtue of being related to them.

Cody continued to study her. "But in retrospect it doesn't surprise you, does it?"

"No." Aware that his nearness was beginning to get to her, Callie turned on her heel and headed back to the campfire. As she shoved her hands into the pockets of her suede jacket, Cody fell into step beside her, his glance turning to a circling eagle overhead. "Sad to say, they'd been running cons as long as I could recall. That's why I wanted out so bad. Because they were pressuring me to start helping them," she explained.

"And I was the mark you were supposed to bait, wasn't I?" This time there was no judgment in Cody's low tone.

Embarrassed, Callie turned away. Feeling near tears, she stared at the dew sparkling like diamonds on the grass. "I admit they deliberately put me in your path by making me get a summer job waiting tables at the diner where you hung out when you were done here at the ranch."

Cody laid his hands on her shoulders, forcing her to turn to face him. "So you deliberately set out to get my attention?" He searched her eyes.

"No." Callie sighed her regret. "I didn't even know what they had in mind." She tilted her head back to better see into the rugged contours of his face and splayed her hands across the smooth chambray of his shirt and the hardness of his chest. "All I knew was that they said if I wasn't going to help them run cons—they had several scams going at the time, one was a stranded motorist routine, the other a fraudulent insurance company scheme—then I had to find out what it was like to work a real job for minimum wage. So they trotted me around from place to place, standing next to me while I asked for work. Because we were new to the area, most places turned me down. When we hit Pearl's diner, Pa started in on me, berating me for my lack of luck in front of Pearl, and she felt sorry for me and gave me a job that she didn't really have to give."

"I remember," Cody recollected softly, tightening his hold on her protectively. "I was in the diner that night, sitting in the booth in the back." His lips thinned unhappily.

"I wanted to cram my fist down your pa's throat, the way he was humiliating you in front of everyone there."

Callie had never wanted Cody's pity any more than she wanted anyone else's. "Well, you needn't feel sorry for me," she replied stiffly. Her face burning with shame, she slipped out of his grasp and turned away. "Pa's blustering and threatening that night was all part of the con." At least, Callie thought, that's what she had kept trying to tell herself at the time. Then and now, she wasn't so sure.

Cody stroked his beard thoughtfully. "I don't know, Callie. Your pa's contempt for you that night seemed real enough to me. But then again," he admitted slowly, "so did the kidnapping scam in Mexico."

"I knew they'd followed us to Mexico. The moment you left me alone they made their presence known and started pressuring me to run a con on you."

"And you refused?"

"Yes. But I knew they wouldn't give up, which is why I had to run away, so you'd be free." Callie paused, her expression perplexed. "There's one thing I don't understand," she said slowly as she struggled to put it all together. "How did they convince you I'd been kidnapped?"

"You were gone. There was no note. All I knew was you were missing. Then they showed up and told me me the kidnappers had contacted them, using a phone number in your wallet, and demanded a ransom," Cody related matter-of-factly.

"So you paid."

An undefinable emotion flickered briefly in his face before he nodded. "And worried myself sick in the meantime," he admitted.

"Did they ever tell you the ransom demand had been a con?"

"No, although they eventually gave themselves away, and I knew I'd been set up from the very first."

"By them, Cody," Callie stressed, curving her hand around the powerful muscle of his bicep. "Not by me."

Cody looked at her and said nothing. Dread welled up inside her. She could see his doubts surfacing once again. "If I'd had any idea what they were up to, Cody, I swear I would have put a stop to it," Callie told him softly, anxiously. "Or at least told you so that you and Max could have put a stop to it." Callie never had been able to stand up to both Pa and Buck on her own with any success. Together, they were too wily. That's why she'd had to run away.

Cody calmly removed her hand from his arm and turned his attention back to the campfire. The flame had been partially doused by the coffee he'd dumped over top of it. He put it out the rest of the way by smothering it with a shovelful of rich Montana soil. The old bitterness and pain were back in his eyes. "I commend you," he said simply.

"For what?" She didn't like the dangerous undertone in his low voice as he packed up his camp shovel and turned to face her again. He stuffed the paper wrappers from the trail-size packs of coffee and pancake mix into one of the saddlebags, then started back to get the camp dishes they'd left drying in the grass, saddlebag still in hand. "This was very convincing, Callie. You're almost as good an actress as your pa and brother were actors."

Callie caught Cody's arm, staying his flight. "I'm not acting here, Cody. I'm scared of Buck and Pa and what they might do to you."

The corner of his mouth quirked up, as if he found amusement in some private irony. "Maybe that would be easier to believe if you hadn't helped set me up so thoroughly before we eloped."

She dropped her hand, recoiling in hurt that he could think so little of her that he would believe she was part of Buck and Pa's sleazy schemes. "What do you mean?"

Cody let the saddlebag dangle at his side. "Telling me you couldn't take it anymore that night, that you were running away."

Callie flushed, recalling her hysteria at the time. "I was running away," she insisted emotionally. Doing so had been the only way she'd known how to survive. "And you didn't have to go with me."

"But you knew I would go with you, didn't you?" Cody persisted, his coldly suspicious glance roving her upturned face.

"I hoped," Callie admitted freely, keeping her eyes locked with his. The seconds drew out tensely. She could feel him starting to believe her. "There's a difference, Cody," she said softly.

In the silence that fell, Callie could feel her heart slamming against her ribs. The relief she'd initially felt as they tried to reconcile themselves to the past had been replaced by the fear she'd had since they'd met—that he would judge her guilty by association, not by what she had or had not done.

"Well, you got your wish," Cody said tersely, looking as deeply troubled as she felt. "And your impetuousness or your cunning—whichever it is, I haven't decided yet—made a miserable mess out of both our lives," he snapped, pivoting away from her once again.

"For a while." Callie hurried after him haughtily, not about to give up on him, not yet. "I, at least, have since recovered."

Cody appeared to see no virtue in that. "Admirably, it would seem," he agreed succinctly as he knelt to stuff the dishes into the saddlebag. "And yet you're back." Finished, he fastened the buckle and dropped the bag onto the grass.

"I guess Uncle Max knew I was needed here," Callie ruminated out loud after a moment. *And I can see why,* she thought passionately.

But her verbal assessment of the situation did not have the desired result. "Needed!" Cody echoed. Jaw rigid, he stood. "For what?" he rasped.

And in that instant, Callie knew. Max had thrown her in with Cody because he loved him, because it was all he knew to do to save his nephew from a life of loneliness, isolation and pain. And Callie was not going to let Max down. Not when he'd always been so good to her, so loving and understanding and kind, even in the most difficult times. And that was, coincidentally, exactly what Cody needed now, too, Callie thought. Understanding. She dropped her voice another tranquil notch. "I am here to help you become the man you were before the hard times hit, to become the man you were destined to be."

CODY STARED AT CALLIE, not sure whether to scoff or applaud. The sad truth was part of him wanted to trust her, but the other part had learned the hard way to regard everything she said and did with the thinly veiled suspicion with which he'd regard any con artist. "So what are you telling me, Callie? That you signed up with the matchmaking agency just like that, without even knowing who exactly it was you were supposed to help out?" he recapped out loud, not bothering to hide the sarcasm in his low tone.

"Yes." As Cody continued to size her up relentlessly, Callie's posture turned stiff and defensive. "As foolish as it sounds, even after all this time, after the heartbreak of our failed elopement, I trusted the people at the agency. So when I got a message from one of the agents, telling me where and when to show up to meet this rancher who so desperately needed my help, I took a blind leap of faith and went." Callie paused and watched the conflicting play of emotions on Cody's face. "Max did not do this to hurt us. He loved you, Cody."

Cody had never doubted that. Although never blessed with children himself, when left with the unexpected guardianship of his niece and two nephews, Max had pulled out all the stops to be a good parent. "He also thought he knew everything there was to know about fixing up our lives." Feeling restless again, Cody moved through the trees to the bank of the meandering stream. "But he was wrong about that, too. He was wrong to encourage me to elope with you to Mexico." He was wrong about Callie and Cody belonging together as neighboring ranchers, never mind as man and wife.

"I'm not so sure about that, Cody. In fact I tend to agree with what Max evidently told the agency." Callie gave Cody a placating grin and surprised the heck out of him by playfully rubbing his beard with the flat of her hand. "You do need some civilizing," she teased.

"The hell I do," Cody drawled back roughly. He had been his own person his entire adult life. Will or no will, he was not letting anyone change that. Furthermore, this conversation of theirs was getting far too intimate. It was making him forget he didn't want her here. That he needed to stay on his guard.

"The only question is where to start," Callie murmured, as she continued to eye him with an almost wifely intent that made Cody think about how much a part of him liked having Callie close again, despite everything. And that, Cody thought, just would not do.

"I've got an idea." Deciding the best way to make Callie understand she was playing with fire in her attempt to get close to him, and stunned by her willingness to inject herself into his life again, regardless of his prejudice against her, he buried his hands deep in her hair and fastened his mouth over hers.

His kisses of years past had been soft and pliant, tender and seducing. In contrast, this one was hard, chastening, a retribution for all the trouble she had caused him and the problems still to come. As he had expected, and, yes, even wanted, she stiffened in his arms and pulled away. Riotous color bloomed in Callie's cheeks. Her breasts rose and fell with every frantic breath she took, and he could feel her heart slamming in her chest. But there was passion in her eyes and a kind of haughty courage in her stance he couldn't help but admire. She was all woman, all passion and temper.

"You're not going to scare me with this he-man act of yours," she vowed, even as she braced her arms between them and he kept his hands upon her waist. "I know you wouldn't hurt me."

Maybe not, Cody thought passionately, but there were times like now when he was treacherously close to falling in love with her all over again, times when he sure wanted to try. Needing to finish what he had started, needing to feel the softness of her slender body crushed against the hardness of his, Cody shifted her close again. Whether she liked it or not, he thought furiously, he was sending her away. And heaven save them both, this appeared to be the easiest, most effective way to do it. "As Max said—" Cody brushed his lips over hers and smiled with satisfaction as he felt her tremble and knew her breath was coming in fast, shallow bursts "—I've changed, Callie. And not," he warned as he buried both hands in the sunflower gold of her hair, "for the better."

No longer was he the young, idealistic kid who believed in the power of love with all his heart. Now he dealt with the tangibles. Desire, which could be sated. Hard work, which was always good for the soul. And land, upon which he made his living. But no more playing games. No more giving his heart. But he wasn't above giving his body, or matching her need, degree by degree.

She averted her head defiantly to the side as his lips forged a steady but determined trail down the softness of her throat. "What is this, then?" she asked in a low, trembling voice. "Revenge?"

"No," Cody corrected softly. "This is revenge."

He bent over her, delivering another long, satisfying, soul-wrenching kiss that had them both trembling from head to toe.

"I'm telling you, Cody, this is not going to work." She put a staying hand on his, keeping him from unbuttoning her blouse, even as she softened against him all the more. "I know you. You're not about to compromise me, especially for dishonorable reasons."

At the moment, with his body aching fiercely and his heart in no better shape, Cody couldn't think of a sweeter way to get his revenge than by making wild, wonderful love to her. He smiled down at her wickedly, gave in to the desire that had been plaguing them both for years now and taunted softly, "Wanna bet?"

Her astonishment at his blatant pronouncement came and went as she kept her eyes on his. "When it comes to sex, I'm still the same innocent girl I was before, Cody."

Cody had been a fool over Callie many times, but he didn't believe that for a moment.

"If you couldn't do it then, when we at least thought we were in love, you sure as heck won't be able to do it now," Callie continued forcefully, with a bravado Cody couldn't help but admire even as he disdained it.

"Aren't you forgetting something?" Cody clasped both hands around her waist and danced her backward, toward a nearby stand of trees. He didn't stop until she was leaning up against a sturdy oak, her arms resting lightly upon his shoulders. "You're not seventeen any longer. And I'm not twenty-four." He braced an arm on either side of her and gazed raptly down into her upturned face, aware that in the time they'd spent apart she had only grown more beautiful. "It doesn't matter what kind of love life or lack of we've had in the past. I'm not going to bend over backward to protect you or treat you with kid gloves anymore, Callie." His voice hardened, as did his attitude. "We're both more than old enough to make love in the cool summer grass, if we so choose."

Callie jerked in an unsteady breath, as shocked as he had meant her to be. The warm blush of color flooded her cheeks. He swiftly noticed she didn't deny wanting him, too. She just didn't want him this way, as part of the price for gaining her part of Uncle Max's legacy. "Just because we're both older n-now..." she stammered, blushing all the more. "Age has nothing to do with this, Cody."

Shifting her arms so that they were no longer between them, and folding her even closer, Cody shook his head in mute disagreement. "Age has everything to do with it," he countered softly. Age was the reason—the only reason—he hadn't made love to her before. Again, and again, and again. But he'd waited, even after their wedding, thinking she should be at least eighteen before he introduced her to the pleasures of his bed. "You're not too young for me anymore, Callie," he rasped as the soft swell of her breasts settled against the hardness of his chest. And then, throwing caution and common sense to the wind, he took her lips again—not roughly this time, but evocatively. Tenderly.

He kissed her until she parted her lips and began to kiss him back, until they lost all track of time, until her knees buckled and she held on to him for dear life. And still it wasn't enough for him. It had never been enough. And it never would be, Cody thought as she whimpered against his mouth and the cellular phone in his saddlebag began to ring.

Damn. Reluctantly, he lifted his head and looked over in the direction of the annoying rings.

Callie shook her head, as if that would make the ringing sound go away. *"What is that?"* Callie gasped as she pulled away, looking tousled and disheveled and—Cody hated himself for noticing—more delectably enticing than he had ever seen her.

"An unwelcome interruption." Frowning, Cody released Callie and, struggling to ignore the unassuaged ache in his body, went to answer his phone.

"Yeah, Cisco... what's up?" Cody listened, and as he did so his mood turned even blacker. Working to control his formidable temper, he tightened his hand on the slim telephone until his knuckles turned white. "Damn it all to hell,'' he said finally, when Cisco Kidd had finished making his report. "Get the chopper here now! Right. See you in a few minutes.''

Callie regarded him anxiously. "What's going on?''

Cody glared at her. The phone call, and the reason behind it, had reminded him of all he would have liked nothing more than to forget. "Like you don't know.''

Her eyes widened in a way that would have won a professional actress an Oscar. "I don't!''

Cody swept up the saddlebag full of camp dishes and paper trash and headed back to the horses. "Gotta hand it to your pa,'' he said as he slung the saddlebag over his horse's back. "He swore he'd get revenge on me, and once again, he's using you to do it.''

Callie stayed clear of the horses. "What the heck are you talking about?''

Cody came around to her side. "This innocent act of yours is getting old, Callie.''

She took a moment to think about that. Her face lost all color. "Cody. My pa is dangerous.''

Cody looked up at the sky and saw the chopper in the distance. He dragged Callie toward the edge of the meadow, where it would land. "And dishonest as hell, as he just proved all over again last night.''

Callie's teeth worried her bottom lip as the chopper gently landed a distance away. "No one's hurt, are they?''

Cody sighed, all too aware of just how easy it would be for him to get sucked into the turmoil of Callie's life again. He was going to have to work harder to keep his guard up. "When your pa and your brother are involved,'' he prophesied darkly, "someone always gets hurt. This time, it just happens to be Gil Guthrie.''

"WHO IS HE?'' Callie inquired anxiously as, heads bent low, they raced to the chopper.

Cody let out his breath wearily as he and Callie ducked the rotor blades. "One of the hired hands who works for me," he yelled.

Once inside the chopper, Cody gave the pilot the thumbs-up sign.

As they went aloft, the roar of the engine and the rhythmic whirring of the blades made it impossible for Callie to ask him any more questions. So Callie was forced to fidget and wonder as they flew over the sprawling Silver Spur Ranch. Had Buck and Pa done this? And if so, what was she going to do? Tell Cody she'd seen Buck that morning, face his everlasting wrath and perhaps put him in danger, too? Or keep silent and pray she'd find a way to protect the man she had once loved more than life from harm again?

Ten minutes later, they were at the scene of the crime.

Bringing order to the melee was the fifty-something Shorty, Cody's bowlegged, frank-spoken crew boss. As Callie had expected, Cody sprang into action immediately.

"What happened?" Cody demanded as he bent over the cowboy leaning up against the side of the Silver Spur cattle barn, where, Callie had quickly deduced, the crossbreeding operation was centered and the prize bulls kept.

The complex, with its brand-new barn and several adjacent, fenced-in pastures, was located in the central part of the ranch, surrounded by rolling countryside. A gravel road led to the crossbreeding center. At one end of the barn there was a small room, similar to a dorm room, where the three cowboys working that part of the ranch bunked.

Gil Guthrie, the injured cowboy, gingerly felt the discernible lump on the back of his head. "I heard a commotion just before dawn and I got up to see what was happening. I musta been hit over the head 'cause the next thing I know, I'm waking up on the ground."

"Which is where we found him at dawn," Shorty, the crew boss, said.

Cody hunkered down beside Gil, who, Callie decided, couldn't have been much more than eighteen. "We better get you to a hospital and have you checked out."

"Sorry, Cody," Gil moaned, more concerned about the theft than himself. "I know how much that new bull of yours was worth—"

"Don't you worry about that," Cody reassured Gil grimly. "I'm just glad you weren't hurt any worse."

So was Callie. She watched as Cody and two other cowboys helped Gil onto the chopper. Callie turned to Shorty. She hated to bother him, since the bowlegged crew boss seemed preoccupied with figuring out how such a calamity had happened at the Silver Spur, but she had to know.

Callie eased closer to Shorty. Not sure the grizzled cowboy would even answer her, she folded her arms in front of her. "Gil said that bull was worth a lot of money. How much money?" Callie asked. She didn't want to think what she was thinking, but if there was money and theft involved, she had no choice but to suspect Buck.

Shorty and the other hands held on to their hats as the chopper took off once again. Once it cleared the barns, Shorty turned back to Callie. He gave her a considering once-over. "A hundred grand now, probably twice that when he gets to be full grown," he answered her question.

Cody, who was in earshot of the tail end of Callie's conversation with Shorty, joined them in their study of the pickup tracks leading to the corral behind the barn. "Though how they loaded Zeus up without getting hurt themselves . . ." Cody queried out loud with a pointed look at Callie.

Callie turned away from the suspiciousness in Cody's gaze. She caught a glimpse of something glistening in the early morning sunlight. Wordlessly, she knelt and pointed to the empty medicine bottle lying hidden in the grass. Although the label had been torn off, Callie recognized it as the kind of bottle used to fill syringes. "This is how."

32:00

"NO PRINTS," the deputy from the county sheriff's office said after he had finished dusting the medicine bottle for fingerprints. "Whoever used this must've been wearing gloves."

"Why does that not surprise me?" Cody said with a sigh.

"I'll send it to the state crime lab and have it analyzed for contents, but we both know it was probably some sort of tranquilizer."

Cody nodded his agreement as he studied the tire tracks leading away from the edge of the pasture. "You're right. There'd be no way to get the bull out without one." He turned back to the deputy. "You'll fax me the results?"

"Sure thing, but it's liable to take a while. Meanwhile, I'd advise you to get the word out to the Montana Cattle Raisers Association. In case that new bull of yours turns up for sale elsewhere."

"Will do." Cody shook hands with the deputy and thanked him for coming out so quickly.

Cody and Callie climbed back into the chopper, which had returned from the hospital, for the ride back to the bull's-eye parcel of land to retrieve their horses.

"You blame me for the theft, don't you?" Callie said after she and Cody were back on the ground. They untethered their mounts and swung themselves up in the saddle, then started back at a very brisk pace, Callie following Cody's lead and riding beside him.

Cody settled his hat more firmly on his head, so the brim was very low across his brow. "Let's look at the facts here, Callie. You're back in my life for what...fifteen hours now, and already it's costing me a hundred grand and the health of one of my best ranch hands."

"I was with you last night—all night!" Callie shot him an outraged glance as his decrepit cabin came into view. "You know that!"

Cody kneed his horse and picked up the pace. "Perhaps we should check for tire tracks around the cabin anyway."

Callie's stomach churned as she thought about Buck's visit to her outside the "powder room" early this morning. Undoubtedly there were tire tracks there somewhere, ones that didn't belong to Cody's pickup truck. Cody couldn't find them. She knew Buck would follow through on his threat. Nothing had changed since she'd run away all those years ago. Buck and Pa still had their hooks in her, but she wouldn't let them get to Cody. It would be too dangerous for Cody to find out Buck was around. She had to do everything in her power to prevent that from happening. Which meant she was going to have to distract him.

Directing her horse to canter slightly ahead of his, which was something sure to annoy him, she jumped on the first source of conflict that came to mind. "We have more pressing things to attend to this morning, Cody."

"Such as what?"

"I was hungry and cold last night," Callie informed him in a tone she was sure would set his teeth on edge. She tossed her head haughtily. The long layers of her hair swirled around her face. "If we're going to continue to live in that cabin together for the next day and a half, I insist we go into town so that I can at least get myself a sleeping bag."

Cody nudged his horse a bit to keep abreast of her. "And if I say no?"

Keeping a firm hold on the reins, Callie squared her shoulders militantly. "Then I'm out of here now and you lose the cattle operation Uncle Max willed to you. The choice is entirely up to you."

Not waiting for his reply, she slowed her horse to a walk and headed for the barn. As she had expected, he quite irritably followed suit. "Assuming I agree to go, how'd you plan to pay for it?" Cody demanded.

"I have my own money, my own credit cards," Callie said, reining her mount in altogether. She wasn't sure how much cash she had left, but she could charge the rest. "I told you I had been working."

Cody looked around suspiciously as they dismounted and hitched their horses next to the barn. Callie strode toward the cabin, but Cody headed back in the direction of the outhouse. She followed suit, intending to escalate their argument to an unreasonable degree if necessary, but before she could think of something suitably incendiary to say, he had spotted and picked up the cigarette butt Buck had thrown aside. He held up the barely smoked cigarette for her to see. "Looks like someone has been here."

With a great deal of effort, Callie faked a carelessness she couldn't begin to feel. "You're imagining things."

"No," he replied evenly. "I'm not."

"Cody, come on. Forget about the disturbed grass. I probably did that myself when I was stumbling around trying to find the powder room this morning."

"What about the cigarette butt?"

Callie shrugged. There was no point in trying to pretend it was hers; Cody already knew she abhorred smoking. "It could have been here for days."

Cody examined the evidence carefully. "In near mint condition? Not very damn likely."

Callie swallowed. They had to get out of here before Cody turned up anything else Buck had left in his wake. "Let me go in and get my purse and let's get going to town, now, Cody."

"You get your purse," Cody encouraged with a distracted air, already heading off toward the woods directly behind them. "I'm going to have a look around." Completely ignoring her, he headed off.

Callie frowned. She could follow him now or sidetrack him again by doing something really outrageous, like trying to drive his pickup truck.

Intending to look for his truck keys as soon as she had retrieved her purse, she headed for the cabin. Her purse was right where she'd left it, on the sofa. Intending to count her cash, she sat down and rummaged through her wallet.

Only there was a problem, she soon realized with mounting frustration. There was no cash in her wallet. No credit cards. Nothing except an old photo of her and Cody taken in one of those amusement park booths. Had Cody done this as a way of limiting her options? she wondered, confused. Or had Buck? Did she even dare ask, when doing so might tip him—if innocent—to the fact someone else really had been there? And what if that in turn led him to Buck?

Swearing beneath her breath at this predicament she found herself in, she stuffed her nearly empty wallet back in her purse and stood up. She had just started her search for the keys when she heard what sounded like someone...something... moving around in Cody's bedroom.

Oh, no. If it was Buck, if he'd bunked down in here, she was going to beat the stuffing out of him!

Agitatedly, Callie started for the bedroom.

Peeked in.

The covers on Cody's bed were deliciously mussed, but it was empty. The room, however, was not. There was an indignant snort from the corner as the beastly intruder staggered menacingly to his feet. Callie took one look at those wild black eyes and let out an earsplitting scream.

Chapter Four

That scream sounded like it had come from Callie, Cody thought, alarmed. As he heard her scream again, he abandoned his search for further signs of disturbance around the cabin, did an about-face and raced toward the sound.

As he reached the cabin doorway, Callie let out another bloodcurdling scream from within. There were several crashing sounds . . . like furniture falling. "Stay away from me!" Callie shrieked hysterically. "Cody—for heaven's sake, where are you? Cody, please! Help me!" she shrieked again.

Through the open portal, Cody caught a glimpse of Callie leaping onto the rumpled covers of his bed. This was followed by an enraged, animalistic snort as the missing Brahman bull lurched drunkenly toward her, a tranquilizer dart still sticking out of his rump. Cody had no time to ruminate on how or why his prize bull had ended up in his cabin. It was plain to see the one-third-grown, four-hundred-pound bull had a heck of a drug-induced hangover and had not appreciated coming to in Cody's bedroom. Nor, given the size of the headache the bull had to have, was he appreciating Callie's startled screams.

"Callie. Be quiet. Now," Cody said.

Callie shot him a baleful look. "About time you got here," she muttered cantankerously beneath her breath, although she was trembling so hard the ancient box springs of his bed were creaking. "What took you so long?"

The bull snorted and pawed the ground.

Cody grabbed a silk shirt from the pile of Callie's clothes on the sofa. He whistled shrilly. "Hey, Zeus! Over here!"

Zeus craned his large black head around. Snorted again.

"Just get him out of here," Callie said, trembling all the harder.

"I'm trying," Cody said, waving her shirt as if he were a bullfighter in the ring. He whistled again, even more shrilly.

Snorting and pawing, the bull staggered toward Cody.

Cody figured all he had to do was get the bull outside, then race back in. When it was safely grazing in the pastureland surrounding the cabin, he could get to the short-wave radio in his truck or the cellular phone in his saddlebag and call for more help.

Cody backed out the door, still waving the shirt. Zeus followed, crashing into the table as he went. Unfortunately, Zeus got only as far as the doorway, when he changed his mind, swung around again, crashing into the sofa as he did so, and headed back for Callie, who was still standing on the bed.

She screamed. Zeus picked up speed. Misjudging the width of the portal, he rammed his shoulder drunkenly into the bedroom door frame, which enraged him all the more.

Zeus backed up and, still glaring at Callie, prepared to charge the bedroom again. Cody swore, wishing he had a rope and lasso handy, but he didn't, so he was just going to have to make do.

Grabbing a handful of Callie's clothes, Cody hurled them at Zeus, one right after another. A shirt landed on Zeus's head, another covered his neck, a pair of jeans fell down to tangle in the struggling, frightened bull's front legs. Snorting, shaking, the bull backed up and tried to get the clothing off his face. When it all tumbled to the floor, Cody hurled more.

Seeing her opportunity, Callie raced past the bull to Cody's side. Figuring it was easier to get themselves out of the cabin than the bull at this point, Cody grabbed her hand, tugged her through the doorway and slammed the oak door behind them. "Now what?" Callie gasped.

"There's a rope in the barn. I'll get it while you get on the cell phone in my saddlebag. Dial one-zero—that'll connect you to Shorty. Explain what's happened, and tell him we need help. Pronto. Probably another tranquilizer dart, too."

Callie ran off. Cody disappeared into the barn. He raced out again, a lasso in his hand. "Shorty's on his way," she told him.

"Great."

"Where are you going?"

"Back in to get Zeus!"

It infuriated her to see him willfully risking life and limb. "Cody, you can't go in there. Zeus is furious. He could trample you or gore you."

His expression pure steel, Cody shrugged off her warning. "He'll calm down once he has a lasso around his neck."

Desperate to protect him, Callie threw herself across the front door. "I'm not going to let you go in there alone!"

The look in his eyes no less determined, Cody merely slung the lasso over his shoulder, picked her up by the waist and shifted her to the side. In a tone that was not to be denied, he barked out his orders. "Go back to the pickup, climb inside and wait for me, Callie. You'll be safe enough there." Without sparing her another glance, he yanked open the door and stepped inside.

IF CODY THOUGHT THE IDEA of running was an option for her, he didn't know her at all, Callie thought, setting her chin. If Cody was going headlong into a battle with a demented, drugged-out bull, he wasn't going in alone.

She owed it to Uncle Max to see that his nephew didn't get hurt or killed in such an ignominious way.

She rushed in after him. Cody did not look happy to see her. "This is not the way you follow orders, Callie," he murmured, his mouth thinning to a disapproving line as he gathered the lasso in hand and moved slightly to the left.

"So it isn't," Callie murmured right back.

Watching as Zeus backed into a table and sent it crashing, Callie leaned down, ever so slowly, and reached for her now empty duffel bag. "On the count of three, I'll distract him, you lasso. One . . . two . . . three." Callie hurled the suitcase so it hit just in front of Zeus. Startled, Zeus backed up just as the lasso swung easily around his neck. Cody tightened the loop. Zeus snorted and tried to go in the opposite direction, then, as his wind was systematically cut off, went promptly down on his side. Callie looked at Zeus nervously. He looked ready to get up and charge again at any minute. "Isn't this the place where you normally tie his legs together with the rest of the rope?" she asked in a trembling undertone.

Cody kept his eyes locked with Zeus's and shrugged. "If he were a calf and we were getting ready to brand him, yeah. We don't do that with an animal this size, 'less of course we got a death wish, and I don't."

Zeus started to move. Cody tightened his grip on the rope and stayed where he was. Zeus, having evidently figured out he was not going to win this battle with Cody, stayed where he was, too, panting loudly.

"Now what?" Callie whispered, trying not to let herself get spooked by the wildness in Zeus's eyes.

"We wait for reinforcements."

As if on cue, a pickup roared into the yard. It was followed by another pickup, dragging a small horse trailer. Shorty hopped out of the first truck and came running, a tranquilizer dart in hand. Cody gave the nod. Shorty aimed. The dart hit Zeus in the rump, just below the first. They waited. Within a minute, Zeus's eyes were drooping.

The dangerous light in them faded. To Callie's amazement, Zeus looked gentle as a lamb. While the bowlegged Shorty turned around and barked out orders to the ranch hands that had accompanied him, Cody turned to Callie.

"Nice work," Callie told Cody. Though her arm and shoulder were aching from her initial tangle with the bull, and his cabin was trashed.

Cody did not look pleased, with either the respect she accorded him or the situation. "I thought I told you to go to the truck," he reminded her harshly, as if a few cruel words could erase whatever camaraderie they had just felt.

So, now that things were back on an even keel and they were safe, they were no longer partners, Callie thought. "I thought I told you not to go in there alone," Callie shot back, mocking his irascible tone. She knew what he was thinking; he didn't want any of the men to think he had been rescued by anyone, never mind the new bride-to-be and coinheritor he considered nothing but a noose around his neck. He didn't want her thinking she could be of any benefit to him whatsoever. Well, that was just too bad, she thought furiously. She had helped Cody, just as he had helped her, and she didn't care who knew about their unwitting and unwilling partnership in temporarily subduing the abducted bull.

The shadows around his eyes deepening, Cody dropped the rope and strode out of the cabin. "You don't give the orders around here."

"Neither do you," Callie asserted, fast on his heels.

"That's news to us," Shorty put in.

Cody wheeled on him, for a second looking every bit as dangerous as Zeus. Shorty, however, did not look intimidated. Which in turn made Callie wonder at the relationship between them. "Shorty, stay out of this," Cody growled.

"Sure thing, Cody," Shorty said with a shrug. "C'mon, fellas, help me get this bull loaded into the truck." With four of them against the newly tranquilized bull, they managed it in short order.

Soon enough, Cody and Callie were alone again. The yard around the cabin seemed awfully still, considering the commotion that had been. They squared off awkwardly. The silence stretched out between them. "Since you were here, and you did lend a hand, I suppose I ought to thank you," Cody said grudgingly at last.

Callie nodded. "Your thanks is accepted." Unable to bear the warring emotions in his eyes any longer, Callie turned. Suddenly, she was feeling a little shaky. Her knees buckled. She felt herself pitching forward.

Before she could do more than draw a breath, Cody was there to catch her. "Sit down," he ordered gruffly as he pushed her onto the sofa, but his hands were gentle on her shoulders. "Put your head between your knees."

"I don't—"

His breath was warm against her cheek as he pushed her down and held her there. "Just do it, Callie, before you flat-out faint on me."

As the room spun around her, Callie gave a low, tortured groan. Maybe this would be best.

She closed her eyes, letting the blood rush to her head. She heard Cody moving around behind her. Somewhere in the bedroom. The sound of a dresser drawer being yanked open, shut. His footsteps neared again. He sat down beside her, the sofa cushions shifting with his weight. "Why didn't you tell me you were hurt?" He sounded annoyed again.

"Because I'm not." Deciding she'd been weak and silly long enough, Callie straightened. Then found she was dizzy all over again, this time for an entirely different reason. As Cody looked her over carefully, then fingered the rip in her shoulder seam, she felt herself quickly becoming both desirous and ambivalent once more.

"Then what do you call this?" he demanded softly.

Callie looked where he was touching. Fighting her reaction to his nearness, she drew in a sharp breath.

His mouth softened as he flipped open the lid of the first-aid kit. "That's a mean-looking cut you've got there."

Callie swallowed. "It's nothing."

"It still needs to be cleaned." As if it were the most natural thing in the world, he took hold of the ripped fabric and with a sharp tug and a brutal tearing sound widened the rip another several inches in all directions.

The thought of being in any state of undress with him, for whatever reason, made her nervous. Panic warred with desire as the blood rushed through her veins; she wasn't ready for this and neither was he. "Cody, for heaven's sake! Did you have to be so barbaric?"

"You're telling me you want to take your shirt off and do it that way?" Half his mouth curved up in a quarter grin as he caught her shocked look, then drawled, "I didn't think so."

Back on task, he was already ripping open a packet of antiseptic.

"I can carry on myself now," Callie insisted, putting up both hands to stop him.

He shook his head in a way that said the argument was closed. "There's no way you can reach your shoulder blade, never mind see what you're doing." He brushed her hands away, pushed them away from the scrape, then moved the cool cloth over the three-inch-long injury. Finished, he brought out a tube of antibiotic cream and, apparently unable to resist, gave her the kind of roguish look she'd been expecting from a hellion like him all along. "Besides, technically anyway, I'm your husband, remember?"

Callie inched forward as he smoothed on the cream. To no avail. The feel of his hands on her skin, caressing so gently, was devastating.

"Forget the technicalities, Cody. As I told you last night, we don't owe each other anything." *At least not anything like this.*

"Oh . . . considering there was a bull just in here—a stolen bull—I think I do owe you, Callie. A lot."

She didn't like the sound of that drawl. She pushed him away. "You're not insinuating I had anything to do with Zeus being dumped in your bedroom!" Was he?

Cody's mouth curled sardonically. "Let's put it this way. He's never visited here before."

"So?"

Cody stood and shrugged his broad shoulders uncaringly. "So you're here less than a day and suddenly he's stolen and then makes an appearance here. In my cabin." Throwing all his weight onto one hip, he towered over her menacingly. "Mighty coincidental, wouldn't you say?"

The depth of her anger invigorating her with new strength, Callie leapt to her feet. "As a matter of fact, I would." She moved forward until they were standing toe-to-toe and slapped her hands on her hips. Tossing her hair back, she smiled up at him with saccharine intent. "Not that this plan of yours is going to work, Cody."

His eyes were smoldering. He let his glance slide down over the rip in her blouse and the curves of her breasts before dragging his gaze ever so slowly and condescendingly back to her face. "And what plan might that be?" he asked in a soft, dangerous voice.

Callie should have been angry at the way he was treating her. She was hurt instead and she faced him boldly. "To scare me off the ranch."

His head shot up. "By putting a bull in my own cabin?" he asked incredulously.

Callie straightened the hem of her shirt with shaking fingers and covered her shoulder as best she could. "You certainly took your time about coming back in here when I first came face-to-face with Zeus. You had no qualms about sending me in first." Even as she said it, it sounded ludicrous. Cody was not a back stabber. If he had wanted to harm her, he would have done so head-on.

Cody faced her grimly. "I did not set you up to get hurt in here."

She studied him. "I believe that. I don't know why, but I believe that."

"Maybe because you know me."

"No, Cody." Callie shook her head. "I never knew you. Because if I had—" Callie stopped herself abruptly. She was revealing too much, and, in the process, setting herself up for even more hurt.

"What?"

She inclined her head at her shoulder, swallowed hard as she reined her feelings in. "I just wouldn't have expected you to take care of me after all that's happened this morning." For a second there, he had been behaving almost like a gentleman.

Cody snapped the lid shut on the first-aid kit. His entire body was rigid with tension. He looked at her as if she had stolen his control, sabotaged his strength. "It's no more than I'd do for any of the hands," he managed to say.

Keep telling yourself that, cowboy.

Just because he was short on manners didn't mean she had to forfeit hers. "Thanks, anyway," Callie said. She didn't know if it was the spirited exchange with Cody giving her strength, but suddenly she was feeling much better. She looked around, unable to believe the damage the bull had done in a few short minutes. And this was a baby bull. She couldn't imagine working with a full-grown bull of thirteen hundred to fourteen hundred pounds.

She shook her head at the mess.

"Now what?" Cody asked, his manner both abrupt and impatient.

Callie regarded him thoughtfully as something very important dawned on her. She stepped closer. "You don't seem very upset for someone who's just had his cabin trashed, all his furniture—what little of it there was—destroyed," she said slowly. Even the sofa they had been sitting on had huge chunks of upholstery ripped out of the sides and back of it.

Yet Cody hadn't once lamented any of it.

Cody gave her a grin. "That's because I don't live here."

THE EXPRESSION OF SHOCK, disbelief and outrage on her face was almost worth it, Cody thought. Though he hadn't meant to give himself away just yet.... Not that this surprised him, either. Callie had a way of evoking emotions in him he didn't even know he had, never mind had any desire to express.

"What do you mean you don't live here?" Callie demanded, her emerald eyes flashing with the fire of righteous indignation.

"Just that. This isn't my home." When she continued to stare at him in rigid disbelief, Cody continued with a casualness meant to provoke. "I live in the original ranch house, where Uncle Max settled when he founded the Silver Spur."

"And that ranch house is where?" Callie knew there were numerous residences on the Silver Spur, some more modern than others. But she didn't know the history of any of them.

"It's in the middle of the cattle operation, about two miles or so from the bunkhouse and the barns, ensuring me, and in the past the family, privacy from the hands."

Rich color flowing into her cheeks, Callie held her arms aloft, the motion lifting and molding the shirt against the soft curves of her breasts. "Then what is this?" she demanded with disdain.

Watching her, Cody was filled with the desire to take her in his arms again. No matter what the past, or her betrayal, he wanted to kiss her senseless. Until she gave him all that she had denied him before. And told him she loved him and only him. And that, he didn't understand. He had told himself over and over he would never forgive her what she had done. Was it possible the shock of seeing her again...touching her...kissing her...had ripped away the protective layers he'd erected to make sure he would never be hurt again?

Callie lowered her arms again. Her breasts heaved with every angry breath as she waited for his reply. Cody had half a mind not to tell her the history of the place, but also knew that she could get the information from just about anyone on the ranch. So it might as well be him. He didn't want her asking questions of the hands or creating more of a stir than she already had.

Having recovered his senses, Cody moved away from her and leaned against the far wall. "This, Callie, is an old cowboy outpost that predates the First World War." He inclined his head at the sturdy walls. "It was originally designed for shelter in inclement weather when cattle were out on the range."

Her green eyes lit up with a compassion he neither expected nor wanted. "But it's so primitive, Cody," Callie said softly.

Cody shrugged and shoved his hands in the pockets of his jeans. He knew this was something she could find out, too, yet he wanted to tell her himself. "After you disappeared on me, I found myself wanting to be alone—a lot. That was damn near impossible at the ranch house at the time—there was always someone dropping by to check up on me. So I started coming out here for days at a time." *So I could make sense of what happened with you, figure out how— and more importantly, why—I'd been duped.*

"Max didn't worry about you?" Callie asked, the gentle understanding in her eyes enough to make him want to drag her back into his arms and hold her there for a very long time.

Cody inhaled a ragged breath. No one had offered him such simple comfort in a long time. He was finding it hard to resist. "He understood that if he and the others didn't leave me alone I'd disappear altogether," Cody revealed shortly, wishing Callie would stop trying to tear down the defenses he'd spent years building. "So he passed the word I wasn't to be disturbed," Cody finished.

Callie fastened the sweet, serious warmth of her gaze on his face. "Weren't you lonely?" she asked quietly.

For you, Callie. For what we'd lost. Realizing what he'd just admitted to himself, Cody shook his head in silent regret. He'd thought he was over all that. Knowing it still cut at him deeply, astonished and disturbed him. She had no right coming back into his life, dredging all this up. Mouth tightening, Cody turned away from Callie and the understanding he saw in her eyes. He knew better than to let her get close to him again. Because if he trusted her again, and she let him down, as he half feared she would, it would destroy him. That being the case, he was going to have to find a way to make sure that she knew it would never work, too. Despite what Max may have wished.

"I found out the rustic atmosphere suited me just fine," Cody continued with feigned nonchalance. Needing respite from her gaze, he found his hat and lowered the brim over his eyes. "When I ran out of supplies or wanted electricity and so on, I went back to the original ranch house, the one where my brother, Trace, and my sister, Patience, and I first lived with Uncle Max. And where Uncle Max had lived before building the new state-of-the-art ranch house where Trace and Susannah are going to live."

Cody looked at Callie's face and knew he'd put some distance between them.

Callie stared at him furiously. "You duped me into thinking this was it! That this was where you had been living...where I was going to have to live if I married you again!"

Cody grinned wordlessly, admitting the chicanery, and Callie flew at him, completely incensed.

Cody caught her arms before she could do any serious damage and held her against him. "I never said this was where I lived full-time," he replied silkily, finding the look on her face almost worth it. "You jumped to that conclusion all by yourself."

Callie yanked herself free, picked up a boot and sent it sailing at his head. Glorious color filled her pretty face. "You are no gentleman, Cody McKendrick!"

Cody ducked to avoid the flying object. It was all he could do not to chuckle at her spirit. "That's not what you said a few minutes ago when I was taking care of the cut on your shoulder!" He lifted a disparaging brow meant to incense her, glad their relationship had landed back in an arena he could handle. "In fact, from the way you were looking at me, you seemed to think I was more than gentlemanly enough," Cody continued, deliberately provoking her all the more. And that, too, had been a problem. Prior to Callie's return to his life, he'd had no problem at all keeping women at arm's length. In the act of protecting and caring for Callie he was becoming more chivalrous again.

He had deliberately been living the life of a hermit. He was not sure he wanted to come back to life again in the way Callie was urging him to. He was not sure he wanted to risk getting hurt again. And she could hurt him. Probably worse this time than she already had.

"A few minutes ago, I thought you had a heart in there somewhere. Now I know I was wrong," Callie stormed.

"And you, Callie, are just as young and immature. But I can handle you this time," Cody said confidently. "Because this time I know who and what you are!"

Callie grabbed up what was left of the clothes from her sparsely packed duffel bag. They were muddy, ripped and smelled like Zeus. "On top of everything else, the only clean clothes I had left are ruined! I've got nothing to wear!"

One glimpse of her soft white skin had told Cody that he did not want her to go around wearing that ripped shirt, either, even if she once again misinterpreted his reason for helping her. "You can borrow something of mine," he said gruffly, telling himself it was no big deal. "I've got plenty of shirts back at the ranch house." A ranch house she had never seen, because during the precious three months they'd dated, they'd spent all their time at Pearl's and on the range.

"I don't— Fine." Callie stopped and, with what looked to him like a great deal of effort, brought herself up short. She raised both hands in a testy gesture of surrender. "I'll take whatever I can get my hands on. Let's just get going."

Figuring they'd stayed more than long enough, Cody decided her idea made sense. He made a sweeping gesture with his hand. "After you."

Chapter Five

"This is where you live?" Callie stared at the white, two-story ranch house with the cranberry red shutters. Victorian in style, with a high pitched roof and painted wood siding, the decades-old ranch house sported long, narrow windows and a raised front porch that ran the width of the house and was edged by a waist-high railing. The house was at the end of a long, tree-lined gravel lane and surrounded by a variety of evergreen shrubs, badly in need of pruning. Wildflower-strewn meadows edged the picket-fenced front yard, and beyond that were woods.

"Officially, yes," Cody replied as he parked in front of the house, which was, as he had promised, a good two miles from the bunkhouse and the rest of the cattle operation. "Is this more to your liking?"

Callie sensed the question was some kind of test. She regarded him, determined to be as honest as she could about as much as she could. "It's better," she allowed frankly, not sure he really wanted to hear the rest of what she thought about his real home on the Silver Spur Ranch.

Cody narrowed his eyes at her. Apparently unable to completely contain his curiosity, he prodded, "But...?"

"You've let it go to ruin a bit, haven't you?" With a disturbed glance, Callie pointed to the flower beds, which were blossomless and choked with weeds.

If Cody felt any guilt about the way he'd let the property go untended, he shrugged it off. "I've got more important things to do than plant flowers," he grumbled irately.

Callie mumbled her dissent unintelligibly, then pointed to the paper taped to his front door. "Let's hope that's not an eviction notice." *For lack of flowers and all forms of tender loving care.*

Cody frowned as he noticed the paper, too. He strode on ahead of her. He ripped the page from the front door.

"What is it?" Callie edged closer and peeked over his shoulder to read the fine, typewritten print.

Cody's scowl deepened ominously. "A bad joke."

Callie lifted her brow. "From?"

"My dear departed Uncle Max, if you can believe that." Cody apparently didn't.

"What does it say?" Callie asked when he shifted, cutting off her view.

Cody read out loud, his skepticism evident. "'Dear Cody, If you are wise, you will swallow your considerable pride and take better care of your bride, as she may need more protecting than you realize.' It's signed, 'Forever watching over you, Uncle Max.'" Frowning his displeasure, Cody handed the computer-generated paper over for her perusal.

Callie looked it over. "Uncle Max was wrong," she muttered.

"About what?"

Because he looked as if he wanted it in his possession, Callie shoved the letter back at him. "I do not need your protection. Or any other man's, for that matter. I am perfectly capable of taking care of myself." And she had been for some time now.

"I'm not so sure about that, Callie," Cody murmured, abruptly looking both distracted and upset.

"Meaning?" Callie snapped her fingers.

"Uncle Max always was at least one step ahead of all of us. Besides, look at what just happened with that bull. Someone obviously wanted us in harm's way."

Callie bit her lip worriedly. As much as she was loath to admit it, Cody had a point. "So you think someone wanted to hurt us?" Or more specifically Cody, since it was his cabin. Someone like Buck and Pa?

Cody gave her a grimly assessing look. "You tell me. Did they?"

"How would I know?" Callie shot back, angry at finding herself accused of being disreputable again. Yet privately, she was worried. If Cody was right, that meant someone was out to get them. She knew Buck and Pa were very capable of mean-spiritedness, particularly where both she and Cody were concerned. The theft of the bull could have been meant as a warning of even more dire things to come unless she changed her mind and cooperated with them in a way she never had before. But there was no sense telling Cody that. He mistrusted her enough as it was.

"Aren't you going to show me inside?" Callie asked anxiously, wanting the subject closed. "I'd like to change my shirt. Actually, I'd like a long, hot bath."

Cody unlocked the door and pushed it open. He motioned her in, then strode on inside. The front hall was long and narrow. Looking the reluctant hellion all the while, he gave her a whirlwind tour of the downstairs. A parlor and study were at the front of the house, both behind closed doors—and the kitchen, dining room and another parlor—this one decidedly less formal and more lived-in—at the rear. Callie had an impression of dark wood and old-fashioned furniture. The placement of lamps, tables, sofas and chairs seemed haphazard at best. Magazines and books were mixed in with CDs, newspapers and personal mail. Dark, heavy velvet drapes shut out the sunlight and added to an overall impression of gloom and disorganization.

"Well?" Cody prompted, able to tell something was on her mind.

"It's very spacious." But not warm or homey at all, Callie thought unhappily. "Sturdy, well built."

"But not as comfortable as you would have expected."

Callie shrugged. Except for his study, which was equipped with computer, fax machine and copier, and the back parlor, which had a television, VCR and stereo system, it looked as if he hadn't updated anything in the ranch house in years.

"There are some advantages to having money, Cody. Having a nice home is one of them." A place that was warm and welcoming and a joy to be in.

"I'm not spending money replacing furniture that is perfectly good," he growled.

Callie hadn't been talking about that, either, but she didn't think he wanted to hear what she would do with this house if it belonged to her, so she kept silent. For now, anyway. She was beginning to understand why Uncle Max had obviously thought Cody needed her in his life. She was beginning to understand what Uncle Max wanted her to do for Cody, if only he would let her.

Upstairs, there were four bedrooms. Cody showed her to a room with a canopy bed covered with a plain white bedspread. "Bathroom's down the hall. Clean towels are in the closet just beside it."

"Where do you bunk?"

"Not here."

As if he had been invited to sleep with her, Callie fumed. "Oh, I know that," she replied with a saccharine smile, then stared at him, still waiting for an answer to the question.

He shifted his weight so it was braced equally on both legs. "In the master bedroom," he said finally.

"Which is where?" Callie asked.

He sighed grudgingly. "At the other end of the hall."

Callie lifted her eyes to his. "You said you'd lend me a shirt?"

Cody nodded. Turning on his heel, he disappeared for a few minutes, then returned, a crumpled flannel shirt in hand. Wordlessly, he handed it to her. "This is the cleanest one I've got. It's been a few days since I've had time to do any laundry."

The soft cloth was redolent with the scent of his cologne and the headier, more masculine scent of his skin.

"But you're welcome to use the washing machine downstairs," Cody continued.

Callie swallowed. "Thanks." It wasn't hot in here but she was suddenly perspiring.

"And while you're at it . . ." He left and returned with a huge pile of filthy laundry and dumped it at her feet. "You can do mine, too."

"I'm not your slave, Cody."

His smug glance was enough to try her patience completely. "No, but you are my wife, at least for the next couple days, so you might as well get used to the long list of chores that come with the job."

Callie humphed and kicked at the huge pile of laundry with the toe of her red cowgirl boot. "I suppose I should be glad you gave me a bedroom to sleep in this time." It was bound to be more comfortable than the sofa she'd slept on a few hours ago.

Cody gave a gusty laugh. "Don't read too much into it. I haven't changed my mind about your character, or shall I say lack of it, one whit." His opinion thusly stated, Cody sauntered off.

"IS THAT A MOUNTAIN of laundry or what?" Pearl asked from the mudroom door.

"Pearl!" Callie dropped the towels in her hand and rushed to greet the woman who had given her her first legitimate job, and through that, the return of her self-respect.

"I hope you don't mind me tracking you down," the fifty-something Pearl said as she let herself in. "I heard you were back and I had to see for myself how you were doing, especially since you'd been hooked up with that rascally Cody McKendrick again.''

"Don't even joke about it."

"Things are that bad?"

Callie shook her head sadly. "He's changed, Pearl."

Unlike the tall, thin Pearl, who still wore her bright red hair swept up into a French twist, just as Callie recalled. In a short pink waitress outfit and white western boots, the bighearted but plainspoken Pearl looked much as she had the day Callie had left her job at Pearl's diner to run off with Cody.

"And not for the better, as we all know and worry over," Pearl said.

Callie sighed and leaned against the washer. Suddenly, she felt so much older than her years again. "Then you know what I'm talking about."

Pearl put an arm around Callie and hugged her. "He never would admit it to anyone, not even Max, but Cody ain't been the same since you left him." Pearl stepped back to give Callie the once-over. "You, on the other hand, are looking mighty fine, gal. You've not only grown up, you've prettied up. And that's saying a lot, 'cause you were no ugly pony when you left here."

"Thanks." Callie blushed.

"It's nothing but the truth."

"You heard about the will . . . and the conditions in it?"

"Shoot. Now that it's been read, everyone in Montana knows about it, I expect. Max always was a wild one."

And, Callie thought, Pearl had always had a crush on Max. She was just surprised the two had never married, as Max had seemed equally devoted to Pearl. But whatever Pearl and Max's relationship had been, the two had kept it very quiet. And very private, at least when Callie had been around.

Callie misted up. "You must be missing Max, too."

She leaned forward to give Pearl another hug.

Tears shimmered in Pearl's eyes. "You're right. I do. But let's not talk about that right now. Let's talk about this crazy situation you and Cody find yourselves in. I admit it's got me a little worried, Max pushing the two of you together this way. Not that the others seem to be faring much better."

Callie set the dials on the washer and turned it on.

She slammed the lid and turned back to Pearl. "Why? What's going on with Trace and Patience and their respective mates?"

Pearl held up a palm. "I don't carry tales from person to person," she declared as if taking a solemn oath. Her voice dropped a conspiratorial notch. "Let's just say they have their hands as full as their little brother, Cody, does."

"Hmm," Callie said as she walked back into the adjacent kitchen.

Pearl nodded at the pot on the stove. "This your doing?"

Callie nodded.

Pearl lifted the lid. "Vegetable soup, straight from the can?"

Callie wrinkled her nose. "I was hungry. I didn't feel like going to a whole lot of trouble."

Pearl rolled her eyes in silent indignation. "Sugar, you will never win Cody's heart this way."

"But—" Callie wasn't sure she wanted to win Cody's heart, not if it meant she had to play tricks and games, even the feminine kind. On the other hand, what was wrong with seeing that the rogue got a little of the tender loving care everyone deserved, especially if said TLC helped Cody return to his former loving self?

"Let's see what we can do to fix it up a little." At home in any kitchen, Pearl quickly found her way around Cody's. In no time, she brought out a potato, some leftover roast beef, a little beef gravy. While Callie diced, Pearl searched the spice rack. "By the time we're done with it, he's going to think it was homemade."

Which was another problem, Callie thought, lest he think she was going to let him get away with his rude, incorrigible behavior. The way Cody was acting, she was not sure she wanted him to think she had gone to any trouble. On the other hand, a great lunch would be nice. And she could always save any leftover soup for later....

"Things must be going okay between you and Cody if you're cooking him lunch," Cisco Kidd observed as he came through the back door into the ranch-house kitchen.

Callie looked at the western-garbed lawyer, who, like her, had been one of Max's unofficial adoptees. The only difference between them was that Cisco Kidd had stayed around to become part of Max's business and personal affairs in an official capacity. "Don't read too much into it," Callie warned sagely.

Immediately interested, Cisco Kidd lifted a brow. "Oh?"

Callie stopped a self-conscious blush dead in its tracks. She held up both hands to ward off further questions. "I'm only fixing Cody lunch because he fixed me breakfast. I don't want to be any more beholden to him than I have to be." She also wanted to be fair, even if Cody wasn't.

Cisco Kidd and Pearl exchanged glances. It was clear, Callie thought, the two were jumping to all kinds of conclusions. "Nevertheless, that is his shirt you're wearing, isn't it?" Cisco Kidd prodded.

Callie sighed and related tiredly, "Zeus—Cody's prize bull—trampled the few other clothes I had with me. I'm going to have to wash and sew before I can wear any of them again."

"You ought to have Cody take you into town to buy some new ones," Pearl said, adding a pinch of thyme to the soup.

Callie ducked her head, loath to admit how little she had in her savings. Working the kind of entry-level jobs she had, she had never seemed to get very far ahead. "I'm a little low on funds," she admitted evasively.

"So?" Cisco Kidd said, as if that were no big deal. "Charge it to his account."

Pearl nodded agreeably. "You are his wife."

Thinking how little that fact meant to Cody, Callie rolled her eyes. "So he said when he handed me that pile of dirty laundry," she muttered dryly.

Cisco Kidd did a double take. He knew her well enough from years past to realize how much she hated taking orders in the domestic realm. "You're washing it?"

Callie tried but couldn't quite hide her amusement as she told her two visitors with mock gravity, "I started right away, with the whites. Of course, they require *lots* of hot water. I hope that doesn't mean that Cody won't have enough for his shower." As the washer in the mudroom switched from the wash to the rinse cycle, there was a corresponding yelp from upstairs.

"Sounds like he's getting the message you wanted to send," Cisco said, slanting a look at the second floor.

Callie's mood turned stormy as she reflected on the past nineteen hours. "I hope so," she said emotionally. "Serves him right for passing off the outpost as his home."

"Actually, that's not so far from the truth," Cisco replied, pulling up a chair at Callie's waved invitation. Cisco exchanged worried glances with Pearl. "I don't know what he's told you, but he's spent a heck of a lot of time out there the past seven years. Isn't that right, Pearl?"

"So much time that I worried about him," Pearl agreed.

Callie was not going to let Max's old friends and trusted confidantes coax her into feeling sorry for Cody. "Why would he do that when he had this house, which is so much nicer?"

Cisco Kidd propped his alligator boots on the bottom rung of another chair. "Max said it was because Cody had never recovered from your botched elopement."

Callie thought of Cody in the firelight, hunkered down in front of the bedroom fire. She thought of him rousing her before it was even light outside, smiling as he cooked her a campfire breakfast as the sun slowly rose in the east. "He looks like he came through in one piece."

"On the outside, maybe," allowed Pearl, who had always been Max's sole female confidante. "On the inside it was a different matter. He swore to his Uncle Max that he'd never give his heart to a woman again, and he hasn't."

Callie paused in the act of stirring the soup, which now looked and smelled homemade. "You're sure about that?"

Cisco Kidd nodded. "The truth is that Cody has been so darn ungallant and unsociable that no woman would go near him, to the point where his Uncle Max had begun to wonder if Cody would ever let himself love again."

Callie wished there was a chance for that to happen. Because if she thought Cody might actually be open to loving her again—loving anyone—it would be so much easier for her to stay and fight.

Aware both Pearl and Cisco Kidd were watching her carefully, Callie shook herself out of her reverie. "About Uncle Max's will. You wrote it for him, didn't you?" When Cisco indicated that was so, she continued warily, "Can it be broken, so that Cody can inherit anyway, even if I don't marry him?"

Cisco Kidd frowned. He put his foot back on the floor and sat forward earnestly. "Listen, Callie, Max really wanted you and Cody to be together."

Callie knew that, but people didn't always get what they wanted. "He also loved Cody," she pointed out. "Max wouldn't want him to be penniless if things between Cody and me didn't work out." Callie looked out the kitchen window and released a troubled sigh.

Cisco Kidd gave Callie a stern look. "What are you saying, Callie, that you don't think things are going to work out between the two of you?" As Max's lawyer and executor of his will, Cisco seemed to think maybe Callie wasn't trying hard enough.

Callie bristled in irritation. Arms folded in front of her, she paced back to the stove. Deciding the soup wasn't cooking fast enough, she upped the burner from low to medium heat. When she was finished, she turned back to face her visitors. "He's changed from when I knew him before."

"So have you, Callie," Pearl said gently. "You're wiser in the ways of the world now, stronger. More independent. If I can see it, so can Cody."

Callie lifted her head. Cisco Kidd was six years her senior, which put him roughly the same age as Cody. She wondered how he saw her. "For the better?" she asked Cisco.

Cisco grinned. "You bet." The way he and Pearl both looked at her, Callie knew she had two allies if she needed them. And she might before this was all over.

"Back to the will." Callie sat at the kitchen table with Cisco and Pearl and got back down to business. "If Cody and I don't marry, according to the will, what happens to the cattle operation?"

"It will revert to a corporation and be managed by that corporation, until which time that corporation is sold."

"What about the profits?"

"Damn, Callie. Ever thought of being an attorney yourself? How do you think of these things?"

Because I have a brother and father who constantly analyze things from every angle. She regarded him impatiently. "Answer my question, Cisco."

"Cody gets the profits."

Callie smoothed a design on the tabletop with her fingertips. "Can he buy the ranch from the corporation?"

Again, Cisco nodded. "If he had the money."

"Does he?"

Cisco didn't answer right away. And from the look on his face, it was clear to Callie that Cisco did not see that as an option. "It would mean getting a mortgage on the land instead of owning it from the outset, free and clear, Callie. It would mean Cody being in considerable debt for the rest of his life."

"But he would still have this place he loves," Callie insisted as her mind raced on ahead to other possible outcomes.

"But he wouldn't have you. Without you, Max was sure Cody could never really be happy," Pearl said.

"Which is why he had me set up his will the way he did," Cisco added.

If only I felt that way, Callie thought. But there were times in the last nineteen hours when she felt that Cody would be so much happier if only she wasn't around. And that in turn made her feel unwanted. She did not like feeling unwanted. In the way.

"Not to mention the fact that you, Callie, would be penniless if it goes down that way," Cisco warned.

But what she stood to gain or lose was the least of her worries, Callie thought.

"Which brings me to my next point," Callie told Cisco. "About the wedding ceremony we had in Mexico. Cody says he doesn't have the marriage certificate. Neither do I." Callie bit her lip worriedly. "Is that a problem?"

Cisco frowned. "It could be, if you want to try and prove you're already married."

"Then our marriage is still legal?" Callie asked. "It's not a sham marriage?" As Cody had implied to her earlier.

Cisco inclined his head thoughtfully. "It's legal to the extent it could be consummated at this point or annulled. Whatever you and Cody want. And you're right to worry about the certificate. You should have it so the situation can be wrapped up properly, either way, at the end of the forty-eight hours Max wanted you to have."

Callie frowned. "If our marriage is already a legal one—and binding—why do we have to show up at the ceremony thirty hours from now to collect on our inheritances? Why not just say we are already married and leave it at that?"

"Because," Cisco Kidd replied in gentle, lawyerly fashion, "Max wanted you and Cody to have a real wedding, with all your friends and family present this time. He felt, at the time he had me draw up the will, that perhaps if you all had stayed here and married instead of running off, as he encouraged you to do, that your marriage to Cody might have worked out the first time around.''

''I don't know about that,'' Callie said, worrying her lower lip again as footsteps pounded in the hallway. As they all looked up in unison, a barefoot, bare-chested Cody strode into the kitchen. He was clad only in a pair of faded, button-fly Levi's that fitted him snugly. Callie bit back a sigh. She had always felt a man clad in nothing but jeans was the sexiest thing.

As for the rest of him, she could see he'd lost no time in getting downstairs to join them. Water still beaded in his beard. His shoulder-length hair was slicked back, away from his face, tied with a rawhide strip at the nape. ''What kind of game are you playing now?'' Cody demanded of Callie gruffly.

Callie saw that the sporadic lack of hot water during his shower had driven home her message that he needed to treat her more kindly if he expected her to do the same. But right now it was time for a little fun....

She splayed a hand across her chest and fixed him with her most innocent look. ''I don't know what you mean.''

Cody glanced at Cisco and Pearl dismissively.

''You don't suppose...the washer had anything to do with it?'' Callie continued in Southern-belle fashion, pulling his leg.

Cody scowled. He knew she had done that on purpose. From the looks of it, he also planned to pay her back. But not, it appeared, while they had company.

Cody turned to Cisco. Apparently convinced he'd made his point to Callie, he now turned his attention to Uncle Max's lawyer. ''What's up?'' Cody asked Cisco, point-blank.

Cisco shrugged and regarded Cody man to man. ''I just dropped by to deliver a message from Shorty. He wants you to know that the ranch hand who was injured this morning was treated and released."

Cody frowned in concern. "Great. What about Zeus? Is he all right?"

Cisco nodded reassuringly. "Yep. He's back in the pen, with two guards and a video cam on him this time. Shorty figured you'd want to know that, too."

Cody's shoulders softened with relief. "I do. Thanks."

"Well—" Cisco Kidd cleared his throat as he leaned over to shake hands with Cody. "Guess I better get a move on and check on Patience and Josh, and Trace and Susannah."

"I'll go with you," Pearl said, also getting to her feet.

"Sure you don't want to stay for lunch?" Callie said to both of their visitors, suddenly eager not to be alone with Cody. Especially after that deliberately-doing-laundry-during-his-shower trick. Suppose he tried to kiss her again and she responded just as wildly as she had last night, or even more so? "There's plenty," Callie continued cheerfully.

"Thanks, but I've got to check on Patience and Trace and their mates." Cisco tipped his hat at her and slipped out the door. Pearl said she had to do the same and headed out after him.

When they were alone again, Cody turned back to Callie. Without warning, Callie's heart was hammering in her chest. "What else did Pearl and Cisco say to you just now?" he asked.

So, he knew they had been talking about him. Callie shrugged. "They were attempting to explain your bad behavior." *I don't think they did.*

Cody stepped closer. Behaving just as unfairly as she had been, he used his height to force her to lean back slightly to look up at him. "I don't see any reason to apologize on my own behalf, and neither should they," he muttered in a low, disgruntled tone.

Callie tilted her head and lifted a dissenting brow. Damn, he smelled good. Like soap and water and that wintry evergreen cologne he had always favored. "I think your Uncle Max might differ with you," she pointed out calmly.

The muscles in his bare chest and shoulders flexed as he folded his arms in front of him. "How so?"

"Max was never rude to a lady."

"You think I've been rude?"

She fixed him with a smile meant to dazzle him silly and perhaps coax him into her way of thinking. "In a word, yes."

"I suppose that means you would change me, and my behavior, if it were in your power."

"Probably," Callie admitted frankly, no longer caring if they were headed for an argument. This needed to be said.

"And how would you start?"

She drew a breath and plunged on recklessly, sure Max would approve. "With the beard. I'd shave it off. You look better without it."

Cody touched a hand to his jaw. "How do you know? You haven't seen me in years," he muttered, running his fingers over his bushy, wheat gold beard.

Callie released a wistful breath and briefly closed her eyes. "I remember your face, Cody." She had dreamed it, night after night. And in those dreams, it was always the same. They were always together. Always happy and in love. She opened her eyes again. "All that beard does is cover it up."

"Fine." Cody shrugged one broad shoulder uncaringly. His ocean blue eyes zeroed in on hers. "But let me make something very clear. You want my beard off, you're gonna have to shave it off."

Chapter Six

28:00

Callie knew a challenge when she heard one. "You don't think I'll do it, do you?" she asserted softly, reading the cool derision in his eyes.

Cody shrugged one broad, bare shoulder. "You said it, not me."

He had just thrown down the gauntlet one time too many, Callie thought. He would soon learn not to do that. She tossed a purposeful smile at him. "All right, we'll do it, as soon as lunch is over."

"You cooked?"

"Soup. And it's great."

Cody made a dissenting sound. Not about to let him get by with that, either, Callie lifted a spoonful of the simmering concoction from the pot on the stove. Keeping one hand beneath the spoon to catch any drips, she blew on it gently, then lifted the spoon to Cody's lips. "Taste it."

Keeping his eyes on hers all the while, he obliged. As the savory mixture melted on his tongue, his eyes lit up appreciatively. "Canned soup never tastes like that when I make it," he murmured, perplexed.

Callie smiled mysteriously. "I'll warm some bread in the oven if you'll set the table," she bartered.

"Deal."

As Cody set out the spoons and napkins, Callie dished up bowls of piping hot soup and carried them to the table. Unable to resist, she asked, "What did your Uncle Max think about your beard?"

Cody filled two water glasses and carried them to the table. "He told me on more than one occasion that I looked like a heathen."

Callie slid the bread in the oven. "So he wanted you to shave it off, too?"

Cody grinned ruefully at the memory. "He thought I'd have had better luck with the ladies if I had."

Callie sank into a chair opposite him and watched as he did the same. "But you didn't."

"It suited me," Cody said as he spread a napkin across his lap and began to eat.

"You miss him, don't you?"

Briefly, Cody's eyes were shrouded in sorrow. "Yes. I do." He fell silent as the timer went off and Callie got back up to remove the bread from the oven. "I know it's only been a few days, but I haven't felt this way since my parents died in that earthquake."

And it was tearing him up inside, Callie thought as she sliced bread for them both and carried it to the table. Sensing he needed to talk about this, she inquired, "How old were you when that happened?"

"Six."

Six. Callie couldn't even imagine what his loss would have felt like. He had been so young...so much a child...a child in need of a parent. She lifted her eyes to his and asked, compassionately, "Where were you living at the time?"

"Butte," Cody replied without inflection, a faraway look in his eyes that was only one of the indicators of the pain he still felt over this. She watched as he blew out a weary breath and pushed on with his story. "My dad had a medical practice there and my mom was a nurse in the local hospital. They had gone down to Mexico City so my dad could demonstrate a new surgical technique he was working on to some doctors there.'' For a second, Cody grew very still. Callie could see him struggling with his emotions.

Shaking his head in silent regret, he went on, ''They were in the hospital when the earthquake hit. Initially, they were one of the lucky ones and were able to get out of the building relatively unscathed. But a lot of others weren't so fortunate.'' Again, he paused, briefly closed his eyes. ''Knowing my folks, they didn't even think about it. They just went back in to deliver medical aid and comfort to whomever they could. Until their luck eventually ran out, too,'' he finished sadly.

Callie could only imagine the horror of what Cody had gone through during that awful time. Still, she wanted to help, even if all she could do for him was to listen. ''How did you find out your parents were gone?'' she asked carefully, wishing they had talked about all this years ago.

''Uncle Max came to the house.'' Cody shook his head, the pain he'd felt then apparently beginning to surface again. ''I knew something was wrong even before he told our baby-sitter he needed to talk to us alone, because Uncle Max practically never left the ranch. But it was days before that would be confirmed for me.''

Cody's expression was so brooding and intent, Callie knew there was more.

''He only told Patience and Trace what was going on. Everyone knew my folks had been caught in a collapsing building during an aftershock and were trapped in the rubble but me. For days I was shut out...feeling there was something terribly wrong...that it was more than just an unexpected communications problem that was keeping my parents from contacting us to let us know how things were going. But everyone kept cheerfully reassuring me that everything and everyone was fine.''

"Only they weren't," Callie said, wishing she could do something to ease the tension in his tall frame and the hurt in his low voice.

"No," Cody confirmed grimly. "They weren't." He pressed his lips together. Again, he had a distant look in his eyes. "By the time the rescue workers were able to reach my parents nearly ten days later, they were both dead, and had been for some time."

"It must have been really hard on all of you," Callie commiserated softly, knowing this was as much, if not more, than Cody had ever revealed about himself to her.

"The worst thing was feeling shut out," Cody replied bitterly. "Like everyone knew the truth of what was really going on but me."

Finished with her soup, Callie put down her spoon and offered what consolation she could. "I'm sure Max only meant to protect you."

The pain in Cody's eyes faded and was replaced by a weary acceptance that tore at Callie's heart. "Whatever his thinking at the time, his actions taught me not to rely on anyone but myself when it comes to discovering and dealing with the truth."

"So that's why you've taken self-sufficiency to new extremes," Callie observed.

Noting Cody was ready for a refill on his soup, she got up to ladle him some more.

"If you don't let yourself rely on anyone else to bring you happiness, you won't find yourself being disappointed. That was true then and it's true now."

Callie put the soup in front of him and sat back down. This seemed a good time to get into his relationship with his whole family. "Surely, after you lost your parents, your brother and sister helped watch over you."

"There's a difference—" He stopped abruptly and began to look annoyed with himself.

"What?" Callie prodded when he seemed loath to go on.

"There's a difference between being watched over and included."

"And they shut you out?"

Cody acknowledged this with a slight nod, explaining, "Patience and Trace were closer in age. They had played together from the crib on. After my parents' death, the two of them were inseparable for years afterward."

"But they were not close to you," Callie said, knowing that must have really hurt.

Cody sighed. "I don't think they deliberately meant to shut me out," he said quietly at last. "They just assumed I was too young to understand or wouldn't be interested in what was happening in their lives. Occasionally they let me tag along with them when they went off somewhere, but most of the time I was politely told to get lost."

"Because you were so much younger," Callie guessed.

"Yes. And couldn't do what they did," Cody allowed.

"And that hurt you?"

"I wouldn't say hurt, exactly." Cody withdrew into himself a little again.

"Then what would you call it?" Callie asked gently, and was rewarded with only silence. But then, he didn't have to tell her his parents' death had had a profound impact on his life. She could see it in his face. "What were you like before your parents died?"

"My memories are sketchy...I was only six...but I think I was a pretty happy-go-lucky kid. I remember being able to talk to just about anyone."

"And after?" Callie prodded.

"After was not good. I was so hurt and angry for being excluded in terms of what was going on that, for a long time after, I didn't talk much to anyone at all."

"Uncle Max must've been worried." *Just like I'm worried about you now.*

Cody shrugged. His expression was grimly nonchalant. "He told everyone more than once that it was just my way of dealing with grief and to leave me alone."

But that wasn't what Cody had needed, Callie thought, then or now. Though there was probably no way that Max, a man who had never had children of his own, could have known that at the time. "And that was okay with you?" she asked as she gathered their dishes and carried them to the sink.

Cody gave her a self-deprecating grin as he stood and followed suit. "To tell the truth, I was kind of like Zeus. So ticked off that I was not really fit for keeping company."

"What about Patience and Trace?" Callie collected the butter and jam and put them back in the refrigerator. "How did they cope with the loss?"

"They moved on, a lot more readily than I did. Or maybe it was just that they were more caught up in the adjustment to ranch life than I was. At the time, we were all city kids. Uncle Max taught us all how to rope and ride and survive out on the range in a blizzard, just in case we ever got caught in one. He kept us pretty busy that first year, and every year after."

Callie looked at Cody and knew it was important she get him thinking about all he had instead of all he had lost. It was important, she thought, that she get him dealing with his grief, not surreptitiously, but out in the open. "I know Max made a lot of mistakes in his dealings with you, but the bottom line is...he loved you very much. And mistakes or no," Callie continued thickly, "that ought to count for something." *Just like what I felt for you—and in some ways still do—ought to count for something.*

Cody drew a long breath, then fell silent, thinking, and the suffering in his eyes began to ease.

Deciding some coffee would be nice, Callie rummaged through the pantry until she found some.

Seeing what she was up to, Cody brought out the sugar and cream and set them both on the table. "What about you? How old were you when your mother died?"

"Fourteen. She'd been ill for quite a while before that. Still, it was a shock," Callie said as she carried the coffee and paper filters back out to the counter. "She and I were a lot alike."

"In what way?" Cody plugged in the automatic coffeemaker and pulled it forward on the counter.

Callie took the water reservoir and added water up to the eight-cup line. "We tended to see things in black and white. They were either right or wrong. My pa and my brother Buck..." Her hands tightening on the water reservoir, Callie paused. She was all too aware they were headed toward dangerous ground. "Well, let's just say they had a whole other way of looking at things," Callie added finally. *One I never could countenance.*

"Did your mother know what kind of man she had married?"

Callie had thought about that herself endless times. "I don't think so," she allowed as she stuffed a paper liner into the filter basket. "Pa was always better when she was alive. He loved her. He didn't want to disappoint her. And he had promised her he would run the hardware store she had inherited from her parents." *And he had,* Callie thought, *he'd run it into the ground.*

Cody watched her measure coffee grounds into the filter. "What happened to change all that?"

"The insurance money he collected upon her death," Callie said as she swung the basket holder shut. Pausing thoughtfully, she switched on the machine.

Comfortable right where she was, she turned around to face Cody and stood there, leaning against the counter. "I don't know if it was the grief or the gambler's instinct that had been in him all along, but Pa had this idea that he could triple the insurance money in a weekend at Las Vegas, if he played his cards right."

Callie shook her head in silent admonition as she recalled, "Buck supported him in the scheme. After that, they had grand plans for moving to California and setting up some sort of fancy nightclub, with a private card room in the back." Callie lifted her hands in a helpless gesture.

"So before I knew what had happened, they'd liquidated everything in the Boise, Idaho store, sold it and the house and packed what was left in a U-Haul trailer."

Cody braced a hand on the counter beside her. His look was unexpectedly gentle and understanding as he studied her upturned face. "You must have been scared to death."

Callie nodded as he looked deep into her eyes, knowing it was true. She had not only missed her mother. Buck and Pa had taken her from the only home she'd ever known. She closed her eyes briefly in remembered misery, then opened them and looked up at Cody again as she told him frankly, "I knew it was a stupid plan from the get-go. I tried to talk them out of it, but they told me to shut up. They weren't interested in my opinion."

She swallowed, and because she needed something to do to keep her hands from trembling, she brought down a couple of stoneware mugs. "The first couple of nights Pa did increase his winnings. I mean they went up and down, but at the end of the night he had more than he'd started with. The third night he lost everything. We got kicked out of the hotel." Just talking about that time made her stomach twist into knots.

At Cody's look of concern, she gave him a watery smile and ducked her head shyly. "I don't know why I'm telling you this." *Especially when it embarrassed her so much.*

"Maybe because I need to hear it," Cody retorted gravely.

Noting the coffee had stopped brewing, he quickly filled their two mugs, then took her hand and led her over to the kitchen table. They sat down opposite each other. "What happened next?" he asked, reminding her that he hadn't met her until three years later, when she was seventeen.

Callie stirred cream and sugar into her coffee. She figured they might as well get as much as possible out in the open in case she had to tell Cody the whole truth later, because it was the only way to save him. "We drove up to Denver. I wanted us all three to look for work." Callie paused, her lips tightening in disapproval. "But Pa and Buck weren't interested in any more dead-end jobs. Instead, they worked out this pool hall scam and hustled enough to get us out of Denver." Callie drew a steadying breath and took a sip of the aromatic brew. "From then on it was just one con or scam after another."

And the scams had gotten more complex and criminal with every turn. And for Callie that was an embarrassment and shame she would carry to her grave.

Looking completely relaxed in his shirtless state, Cody folded his arms in front of him, leaned toward her and studied her intently. "You had nowhere else to go, no one to turn to?" Surely, he seemed to feel, she could have done something.

Callie shrugged. "Buck and Pa were the only family I had left. I wanted to love them. I think maybe at one time I did." But looking back, she could see she should have done something, too, even if it had meant carting herself off to the child welfare authorities.

"But you don't love them now?" Cody guessed, pausing to take a drink of his coffee.

Callie couldn't and wouldn't lie to Cody about that. "You can't love someone you don't respect," she replied quietly.

He nodded slowly, put his mug down. "Do you ever have any regrets about what happened to us?"

Judging by the look in his eyes, he was feeling as confused about being thrown together this way as she was. He liked it and he didn't. Most of all, though, he wanted to find peace. As did she. They had both been carrying the burden of their breakup and sham marriage for too long. "I wish we'd waited till we were a little older to run off," she said frankly. And thought wistfully, *Maybe it would have worked out if we had.* "What about you?"

"I wish that, too. Maybe then—" He shrugged and his voice trailed off.

She knew he didn't want to go on, but Callie wasn't about to leave it at that, not when they had already talked about so much. "You think it would've made a difference if we had stayed here and gotten married or simply waited for a less stressful time to commit to each other?" she ventured.

"Don't you?" Cody shot right back.

"I don't know." Callie studied her hands. So much had been taken from her already. She hated to let go of the last of her illusions, or find out she and Cody were not meant to be together after all, which was, she knew, what they were risking in trying to take this any further. She leveled a contemplative look at Cody and admitted honestly, "I just wish we had talked this openly then."

"Me, too," Cody agreed gently. "I think it would've made a difference."

Maybe it would still make a difference, Callie thought optimistically, knowing she felt better already.

"And speaking of differences—" Callie pushed away from the table cheerfully "—we better get to that shave." *Before you change your mind.*

Not waiting for his reply, Callie hurried up the stairs. Three minutes later, she returned with a washcloth and towel over one arm, a pair of small barber scissors she'd found in the medicine cabinet, an old-fashioned straight razor and some shaving powder in a barber's mug with a brush.

Still barefoot and bare-chested, Cody was straddling a kitchen chair. His brawny arms were folded over the ladder back of the chair.

"I didn't know guys used this kind of razor anymore," Callie said as she set her barber supplies out on the table.

"Most don't." Cody eyed her skeptically as she began to get set up.

"Then?" Callie cast Cody a questioning glance as she moved to wrap the towel around his shoulders.

"Patience gave it to me for Christmas a couple years ago. She knew I'd thrown my other razors away when I decided to stop shaving and she thought the novelty of trying that straight razor might tempt me to shave off my beard."

"But it didn't," Callie guessed.

"Nope."

He eyed the scissors she'd brought down. "Planning to give me a new haircut, too?"

His face showed no clue as to what he thought of that idea.

Callie moved to the sink. "I will later, if you want. Although I wouldn't cut off much," she allowed as she added shaving powder then water to the cup, then swished it around into a creamy lather.

"No?" Cody watched as she set the shaving cup aside.

"I like it long," Callie admitted with a smile as she turned toward him urgently. "It suits you. But we can do that later. Right now I want to get started on this beard." She wanted to see if he still looked like the old Cody without it.

Callie cupped his chin in one hand and tipped his head back. As she touched him, their eyes met. Initially, his glance was speculative, almost playful, then abruptly— raptly—fascinated. But as she continued to touch him, that too faded. He became oddly vulnerable. As did she. And as they continued to look deep into each other's eyes, it was as if she could see directly into the depths of his bruised soul. All the hurts he had suffered, all the dreams that had escaped him, all the dreams he still had were reflected in his dark, tormented eyes.

It took an enormous amount of willpower for Callie to proceed with the barbering challenge.

There was still a part of her that wanted nothing more than to take him straight to bed and kiss him and hold him until all the pain in his heart went away, for good this time, and another part of her that wanted nothing more than to run from the possibility of tangling with Cody in any truly intimate way. She had already lost her heart to him once, only to have to leave him to protect him. She didn't want it happening again. Not unless she knew for certain that he could and would return the feelings she still had and always would have for him, and that in the end she would be free to be with him.

But it was too late to back out on him now, Callie told herself firmly as Cody continued to regard her solemnly. He had challenged her to do this and she had accepted. It didn't matter that being so close to him made her pulse race and her senses swim, Callie thought nervously. She had to go through with this or be seen by him as weak and fickle once again. And that she couldn't countenance.

Taking solace in the fierce concentration required for the task, and the sudden absence of any real conversation between them, she began carefully snipping off thick chunks of dark, wheat gold beard, discarding them barber-style onto the floor. As she worked, Cody continued to watch her unremittingly. Rather than resenting the way she was touching him, he seemed to enjoy it. "Do this a lot, do you?" he teased softly, in his old, roguish way.

As Callie moved from the right side of his face to the left, she inhaled the scent of his cologne. The brisk masculine fragrance reminded her of all the times they had kissed.

Avoiding his ocean blue eyes altogether for fear she would lose all track of what she was doing if she didn't, she concentrated on his chin. "Actually, this is my first time."

His eyes twinkled with sudden mischief and he chided her gently, "My first time, too."

Callie blushed as he meant her to, then put down her scissors and picked up the shaving mug and brush. "Behave," she scolded.

He settled his hands on her waist, caressing gently. "Tall order."

How well Callie knew that! "Do it anyway," she said, willfully injecting more sternness in her tone than she felt.

Pushing his hands away, she stepped in front of him so that his long legs were on either side of her. With a nonchalance she couldn't begin to feel, she began to lather the sides of his face and the underside of his jaw, then his upper lip. Still watching her intently, Cody angled his head back. Callie picked up the straight razor, scraped the blade down his face and was rewarded with her first glimpse of rugged male skin. The planes of his face were every bit as beautifully sculpted as she recalled. Anxious to see the rest of him, Callie wiped the excess lather on the edge of the towel. Then, still concentrating fiercely, she did the whole process again, and then again, and then again.

Finished, Callie put down the razor, picked up the washcloth and went back to the sink. She soaked the cloth with hot water, then went back to Cody. She gently finished her barbering by washing the last bit of shaving cream from his face, then stood back to get a glimpse of her handiwork.

And found, in her growing sense of wonder, that he looked incredible. Absolutely incredible. The absence of the beard had opened up his face, showing him to be classically handsome in that rugged, Montana rancher way. His blue eyes, with their thick fringe of golden lashes, somehow seemed more intensely alive, his cheekbones higher and more prominent, his lips more sensual. But there were other, more important changes, as well, Callie thought as the satisfaction deep inside her built and built. It was as if something else...some private stock of pain and grieving...had been released. As if Cody were free again, of so much. As was she.

"Well?" Cody drawled as he ran a hand along his smoothly shaven jaw. "What do you think?"

Grinning, Callie smoothed a hand across his cheek. She hadn't felt this lighthearted in years. "Much better." Reminded he hadn't seen the way he looked yet, Callie linked arms with him and retorted happily, "But the real question is, what do you think, Cody?"

Cody ran a hand across his face again, then shrugged his broad shoulders negligently. "It feels great. I don't know if I'll recognize myself, though." He headed for the bathroom mirror upstairs, Callie by his side.

"Well?" she said as he studied his reflection in the mirror. She knew she was deeply prejudiced in his favor but she thought he had never looked more handsome. Not boyishly so, as he had when she had known him before. But handsome in a mature sense, rugged and wild in that Montana cowboy way. She could still see he had suffered, just as she had. But he had also found the strength to pull himself up by the bootstraps and go on. As she had. Perhaps, she thought, encouraged, they had more in common than they knew.

Cody touched a hand to her shoulder. "You did a great job for me," he said, his low voice reverberating with a distinctly sensual pleasure. "I don't know after all this time if I'd have had the nerve or will to do it. Thanks."

Callie nodded, almost shyly, and their eyes met and held in the reflection of the mirror. "You're welcome," she said softly. And suddenly there was no more need for words. Because it was all there, on his face and in her heart.

He wanted her as much as she wanted him.

And suddenly, despite all her effort to the contrary, they were headed into dangerous territory anyway.

They tore their eyes from the mirror's reflection. Cody's eyes darkened sensually as he swung around to face her. He slanted her a sexy half smile, and suddenly she knew what was coming, even before he offered up in a lazy drawl, "As long as we're into experimentin' this afternoon, let's try this, too."

As if it were the most natural thing in the world, he captured her in his strong arms. Leaning against the sink, he drew her between his spread legs and wrapped his arms around her waist.

Callie's heart skipped a beat. "Cody, I—I'm not—this is—what I—uh—"

Callie's words were cut off as his lips brushed hers, softly, tantalizingly at first. She heard herself whimper and then instinct and desire took over. She let herself go. Let herself surrender to the inevitable. Her lips opened to his and the deep, evocative plundering of his tongue.

Cody had learned, years before, just how to kiss her, she recalled. And as he held her and kissed her and kissed her, his hands smoothing down her spine and over her hips, he drew on that knowledge to devastating effect, involving not just her lips and her body but her heart and soul, too. "Oh, Cody," Callie whispered shakily at last. Too much was happening too soon, and she wasn't even sure it was for anything near the right reasons, the right reasons being love not lust. But she was powerless to resist as he wrapped her against his hard frame. It all felt so damn good. So damn satisfying.

"Cody what?" he prodded gently as he lifted his head and looked at her, the hungry, watchful expression in his eyes so different from the tender evocativeness of his hands.

Buying time, Callie stroked the brawny width of his shoulders, the warm, rock-solid muscles of his hair-whorled chest. She couldn't help but notice that the lines around his mouth and eyes had eased in the moments since they had begun to touch and kiss. She didn't want them coming back again; he had already suffered far too much. "Don't do anything you'll regret," she warned in a soft, caressing whisper. *Don't do anything I'll regret.*

Cody's eyes gentled even more as he pressed a light kiss to her brow. "I'm not going to regret this, Callie. And neither are you. And why should we? I want you. You want me. What could be more natural than that?"

From the sound of it, he wasn't offering her much more than an affair. And that was such a tenuous thing, whereas she had always wanted something permanent, something lasting. Like marriage. But not to just anyone.

Before she came to her senses, he swept her into his strong arms and carried her to his bedroom. Callie drew a shaky breath as he unbuttoned the shirt she had borrowed from him and drew it over her shoulders.

"Don't you want to make love?" Cody asked, already caressing her breasts.

Callie trembled as her flesh came to life under his questing fingertips. "Yes, but it still doesn't mean we should do this."

Cody merely smiled. There was a whimsical gleam in his blue eyes. "Doesn't it?" Not one who was easily dissuaded about *anything,* he unfastened her bra with one hand, then cupped her breasts in his palms, stroking them, tracing her nipples until she moaned. "When was the last time you felt like this, Callie?" he inquired huskily as he eased her jeans and panties down her legs. "When have you ever felt like this?"

Seven years ago, Callie thought dizzily. He laid her on his bed and wedged a leg between her thighs. His jeans were enticingly rough on her bare skin as he stroked her intimately. A fire raged through her veins as he kissed her again and again, leisurely exploring the erotic potential of his lips when locked against hers. And as they continued to kiss, she couldn't help but marvel over the miracle of finding him again, of feeling their anger and disappointment begin to dissolve—even if it was only through sex—and a burden begin to be lifted from her heart.

She had missed him. Not willing to waste an instant of the incredible passion that had often seemed more dream than memory, she wreathed her arms about him, moved against him sinuously and released a tremulous sigh. "I knew you were trouble the first moment I laid eyes on you again."

"You know what they say about trouble," he murmured as he continued to kiss her in the same slow, deliberate way, shattering what little reserve of caution she had left. He paused only briefly to remove his jeans.

"What?" She forced her gaze up until it locked with his. She smiled at the tightening of his muscles beneath her fingertips, the heat flooding into his bare skin, and knew, even though it was a terrible risk, that she didn't have the strength or will to pull away.

"There'll be hell to pay when it's over." He slid down her body, kissing the hollow of her stomach and stroking the soft insides of her thighs. He traced her navel with his tongue, then slid lower, to deliver the most sensual of kisses.

His fingers were warm and demanding as he brought her to the brink of ecstasy. She parted her lips, her breath catching as he dipped his tongue into her mouth. She had never experienced anything like this intense, aching need. She had never wanted so much to be kissed, touched, held.

She closed her eyes, reveling in the warm, heavy weight of him, the hardened muscle and smooth skin feathered with tufts of soft, whorling hair. The longing inside her was fierce. Was this what it would be like to make love, to become one with Cody, body and soul?

Her fingers gripped the muscles of his upper arms as he eased her legs open with his knee. As his body sank into hers, she felt a moment's panic, a moment's brief, searing pain, which was soon obliterated by the thrill of having him inside her. She was pulsing all over, inside and out, and the hunger that had always been between them flared to life. They moved together as if they had been lovers for many years, their coupling bringing her the most riveting pleasure she had ever known.

And still it wasn't enough for either of them. Moving in primal rhythm, she sheathed him tightly. Whispering his name, she arched upward, again and again.

The depth of her passion pushed him into oblivion. With a final thrust, he brought them both to ecstasy. She surged against him once more, fitting her mouth to his. Gathering her close, he kissed her sweetly, languidly, until finally the shudders drew out, their emotions were drained, and they lay spent, trembling and exhausted.

Chapter Seven

Cody had dreamed of having her in his bed, in his life again. Sometimes, some long, lonely nights, it seemed that was all he ever dreamed. But nothing could have prepared him for the softness of her surrendering body against his, the sweet give of her lips, the flinch of pain. The knowledge he was the first to make love to her—that she had waited all this time for him as he had waited for her—lit fire to his own aching, overwhelming need. In slow, purposeful consummation, he had let her know with every touch, every kiss, every stroke that she was his, and only his.

But he had thought—hoped—he was over Callie by now. Considering all that had passed between them, he certainly should have been.

His feelings in turmoil, his body still humming with the aftereffects of their lovemaking, Cody levered himself away from her. He rolled onto his back, staring at the ceiling above his bed. When she had duped him and run away, he had sworn to wreak his revenge on her if he ever caught up with her again. And now... Cody groaned and passed a hand over his eyes.

"Cody? What is it?" Callie asked in a voice that quavered slightly.

Cody ran a hand over his jaw. The smooth skin that had lain beneath his beard felt as unfamiliar to him as having Callie in his bed.

He rolled onto his side and propped himself up on one elbow. "Ah, Callie..." Damn, he wished she wasn't so beautiful. That her hair was not so soft and clean and touchable, or cut in such a sexy, tousled way. If she kept looking at him like that with those wide green eyes full of shimmering wonder and desire, that trembling lower lip that just begged to be kissed again, he was going to be a goner. Unless, of course, Cody thought as he reined himself in hard, he worked swiftly to inject some distance between them again. And if there was one thing he knew, Cody thought, beginning to get himself back on track again, it was how to push people away.

Cody sat up lazily. "We finally consummated our marriage."

Callie tugged the sheet up to cover her breasts. "Is that the way you see it?"

Cody tore his eyes from the soft curves of her breasts and shrugged. "I don't know what else to call it." He let his eyes move over her. "Except maybe satisfying our curiosity about what it would be like to be with each other in the most intimate way possible."

Callie's eyes flashed fire. "Well, now we know for sure that we're all wrong for each other, don't we?" she snapped.

This was the Callie he knew, her temper in full flame. "I guess we do at that," Cody drawled, tossing off the sheet. Naked, he reached for his clothes, while Callie wrapped herself toga-style in the sheet.

"So we won't have to be doing this again," she vowed.

Cody tugged on a clean pair of socks. "I'm all for that." He pulled on his boots, one after the other, then became aware of the scent of something burning. He looked at Callie as she slipped on her own jeans and shrugged back into his shirt. "You smell something?"

"Oh, no!" Callie clapped a hand to her mouth and raced for the kitchen. "The soup! I forgot to take it off the stove!"

"SO MUCH for your housekeeping skills," Cody said as Callie studied the blackened bottom of the pan.

Callie dropped the scorched pan back onto the stove with a bang. Both fists planted firmly on her waist, she tilted her head up and glared at Cody pointedly. She didn't know what had happened to him in the few minutes since they had made love with an incredible mix of passion and tenderness, but in the interim he had undergone a metamorphosis she most certainly did not like. "Cody," she warned tightly, her notorious temper fast approaching the danger zone, "if you value your life, don't start."

Taking that as an invitation, he rocked back on his heels and folded his brawny arms in front of him. "Wish you'd said that to me a mite earlier, Callie darlin'," he drawled.

He is not going to get to me, no matter how much he goads.

Her head held high, Callie shouldered her way past him and carried the scorched saucepan to the sink, slapped it down, then added a generous squirt of dishwashing soap.

Cody lingered next to her shoulder as she turned on the hot-water spigot. He was standing annoyingly close.

"Hate to break it to you, but I seriously doubt you're going to be able to wash that pot clean," Cody said, buttoning his shirt.

Callie turned to glare at him. En route downstairs, he had tied his hair back with the familiar rawhide strip. He hadn't bothered to comb it first, he had just smoothed it with his hands, and it had a rugged, sexy look to it she found even more annoying. Plus, his beard had been a constant reminder of the less-than-desirable changes he had undergone in her absence. Without it, he looked more like the man she had fallen in love with. The man she might still be in love with, as much as she loathed even thinking about that possibility, considering the way he was acting.

"Then perhaps you can try," Callie said stonily, resisting the urge to cry.

"Nope," Cody refused politely. "House rules. Whoever dirties a dish cleans it up. Max taught us that." He looked her up and down.

Barely restraining the impulse to bean him with the aforementioned pot, Callie slammed it back into the sink. "Too bad Max didn't teach you how to be a gentleman," she shot back.

"Oh, he tried, in his own unconventional way."

"But it didn't take."

Cody flashed her a devastating smile. "You'd be the expert on that. You being my now-considerably-more-than-in-name-only wife and all."

"Don't remind me," Callie drawled back sarcastically as she flung a wet dishrag at his chest. "Well, I hope you enjoyed having me in your bed, Cody McKendrick, because that is all the 'wedding night' you are ever going to get from me."

Looking suddenly as dangerous as a mountain lion on the prowl, Cody shoved away from the counter. He peeled the sudsy cloth off his shirt with two fingers. Callie could see he was spoiling for a fight, too. Anything to diffuse the charged atmosphere between them. "Is that so?" he taunted with the soul-deep recklessness she had always loved.

"You bet your bottom dollar it is!" Callie shot right back.

He slanted her a knowing half smile that indicated he had half a mind to seduce her again just to prove her wrong.

A long silence passed. Callie drew a shaky breath, wondering if they would ever be able to get back to where they'd been when they first met—to a consistent level of friendship and fun. "You really have changed," she said finally.

"And not for the better, right?" he goaded.

She thrust her hands through her hair. She felt as if she were going to explode. And the way he kept studying her only made it worse. "Would you just get out of here?"

Cody shook his head and stubbornly held his ground in the face of her recalcitrance. "Uncle Max wanted us to stay together," he reminded.

Callie drew a tranquilizing breath and passionately replied, "He gave us three thirty-minute breaks. I vote we use one now." *Before we say or do even more things we'll regret.*

Abruptly, Cody seemed to have second thoughts about staying with her, too. "Maybe you're right," he allowed as he reached for his hat and slapped it on his head. "Maybe time apart is what we need."

Looking suddenly as if he hadn't a care in the world, he swaggered out the kitchen door.

25:30

CALLIE WENT BACK UPSTAIRS to restore some order to her hair and makeup. Wanting no reminders of their tryst, she also remade the bed. Still feeling a little guilty about the mess she'd made with the boiled-over soup, she went back down to the kitchen. At the sink, she stared at the pan.

She and Cody hadn't even been together twenty-four hours yet, and though there had been moments of real closeness, they had also spent much of that time at each other's throats. What was Max thinking, putting them together this way? Sure, she and Cody had had some nice moments, some sexy and romantic moments, Callie reflected wistfully. But the way things were going now, they'd never survive to make it to the wedding, never mind actually be able to stay married once their vows were said again before family and friends, as Max wished.

The back door opened and shut. Thinking Cody was feeling the same way she was and had come back, if not to apologize, to sort of make some amends, she rushed toward the sound. "Cody?"

"Wrong again, gal."

Callie sucked in a startled breath. She felt her face turn white and red simultaneously. "Pa."

"I see you still remember me. Not that you've bothered to call." Al Sheridan walked toward her. At age fifty, he looked much as he had when Callie had last seen him seven years ago. Tall like her brother Buck, and solidly built, his face prematurely weathered by overexposure to the sun. In muted plaid shirt, worn dusty jeans and hand-tooled boots, a cowboy hat drawn low over his brow, he looked like any of the hands that worked the cattle operation on the Silver Spur Ranch. Except for his hands, Callie thought. His hands had never done an honest day's labor, and it showed.

Callie gulped. "What are you doing here?" she choked out, even as guilt flooded her anew. She knew she ought to feel something other than dread for the man. He was her father, after all. But deep down all she wanted was for him to go away and never darken her door again.

Pa's gray eyes grew dark as pewter, his smile unforgiving. "Why, I came to see you, of course."

Panic set in as Callie noted the deliberate undertone of intimidation in his voice. Pa wanted something. He was here to make her pay for deserting him and her brother.

He walked over to the coffee machine and paused with an expectant look.

She would give him a cup of coffee, because it was the least her mother would have expected her to do for her own flesh and blood, but then she was sending Pa on his way. Not that it would be easy doing so.

Callie headed for the coffeepot, which was still half-full. Wordlessly, she poured her father a cup of the strong brew. "You can't stay," she said as she handed it over. With effort, she mustered her courage and met Pa's eyes. "Cody—"

"Hightailed it over to the bunkhouse in his pickup, from the looks of things."

Silence fell between them. Callie watched as Pa took a sip of the too strong brew. He swore, spat and poured it in the sink. "This'll never do, gal. Make me some fresh. Now."

Callie saw the cruelness in his eyes, the complete disregard for others, and recalled full well why she had run. Pa had only backhanded her once. It had been enough. "Where's Buck?"

"Taking care of some important things." Pa watched as she set about making a fresh pot of coffee. His lower lip curled into a sneer. "I'll tell him you asked about him. I'm sure he'll be glad to hear that."

Callie switched on the machine and waited impatiently for the coffee to brew. "Cody can't find you here," she said shortly.

Pa studied her contemptuously. "Why do you care? It's not as if you wanted to marry him anyway, did you?"

Callie was silent, staring at the man whose blood she carried in her veins. She might as well have been delivered from aliens. She just knew she felt no kinship with Pa or Buck. She'd never felt she belonged with them.

"And it's not as if I have any affection for the young stud," Pa continued gregariously. "After all, it's because of him that you ran away from me and your brother in the first place. Interstate kidnapping, I believe they call it in this country, since you were under age."

Callie swallowed at the implicit threat in Pa's low voice. It hadn't been kidnapping; they both knew that. But if Pa saw to it that Cody was charged or even simply accused, she and Cody both would be in a helluva mess while they were proving otherwise. They would be in the midst of a public scandal. Neither she nor Cody would appreciate that. It would be just one more reason he'd have to hate her.

She folded her arms in front of her, mustered her courage and stood her ground. "What do you want?"

Pa smiled and helped himself to some of the fresh brewed coffee. "Control of the Silver Spur cattle operation, of course."

Callie released a quavering breath. "Cody'll never give that up."

"Maybe not voluntarily," Pa allowed.

Callie narrowed her eyes at him. "You're planning something, aren't you? Another con?"

Pa smiled evilly and quaffed the rest of his coffee in a single gulp. "Now you're catching on."

Callie swept her hands through her hair. Her mother could have talked Buck and Pa out of this. Put them back on the path to redemption. Out of respect for her mother's memory, Callie knew she had to try to do the same. "Pa, please. Cody's never done anything to you—"

"The hell he hasn't." Pa's face turned dark as a thundercloud. "The one time I asked him for a handout, he told me to go to hell."

"When was this?"

"After he paid the ransom and came back to the States. He was in one foul mood, that boy was, 'cause you hadn't been found."

"Did he know you and Buck conned him?"

"He was beginning to figure it out, which is why he said no. Not to worry, though." Pa angled a thumb at his chest. "Now that you're back, Callie, so is our gravy train. Me and Buck have worked out a way to pay him back for all the misery he cost us, Callie."

Callie didn't like the sound of that, either. "How will you do that?" she asked warily.

Pa's eyes gleamed with the need for revenge. "By robbing him of his inheritance, of course," he said in a low, oily voice.

Callie knew that to be a party to anything less than honest would eat her up inside. "You can't do that," she told her pa firmly. "Max McKendrick left the cattle operation to Cody."

"Cody only inherits if he marries you at four o'clock Saturday."

"Right. And he's planning to do that."

Pa gave Callie an evil smile as he handed her his empty coffee cup. "Maybe he is now," he allowed. "But Buck and I feel he's going to change his mind about going through with the ceremony."

Callie did, too, though for totally different reasons than what Pa was thinking, she was sure. "How do you figure that?" she asked uncomfortably.

"Because we all know how he feels about dishonest women."

Callie's back went rigid with dislike, even as her antennae for danger went up. "Everything I did, I did for him."

Pa smirked, and Callie found his confidence sickening. "It doesn't matter if you have or haven't," he advised. "All that matters is what *he* thinks you did."

Callie drew in a jerky breath. "What are you planning?" she demanded, and was met only by silence. "Damn it, Pa." Tears of frustration burned in her eyes. She'd thought she was through having to feel ashamed—as though a piece of her were sullied—just by being related to her father and brother. But here it was, happening all over again. She faced her pa angrily. "If you implicate me in another one of your schemes, I swear I'll—"

"You'll what?" Pa interrupted smoothly, his look warning her not to cross him again. "Tell Cody you're not a con artist?" When she would have turned away from him, he grabbed her by the arm and twisted. "Think he's going to believe that, knowing that the talent for a good con runs in the family?" Pa demanded until Callie's eyes smarted from the painfulness of his grip on her.

"He'll never marry a thief, you know," he continued viciously, making his point before pushing her away abruptly. "Never mind a thief who duped him years before, even if it means giving up his claim to the Silver Spur cattle operation," he finished spitefully. "After all, he can always say to hell with Max's plans and start anew somewhere else. Getting his reputation back, on the other hand, would be a lot harder to manage."

"You're going to try to make him refuse to marry me, is that it?" Callie felt sick inside at the possibility of Pa interfering with her relationship with Cody again. It was bad enough, what Buck and Pa had already done.

Pa shrugged uncaringly. "Nothing dishonest about that. The possibility for said occurrence was even in Max's will."

"How do you know about that?" Callie's voice cracked nervously.

"News of the terms of Max McKendrick's will went out with the quickie wedding invitations. Most of which were hand-carried, by the way. And those that didn't hear about it that way heard it from Susannah and Trace's kids. Seems they can't stop talking about it, either. There's even talk that Patience's photo is about to show up in a tabloid, her being a syndicated newspaper columnist, semicelebrity and all."

Callie sighed. With Pa and Buck both on the scene, this had all the makings of a real disaster!

Pa's voice turned low and soothing as he tried to talk her into cooperating. "Not to worry, gal. All you have to do is want to marry Cody. If he refuses to marry you, you inherit the ranch, he gets the bull's-eye. And then you, Buck and I can live off the ranch profits for the rest of our lives. Think of it, Callie," Pa dreamed aloud, an avaricious gleam in his gray eyes. "None of us will ever have to do another lick of work."

I like to work, Callie thought. I like earning an honest living. She shook her head, said flatly, "I'm not going to be a part of this."

"I thought you'd say that." Half of Pa's mouth turned up in a knowing smile. "But I think you'll change your mind when you see what happens when you don't help us out."

"What are you talking about?" Callie demanded uneasily. "What have you done now?"

Pa merely smiled and refused to tell. Wordlessly, he grabbed his hat and planted it back on his head. "I better get out of here before Cody gets back. Oh, and, Callie, when he does, you might want to ask him to take you to see where he grows his winter feed.''

Pa moved through the house and slipped out the front door.

Callie stared at the ruined pot she had yet to scrub.

The back door slammed. She jumped a mile as Cody came striding in. She went even whiter as she realized Cody and Pa had just missed each other. ''You look like you've seen a ghost,'' he said.

In a way, she had, Callie thought wearily. ''Where've you been?''

''Checking on Zeus, and talking to Shorty over at the bunkhouse. Why?''

Callie swallowed as she thought about what Pa had said. ''Would you mind showing me where you grow the winter feed for the cattle?''

Cody narrowed his eyes at her suspiciously. ''What brought this on?''

Callie shrugged and went back to scrubbing the pot. Deciding it was ruined beyond repair, she dumped the excess water out of it and tossed it into the trash. ''It's just something I should know.''

''Max didn't leave you any cropland, Callie.''

''I know, but—'' Callie bit her lip, not sure she should say anything else for fear she'd let on more than she intended.

''But what?'' Cody demanded when she didn't finish.

''I just want to see it,'' she continued stubbornly as the air between them crackled with electricity.

''Fine,'' Cody said, his determination not to make anything the least bit easy on her apparent. ''We'll go later.''

''No,'' Callie said sharply. That would not do. It would not do at all. ''Now, Cody.''

He studied her a moment more. She knew he knew something was up. He just didn't know what. And that scared him, too. His sensual lips flattened into a tense white line. He gave her another long, hard look. Then said simply, a muscle working convulsively in his cheek, "Let's go."

They rode out in silence, each in their own corner of the pickup. The tension between them was so thick it could have been cut with a knife. "How far is it?" Callie asked finally, unable to completely hide her impatience or her anxiety.

"Four miles from the original ranch house." Cody slanted her an interested glance. "Why do you ask?"

"No reason," Callie muttered without inflection, unwilling and unable to meet his probing gaze.

But when they got in view of the fields, to her dismay, he knew why. They both did.

Chapter Eight

Cody turned his glance from the smoke billowing from the field to her. Accusation hung in the air between them. Callie knew he was not going to rest until he knew precisely what part she had played in this. And when he found out, he was not going to forgive her. But all that would have to wait until they dealt with the emergency at hand.

"Get on the truck's shortwave radio now and and call for help," Cody ordered briskly. Mouth thinning, he turned away.

"What are you going to do?" Callie said, aware they were on the brink of disaster here, and her pa and brother Buck were responsible. Damn them!

"My best to put the fire out!" Cody vowed grimly as he circled around to the back of the truck. He grabbed a small fire extinguisher out of the metal toolbox in the bed of the pickup, located just behind the passenger compartment, and sprinted purposefully for the smoldering wheat.

So far only a half acre was burning, but who knew how long that would be the case if the wind picked up, Callie thought. Ten to one, Cody didn't have nearly enough fire-fighting foam to put the entire fire out. Callie turned on the radio, all the while eyeing what was left in the pickup's toolbox. She got the bunkhouse. In a voice that shook, she quickly related what was happening, then, signing off, grabbed anything else she thought might help—a shovel, pickax and small wool blanket—and rushed off to help Cody.

"The hands are sending a fire truck," she shouted as the billowing smoke stung her eyes and throat.

Cody nodded his understanding and finished spraying the last of the foam around the perimeter. "Get back to the truck," he ordered as his extinguisher made a dry, sputtering sound and then fell silent. He tossed the empty extinguisher into the dirt.

Ignoring his order—Cody needed her help whether he wanted it or not—Callie grabbed a shovel and began to help. Intending to dig a ditch around the perimeter of the still-burning acre, she picked up a shovelful of dirt and tossed it on the fire.

Cody scowled at her. Then he moved on ahead of her and with a powerful motion of his arm began to rake the pickax through the dirt, loosening the soil ahead of her. The digging and shoveling began to go faster for Callie as Cody then picked up a blanket and beat at the flames.

Some fifteen minutes and much backbreaking labor later, they had the fire pretty much contained. And it was then that the hands came barreling into the wheat field in a convoy of pickups. Jumping out of the truck, with the crew boss Shorty in the lead, they carried other fire extinguishers over and quickly put out the rest of the flames.

Cody was already moving off through the fields, studying the crops. "What are you looking for?" Callie asked, jogging after him breathlessly.

He shot her an angry glance over his shoulder. "Like you don't know."

Callie was covered with dirt and soot. Perspiration streamed down her face and chest. She found a relatively clean square of shirtsleeve and wiped her face. "You think there's more fires starting?"

"I think that a fire like this doesn't start by itself, not on a green wheat crop."

He hunkered down. Callie paused beside him.

He was studying an empty gasoline can, turned on its side. It was the kind used to carry fuel for a lawnmower and it was drained completely dry, and not the least bit weathered.

Buck and Pa had left quite a calling card. And unfortunately, because she had been compelled to follow through on their hint, she had implicated herself in the malicious mischief, as well.

Cody glanced back up at her. "You want to tell me what you know about this?" he demanded furiously, as a short distance away the hands began the job of cleaning up.

Callie swallowed and knit her hands together nervously. "I had nothing to do with what happened here."

"And yet you knew about it."

What could Callie say to that? It was true. Unable to bear the hurt and betrayal she saw in Cody's eyes, she turned away. She did not want to have this conversation. Now or ever. She did not want to be in a position to have to turn her own family in to the authorities. Let someone else do that. The way Pa and Buck were popping up and taking chances, it wouldn't be long before they were caught doing something.

Cody followed her, refusing to let the matter drop. When he spoke, his voice was dangerously soft. "You urged me to come out here." He grabbed her shoulders roughly, shook her slightly, as if that would tumble the truth out of her. "Why, Callie?"

Callie drew an enervating breath. She felt hopelessly torn. The truth was, she didn't know what to do. She knew her mother would have expected her to protect Buck and Pa, to somehow put them back on the right path as she had time and again. They were her family, after all. But Callie had tried to get them to do what was right and failed in that endeavor countless times years ago, and she had finally come to the conclusion it wasn't going to happen, not in her lifetime, not in Cody's. So what was she supposed to do? Tell Cody her pa and Buck were back around, causing trouble for him, and have him think she was in on it, too, and turn her into the police? Or keep silent and pray Buck and Pa would either get caught and turned in by someone else or go away when they didn't get what they wanted? Either way, her relationship with Cody was ruined almost before it had even been rekindled.

Aware Cody was still waiting for an answer, Callie swallowed and looked up at him in desperate appeal, answering him as truthfully as she could. "I had a bad feeling. All right?"

The accusation in his blue eyes deepened. "At precisely the time the fire here was starting," he concluded disbelievingly. "What next, Callie?"

That was it, Callie thought, her own despair increasing by leaps and bounds. She didn't know. And wouldn't until it happened.

Before she could respond, Shorty came up to talk to Cody. "Looks like everything is under control here," Shorty reported.

"And elsewhere?" Cody inquired as Callie looked on with bated breath, hoping nothing else bad had happened.

"Nothing much," Shorty reported, looking from Cody to Callie and back again. "We've got a maverick calf out in pasture ten twenty-six. I was about to go out and pick him up and return him to the rest of the herd when I got your call."

"I'll do it," Cody was quick to volunteer. He still looked as if he wanted to explode.

Shorty nodded. "I'll get you the stuff." He returned to his truck and brought back a first-aid kit, a rope with a lasso on the end of it and a bottle of formula.

In silence, Cody turned and headed for his pickup truck, his strides long and angry. Silent and upset, Callie followed him and got in, too.

Cody shoved the key in the ignition and started the truck up with a roar that had everyone turning to look their way. "I don't know what my Uncle Max was thinking when he tried to fix me up with you." He thrust the truck into gear and roared off, out of the pasture. "You don't have a heart. You don't even have a conscience!"

"That is not true!"

Ignoring her, Cody floored the accelerator. They flew over the gravel lane, bouncing back and forth and up and down. Cody's hands gripped the wheel fiercely as he shot her a debilitating look. "'Course, Uncle Max was probably right to think that you'd want to marry me, if for nothing else than to get your hands on my money and thereby enhance the quality of your own life. But as for you knowing anything at all about being a good wife to a man like me..." He shook his head disparagingly.

Callie flushed. "So I forgot to turn off the stove and boiled the soup pan dry," she railed. "That was your fault as much as it was mine."

Cody's sensual lower lip curled in remembered satisfaction. "The lovemaking, maybe. But you forgot the stove first," he swore as he took a hard right turn, then screeched to a halt that sent them both tumbling forward. Thrusting the vehicle into park, he caught her up short and hauled her close. "Or was that your intention?" he wondered, his fingers tightening almost painfully on her upper arms. "First, burn my house down, then my crops? God knows you've already trashed the old outpost, which was my home away from home!"

Callie put a hand square on his chest and pushed until he released her. "I told you I had nothing to do with the theft of your bull." She scooted back to the far corner of the pickup cab. "Furthermore, your theory doesn't even begin to make sense. *If* I had known about the bull being inside your cabin, why would I have put my own life in jeopardy by going in there?"

"How the heck should I know?" Cody shrugged. "Maybe you wanted to make sure no clues were left that would point to your partners in crime. Though I think it is pretty clear who those fellas are."

Callie couldn't disagree with him on that. So she jutted her chin out stubbornly and changed the subject back to her domestic skills. "Furthermore, I do too have what it takes to make a good wife." It had been wrong of him to say otherwise.

His left arm casually looped over the steering wheel, Cody sat back against the driver's door. "It's more than making a man happy in bed."

Now this, Callie thought, was getting interesting. "Go on."

Cody exhaled an exasperated breath. "It's more than simply cooking and cleaning, too. It's making a place a home," he said wistfully. "Making it warm and cozy."

Callie rolled her eyes. He sure had strange ideas about what he wanted in a wife. "A decorator could do that for you, Cody," she said dryly.

Cody frowned. "I'm not talking about spending money here, Callie. I'm talking about a gift from the heart." He paused to dramatically palm his chest. "I'm talking about creating the kind of warm, loving ambience you can't buy in any store or read how to do in any magazine. Being able to do that comes from in here." Cody pointed to her heart. Finished, he started the engine and thrust it roughly into drive again. "Although now that I ruminate on it a bit, I think I know what all this homegrown terrorism is about."

Callie narrowed her eyes at him. "Excuse me?"

Cody slanted her a complacent glance. "You're trying to get me to refuse to marry you so you can have the lion's share of the ranch. Well, it's not going to work, Callie," he warned decisively. "You stole my happiness years ago. You're not robbing me of anything else, no matter what you do or say."

"Well, you stole my happiness, too!"

"Then we're even."

No, Callie thought as Cody stopped at a pasture gate marked 1026. But one day soon they would be.

He got out, unlocked the padlock on it and swung it open. He drove the truck through, then continued on until he spotted a bawling calf, no bigger than a full-grown golden retriever, tangled up in a section of fence.

Cody got out of the truck, grabbed the lasso, the first-aid kit and the bottle of formula. As he looked toward the maverick calf, his face softened compassionately. It was clear he identified with the calf, and Callie could see why. The maverick had been accidentally separated from the herd through no real fault of his own. Now, miserable, alone, frightened, the calf had no idea how to find his way back to the herd. Just as Cody had no idea how to find his way back to her or the people he loved.

"How'd he get stuck out here all alone?" Callie asked.

Cody frowned and shook his head, the distant look still in his eyes. "Probably got scared by the sound of the trucks and ran off and hid while we were rounding the cattle up a couple of days ago. We move them from pasture to pasture in trucks nowadays," he explained.

Callie struggled to keep pace with Cody. "How come?"

"It saves time and money and is a lot easier on the grass and the horses. Anyway, my guess is this maverick calf is missing his mama desperately by now. And from the looks of it, he's gotten a little banged up, too."

Callie squinted at what she thought was blood. "Are those cuts on him?"

Cody nodded. "Probably from the barbed wire," he said tersely, already waving her off. "You don't have to help me out with this. You can wait in the truck."

Callie grabbed his arm, momentarily slowing but not entirely stopping his headlong pace. "I want to help," Callie insisted. And it was true, she did.

Cody looked as though he had neither the time nor the patience to argue with her. "All right. But don't get in my way," he growled. "And do exactly as I tell you. This calf is not used to being handled. He may only weigh seventy pounds or so, but he can still wield a mean kick."

As they neared, the calf stumbled to his feet and, still bawling, tried to run away, dragging a section of downed barbed wire with him. Cody handed Callie the first-aid kit and formula. Swirling the lasso around his head, he threw the rope. It landed neatly around the calf's head. He tightened the noose, which subdued the maverick calf enough that they were able to get close.

"Just as I thought," Cody said, looking at the calf's untagged ear after he had untangled the bawling animal from the barbed wire. "This one missed the branding. He looks a little dehydrated, too. Get the bottle, Callie. See if you can't feed some formula into him."

Callie moved around as directed, finally sitting so the calf's head was in her lap. The animal's steady bawling was so plaintive it brought tears to her eyes. Offering the bottle, she stroked his head softly. After a moment, the maverick calf began to suck greedily on the nipple. As he did, his bawling ceased.

"Poor calf," Callie said.

"Probably was frightened," Cody agreed, getting right to work, cleaning the jagged cuts and applying antiseptic cream.

"He's not going to like being branded and innoculated, either, but it has to be done."

"Now?"

"No. I'll have Shorty send someone over to do it later." Finished, Cody stroked the calf's side. "Right now we have to get him reunited with the herd. He's too young to be weaned."

While Callie gathered everything else up, Cody carried the calf over to the bed of the pickup and set him inside. Callie and he climbed into the truck and took off again. Moments later, they were at another pasture. Cody unlocked the gate and set the calf inside. "What if he can't find his mother?" Callie asked. There were more than one thousand cows inside the vast, rolling pasture.

"He'll know what to do," Cody told her confidently.

And sure enough, the calf took one look at the other cows and immediately began bawling at top volume again, almost as if he were calling for his mama to come and get him. Cody closed the gate again. As he and Callie leaned against the fence and watched, a huge cow came lumbering out of the herd toward the calf.

Cody smiled. "That's his mama, I'll bet."

"She must've wondered what happened to her baby," Callie said as the calf stopped bawling and began to nurse.

"They both look happy enough now," Cody said. "It's funny how Mother Nature is a powerful force in animals." His mouth tightened, and a distant look came into his eyes.

Cody settled his hat lower on his head so his eyes were shadowed by the brim.

"Are you angry you lost your parents?" Callie leaned against the pasture gate and looked up at him.

Cody continued studying the horizon. "I don't know that *angry* is the right word, but I do regret that my brother, sister and I had to grow up without parents." His voice dropped a husky notch as the afternoon sun warmed their shoulders and the gentle June breeze stirred their hair. "I regret the opportunities to be close to each other that were lost to us when my folks passed away."

Callie had the distinct feeling he was talking about more than just his parents. He was talking about the loss of their marriage, too. He felt she had walked away from him, not caring about what she left behind, when nothing could have been further from the truth. But how to convince him of that, she didn't know.

Silence settled upon them like an unseen weight. Their work in rescuing the maverick calf done, they made the drive back to the ranch house in silence. Once again, Callie yearned to tell Cody everything, but she knew that even if she did he would never believe she was innocent now. Which had, of course, been Buck and Pa's intent. That left her only one choice. She had to marry Cody, and then she had to leave.

And she had to find a way to prove to him that she wasn't what he thought she was, and make up for at least some of what had occurred in the last eighteen hours.

21:00

CODY STOOD AND STRETCHED. Working on the ranch books for the last two hours had proved therapeutic. Playing his stereo at a volume matched only in his college days had also aided in dissipating his foul mood.

Cody grinned, wondering what Callie had thought of that last Van Halen song, which—thanks to his programmable CD player—he had played a record twenty-three times in a row. It didn't matter where she was in the ranch house or what she was doing, he thought as he moved away from his computer. She couldn't have missed either the music or the lyrics, which had suggested that the dream they had once shared was over and it was time for them both to move on.

And that, Cody thought as he switched off his computer, was exactly how he felt about their romance. Once, a very long time ago, it might have worked. But not now, no matter what his crazy Uncle Max had thought.

Deciding to see if his music had managed to get his point across to Callie, he strode over and swung open the study door.

The first thing that hit him was the incredible glare of light in the normally dark hallway. The second was the fresh, early summer breeze wafting through the entire downstairs.

"What the heck—" Frowning, Cody crossed the hall and stopped dead in his tracks. He stared at the back parlor. If he didn't know better, he'd swear he was in a different house. The heavy drapes had been removed. Sunshine streamed in through the windows. The ancient black cherry sofa and matching overstuffed leather armchairs had been moved around to form a cozy conversation pit facing the sandstone fireplace. The books in the shelves on either side of the fireplace had been lined up in an orderly fashion that was both sensible—they were sorted by subject—and appealing to the eye. Another, smaller bookshelf, dragged down from one of the upstairs bedrooms, now contained neat stacks of magazines. The captain's desk and matching swivel chair had been moved to the opposite wall, between the two windows. The desk's contents were also neatly organized. The ugly, mud brown rug had been removed, the wooden floor polished to a golden glow. The rug's absence opened up the room, just as the white afghan tossed over the back of the sofa and the vases of strategically placed wildflowers warmed it with a woman's loving touch.

Callie came in, looking very fetching in another one of his shirts, jeans and red western boots. She had washed up after their fire-fighting, calf-tending chores and braided her hair in one loose plait that fell midway down her back. Tendrils of hair framed her piquant face. She had two freshly polished silver candlesticks in her hands.

Seeing him, she drawled, "What happened? Did you finally go deaf?"

Ignoring her gibe, Cody pointed to the straight-backed rocking chair next to the fireplace. "Where did that come from?"

She met his gaze equably and gave him an innocent smile. "The attic," she said simply, her look just daring him to complain.

Cody had thought that getting her out of his mind and his heart the last time she had left him was impossible. Now, thanks to what she had done in transforming his house into a home, it was going to be even worse. Even if he were to put everything back exactly as it had been, he would never forget what she had done this afternoon.

He scowled at her, letting her know with a single glance this was not a change he welcomed in his life. "You were up there, too?"

"Looks like."

"Where'd you get the flowers, then?"

Callie smiled happily. "One of the hands stopped by and volunteered to pick them for me. Don't worry." She put up a staying hand before he could interrupt. "I didn't violate Uncle Max's stipulation about us staying under the same roof."

Cody's scowl deepened. He didn't want anyone picking wildflowers for Callie but him. "If you threw away any of my magazines..." he threatened, working hard to hang on to his foul mood.

Callie breezed past. "I merely organized them. And from the looks of things around here, it was about time somebody did."

Cody folded his arms in front of him and struggled to stay ticked off at her. "I knew exactly where everything was."

Callie made a disbelieving face. "You did, did you?" she drawled.

"You're darn right I did," Cody shot right back, daring her to try to tell him otherwise.

"Somehow I thought you'd say that," Callie murmured, looking completely nonplussed. She dug into the pocket of her jeans and pulled out a scrap of paper. "Okay, where was the October issue of *Newsweek* before I moved it? Can't tell me, huh. Let's move on to the next item. Where was the novel *Patriot Games?* Can't tell me that, either."

Cody snorted in exasperation. "You're missing the point."

"Which is?"

He stalked nearer, wishing her lips didn't look so soft and kissable in the fading, late afternoon light. Wishing he didn't want to kiss her again so much. How could he feel this way about a woman he didn't even trust? A woman who might be trying to destroy not only his past and his future but the barely happy, lonely-as-a-prairie-dog existence he had now!

Cody swiftly realized that unless he wanted to be made a fool of a hundred times over, he had better get more barriers between them, fast. And toward that end, Cody knew just where to start. "How am I going to find anything?" he demanded as he looked down into her upturned face.

"Gee, let's see." Not the least bit dissuaded from her mission by his foul mood, Callie tapped her index finger against her chin. "Books in the tall bookcase, this month's magazines over there in a basket, personal mail, stamps, stationery and envelopes in the cubbyholes in the desk. I see what you mean. It is a lot for a dumb ol' cowpoke like you to recall. Perhaps we should write you a list?"

Frustrated that his attempt to quell her delight in her accomplishments had failed, Cody scowled. Afraid that if he stayed as close to her as he was, he really would take her in his arms again, he stepped back a pace, and then another. "You're not staying," he warned.

Callie shrugged nonchalantly. "I never said I was," she allowed just as bluntly. And he could tell from the look in her eyes she meant what she said.

Another silence fell. Despite his fierce efforts to the contrary, Cody could feel himself softening toward her again. "Then why did you do all this?" he demanded, struggling to understand.

Callie's eyes gentled in the way he had always loved. "To prove a point," she retorted passionately, closing the distance between them once again. "You said I didn't have it in me to be a good wife or make anyone a home. Well, I did it all on my own and without spending a lick of your money or anyone else's. And I defy you to tell me, Cody McKendrick, that this room isn't the kind of warm, cozy environment any man in his right mind would be proud to call home."

"It looks good," Cody said grudgingly after a moment. Worse, this was what he had imagined marriage to Callie would be like . . . that she'd bring sunshine and warmth to his life . . . the kind he hadn't felt in a long time. And that in turn made him feel his whole world could come crashing down again if he let himself get too comfortable in his refurbished surroundings with Callie.

It scared him, this feeling of being vulnerable to hurt again. "Thank you," he said stiffly, finally remembering his manners. "But I like it better the way I had it," he continued stubbornly, seeing no reason to lie to her about that, else she might try her way with the rest of his house, too. "I want you to put everything back the way it was before you leave. Since you wrote everything down, it shouldn't be a problem."

As Callie's ebullient mood faded, and hurt and anger flashed in her eyes, Cody had never felt worse about disappointing anyone in his life.

"I most certainly will not put it back," she said.

Cody exhaled wearily and tried to reason with her. "Callie—"

"If you want it put back, you're going to have to do it yourself." She stormed past him and headed for the stairs.

Chapter Nine

Callie stormed in from the mudroom, stood in a square of dying sunlight that brought out the prettiest glints in her sunflower gold hair and glared at Cody. "Just so you know," she said dramatically, propping both fists on her slender hips, "I am *not* laughing at your latest uncouth behavior, cowboy."

Cody paused in the act of unpacking the groceries that had just been delivered via a store in town. "Well, I'm not guffawing, either," Cody retorted tongue-in-cheek as he paid the apple-cheeked teenage delivery boy and sent him on his way. Of course, he thought, mildly amused, he hadn't a clue what she was talking about, either.

Hands on her hips, Callie watched as he shut the door, locking them in together once again. "All right. What have you done with them?" she demanded irately. Clearly, he thought, her patience with him was just about gone.

Cody set a head of lettuce and a package of broccoli on the table, then tilted his head to the side. "What have I done with what?" he asked as their glances collided like firecrackers on the Fourth of July.

"My clothes!" Callie stormed in something akin to a fishwife's screech. "They were in the dryer, along with yours. Now there are only yours there," she elaborated when he continued to regard her with an irritatingly innocent look.

Cody shrugged, telling himself he could have cared less what she wore—or in some cases, didn't—and continued to unpack the groceries, pulling out a luscious porterhouse steak, a bag of potatoes and a loaf of fresh bread. "Don't look at me." Though who else might have taken them was certainly something to chew on....

"Who else should I look at?" Callie demanded hotly as she edged closer to Cody, who was putting the milk, butter and mushrooms in the refrigerator. "We're the only two people here and those clothes couldn't have just walked off by themselves."

True. "Did you check your closet upstairs?" Cody calmly folded the paper sack and put it in the recycling bin. "Maybe you took your clothes up there and forgot."

"I think I'd remember that if I had done it," Callie snapped back.

Cody begged to differ. "Maybe not. You have been behaving pretty curiously," he drawled. Which was exactly what had him so worried. If Callie wasn't up to something herself, someone clearly was. The real question was, was she involved up to her pretty little neck, as circumstances and evidence thus far indicated.

"Fine. You want me to show you my closet upstairs and prove that my clothes aren't there? I'll show you!" Callie raged. And she headed off to do just that.

CALLIE DIDN'T EVEN KNOW why she was doing this as she dashed up the stairs and Cody followed, fast on her heels. But if he wanted to play this farce to the bitter end, then so would she. But one way or another she was finding something else to change into! The scent of his cologne on the shirt she wore was driving her wild, making her recall with disturbing clarity all she would have preferred to forget about their noontime activities.

Once in her room, she threw open a bureau drawer. "You see," she demonstrated hotly. "My clothes are not—" She stopped in shock and stared at the array of lacy, very transparent, very sexy lingerie. Aware she had not put the sexy garments there, she slammed the drawer shut and glared at him, wondering what kind of hellion's game he was playing with her now.

He lifted his brow in silent query. "What's wrong now?"

Ha! As if he didn't know. Callie tossed her head and stormed over to the closet. She flung open the door. Previously, the closet had been completely empty, as she hadn't had anything clean to hang up. Now it was filled to the brim with western wear in just her size. The clothes were beautiful, but after the way he had just treated her, resenting all she had done to make his home a little cozier and a lot more welcoming, she was not happy to see them hanging there. "I suppose you're going to deny having a part in this, too?" she said softly. Was he trying to make her think she was crazy? Pay her off and assuage the conscience she was sure he still had in there somewhere for the lovemaking? Or did he just hope to buy her cooperation for future escapades, since he seemed to be laboring under the considerable misconception that it was money, not love and self-respect, that drove her.

"You're darn right I'm denying it," Cody growled back, apparently, Callie thought, having his own reasons for being upset. His jaw set, he swung away from her and stalked furiously toward the door.

Exasperated, for now she felt she was really in the dark, Callie fell in line behind him again. She was getting very tired of this game of chase. "Now where are you going?" she demanded. She didn't like the fact he was now behaving as shocked, upset and disgruntled by this latest turn of events as she felt.

Cody rapidly tackled the stairs, two at a time. "Downstairs, to call Cisco."

Callie sprinted after him. Did Cody know something she didn't? And why was he suddenly so angry? "Why Cisco?" she asked.

"I don't care if he is Uncle Max's attorney." Cody spoke through clenched teeth. "He has meddled in my life, in my uncle's stead, for the last time."

CALLIE RETURNED to her room, shut the bedroom door and went back to the closet. Since the clothes weren't from Cody, and she knew they weren't from Buck and Pa—it wasn't their style to ever give her anything—she supposed it was okay to put them on. After all, they were beautiful garments and they were obviously meant for her. The question was, What should she wear? Her glance traveled over the dizzying array of quality garments, finally settling on a soft, doe-colored split skirt, ecru silk blouse and red, gold, beige and bone tapestry vest. It would go perfectly with her red cowgirl boots.

As she took it out of the closet, a note fell out of the pocket. It was on Uncle Max's personal stationery and had obviously been written at the time he concocted his plans to see both his nephews and niece wed.

Dear Callie,
You always were a spunky gal and, whether Cody knows it or not, just what an uncivilized cowpoke like him needs. Use the cowgirl duds like the lethal weapon they are, and go for the brass ring. Remember—I'm a-rootin' for you. I always was.

                                                    Max.

Recalling how kind Max had always been to her, Callie's eyes welled with tears. Oh, Max, she thought, if only it was as simple as me wanting Cody, I'd go after him in a Montana minute.

But Cody didn't want her or anyone else. He'd made that clear by the cruel and ungrateful way he had reacted to her efforts to brighten up at least a small part of his ranch house.

And yet, Callie thought, recalling the way he had leapt to protect her from Zeus, there was a part of him that was still gentle and kind. A part of him that didn't hesitate to aid her in bandaging her wounds. A part that made love to her with incredible passion and tenderness, even when he didn't want to desire her.

Cody had so much to give, if only he would allow himself to do so. Max had been counting on her to civilize Cody, to bring that part of him back to life. It was why Max had brought her back to Montana, why Max had left her the bull's-eye property. If she was entirely honest with herself, Callie knew there was a part of her that yearned for Cody's complete recovery, too. She didn't want to go through life feeling responsible for his downturn. She wanted to bring him back to the way he was when they'd first met: happy-go-lucky, if a bit on the shy side when it came to revealing himself, and chivalrous to the core. She wanted him to have the full, happy life he had always wanted for himself. And initially those plans of his had centered around the two of them and the ranch they would build, the marriage they would have, the kids they would bring into this world.

Deep down, Callie felt Cody still had all those dreams, just as she did. Getting him to admit any of that wouldn't be easy, but then, when had anything worthwhile ever come easily, Callie wondered with a smile as she began to undress.

CALLIE HAD ON her fighting clothes as she swept down the stairs some thirty minutes later. A movement on the front porch caught her eye. Pa? Oh, no, she thought. Please—

Callie glanced toward the rear of the house. Cody was in the kitchen. She could hear him moving around. Cooking.

Hoping she could get rid of her father before Cody noticed they had company, Callie eased open the front door and slipped out onto the porch. "I was just getting ready to ring the bell," Pa said.

Callie stood her ground as fiercely as a marine sentry. "You have to go."

"Now, Callie, is that any way to treat your kin?"

"I mean it, Pa." Callie looked him straight in the eye, distressed at the lack of morality she saw, the lack of concern for anyone but himself and his own comfort. "Cody will have you arrested if he catches you here."

"For what?" Pa gave her a sly look.

Callie clenched her hands as she thought of the destruction Pa and Buck had already wrought and would not hesitate to do again. "Trespassing. Arson."

Pa mocked her smugly. "So you noticed our little blaze?"

Callie trembled with anger and fear. "That was a rotten thing to do," she asserted in a low voice.

"It got your attention." Pa reached behind him and pulled a small black handgun from his pants. "We wanted you to know we mean business. We want a lot more dowry from Cody than a puny hundred-grand bull."

Her insides turning to mush, Callie stared at the gun in his hand. Since when had her pa started carrying a weapon on him? "I don't have any money." Bravado lent a defiant edge to her voice. "I'm not going to get any, either."

Pa grabbed her roughly by the arm and squeezed until she winced. "Don't snow me, gal." He put the muzzle of the gun against her chin and cocked the trigger. "That groom of yours is loaded."

"Maybe in terms of cattle and land," Callie countered, beginning to perspire, "but not ready cash."

Pa released her as suddenly as he had grabbed her. "I'll take a big hunk of land." He looked around him with appreciation and without warning became very genial. "Say the whole ranch. Then I can sell it off piece by piece. I can get me plenty of cash that way."

"Why are you doing this?" Callie asked miserably. She hid her fingers in the folds of her skirt so he would not see her trembling.

Pa merely smiled at Callie as if they were discussing the weather and continued to thoughtfully stroke the barrel of his gun. "Because Cody McKendrick owes us for the low-down trick he pulled on us in Mexico." He lifted his gaze and glared at Callie meaningfully, letting her know in a second just how far he'd go to extract revenge. He straightened the brim of his hat with a dapper touch. "What goes around comes around, I always say."

Callie's blood boiled. Before she knew it, she was speaking her mind. "What happened in Mexico is not his fault. After all, you started it," she accused, then realized too late she had just revealed to Pa how much she cared about Cody. Big mistake, she thought miserably. Now that he knew, he would use it against her. And once again, Cody would be hurt just by his mere association with her.

There was a long, deadly silence. "And your brother Buck and I are gonna finish it." Pa smiled complacently, having found her vulnerable spot in Cody. "With or without that man of yours." Eyes gleaming greedily, sure now he was going to get what he wanted, he pocketed his gun casually. "Remember what I told you, gal. You find a way to get us a big cash settlement as dowry, or else."

His threat delivered, Pa slipped off the porch and moved away from the house.

"Callie?" Cody's voice sounded behind her.

Her heart jumping in her chest, Callie whirled around. Smoothing her hair, she fixed a bright smile on her face and headed for the door. Cody could not know what had just gone on. She had to have time to think. She had to have time to devise a plan. She was going to fight for Cody like she had never fought for him before. She was going to protect him like he had once protected her. She owed that to Max and more.

He looked at what she knew must be the unusual paleness of her face. His tone gentled. "What are you doing out here?"

Callie shrugged self-consciously and did her best to act nonchalant. "I wanted to take a look at the sunset." She smiled at him blithely. "There's nothing like the sun going down in a blue Montana sky."

His eyes drifted over her soft, doe-colored split skirt, silk blouse and tapestry vest before moving back to her face. He stared at her as if he had never seen her dressed up before. As his eyes roved over the just brushed softness of her hair and the hint of color on her lips, something in him gentled. "That's the way I feel, too."

"About the clothes in my closet, the clothes I'm wearing now..." Callie struggled not to get lost in the ocean blue of his eyes. "They're from Max."

"I know," he said. "Cisco Kidd told me."

"I found a note."

He struggled to break the spell that had them so aware of each other. "Mind if I see it?"

A self-conscious blush heating her cheeks, Callie pulled the note from her pocket and handed it over to Cody for his perusal. As she watched him scan the note, she noticed he did not look surprised or even displeased at anything in it.

"So," Cody said eventually, the barest hint of a smile tugging at the corners of his lips. In no hurry to go back inside, he leaned against one of the square posts that supported the porch roof. "Max is a-rootin' for you."

He's a-rootin' for us, Callie thought.

"And he wanted you to have a trousseau."

And quite a trousseau it was, Callie thought, mulling over the sexy nature of some of the nightclothes that had been provided for her. She leaned against a post opposite him, marveling at the fact Cody didn't seem to resent the sentiment plainly displayed in Max's note. "How did the clothes get in there?" she asked, wrapping her arm around the sturdiness of the wood. "And when? Were you able to find out?"

Cody nodded. "Cisco brought them over while we were out at the wheat fields this afternoon. He has a key to the ranch house, since technically it still belongs to Uncle Max and is part of the estate, so it was no problem for him to let himself in.''

''And my old clothes?''

''That's the funny thing.'' Cody gave Callie the note back, his fingers brushing hers in the process. He shoved his hands in the pockets of his jeans, the unconscious action drawing the fabric tighter across his lower torso. ''Cisco said he wasn't anywhere near the utility room.''

Callie sighed and tore her glance from the front of his jeans.

''Any idea what might have happened to them?'' Cody asked curiously.

Yes, Callie thought, blushing all the harder. Pa or Buck could have stolen into the house and removed them from the washer and dryer. They would probably think a prank like that was downright hilarious.

But not wanting to share her suspicions with Cody for fear it would spoil his newly amiable mood toward her, Callie shook her head. ''Maybe Max arranged that, too. With someone else like Pearl or Shorty. With Cisco running interference for all three couples, he has a lot to do.''

''You're right about that,'' Cody said, mulling the possibility over.

And speaking of the others, Callie asked, ''Have you talked to Patience or Trace?'' She wondered if things were faring any better for the other two McKendrick heirs.

Cody shook his head. His eyes locked on hers. It was clear he had noticed the pains she had taken with her appearance and appreciated the way she looked; he could barely take his eyes off her. Max was right. These clothes were lethal weapons.

Cody lifted a hand and tangled it in the ends of her hair, caressing the tousled waves gently. It was a teasing gesture, one he had bestowed upon her often in the past. ''Dinner's almost ready. Come on in the kitchen.'' He took her hand, tugging her forward playfully when she hesitated, and led her into the house and back to the kitchen.

The table was set for two, Callie noted. Another good sign. Or was it? she wondered, considering that Cody still suspected she'd had a part in the prank involving Zeus and the fire in his wheat field. She studied him warily, hoping she wasn't falling into a velvet-lined trap. "You cooked for both of us?"

Cody lifted his broad shoulders in a careless shrug. "Thought I owed you for what you did to make the ranch house more of a home. One good turn deserves another and all that."

Callie looked into his eyes again and was immediately disappointed. Cody hadn't done all this because he loved her. He had done it because he didn't want to be beholden to her. And because she had made him feel ashamed of his bad behavior.

Score one for her civilizing influence on him.

"Besides," Cody said over his shoulder as he checked the meat for doneness and took the sizzling steak out of the broiler, then teasing her with a lighthearted wink, "I figured it was safer than letting you near the stove again."

Callie made a face at him. "Cute."

She edged closer, knowing she probably should not be so quick to forgive his rude behavior, and yet she figured any reason for a truce between them was better than none. After all, she reasoned, every journey began with a single step. Maybe Max was right. Maybe there was reason for them to hope for a happy ending after all, since their mandatory prenuptial period was only half over. Cody had done this much. She could go the rest of the way and at least try to make this a civil, if not downright romantic evening. "Can I lend you a hand?" she asked quietly.

"Just have a seat." He slid the sautéed mushrooms onto the steak with the ease of an accomplished cook, brought out twice-baked potatoes, broccoli and a tossed salad.

"It all looks delicious," Callie said as Cody poured the wine. He had gone to an awful lot of trouble, she thought appreciatively. Was it simply to make up for his unkind words to her earlier? Or because, deep inside, he was tired of fighting, too?

CODY DIDN'T WANT TO SEE the admiration in Callie's eyes as she propped her elbow on the table and rested her chin on her palm, any more than he wanted to notice how intimate sharing quarters with her had become. But there was no denying either.

"Where did you learn to cook like this?" she asked softly, looking as if her simply being there with him like that, so romantically, were a dream come true.

Welcoming the chance to talk about something not connected with their forced marriage, Cody spread his napkin across his lap. "Susannah, Trace's first wife, got me started when the two of them were first married. I was only twelve at the time, but she took a special interest in me and showed me the basics. We were both a little lonely at the time— Trace was almost never home—and it was a way for us to pass the time. Max liked it, of course, 'cause it kept me out of trouble. Later, when I began spending a lot of time on my own, it just made sense to be able to cook something for myself besides freeze-dried camping food and frozen TV dinners." And it had taken the edge off the loneliness, Cody thought as he spread steak sauce liberally on his meat. "What about you?" he asked curiously as he cut into his meat. "How come you never learned to cook?"

Callie shrugged. "I don't know. I always meant to, but I never got around to it." She paused, a dark cloud passing across her face. "I guess it just seemed like an awful lot of effort to go to for just one person."

Cody stared at her. Had she been as lonely as he had been all this time? The notion was as comforting as it was distressing. Silence fell between them.

"Cody?" Callie asked finally.

"Hmm?"

"I have something to ask you." Something she did not seem to think he would appreciate being asked, Cody noted emotionlessly. Curious as to what that could be, he gave her the go-ahead with a single look.

Suddenly looking a little nervous, Callie wet her lips, put her fork down and forged on. "What did you do to my pa and Buck in Acapulco to make them so angry with you?"

Cody gave Callie a considering look, his mouth set in a grim line. "I thought you had nothing to do with all that."

"I didn't."

He waited.

Callie toyed with a piece of broccoli. "I guess I want to know how much I was worth. What kind of ransom did you have to pay to get me back?"

Not a lot, she obviously hoped. Cody didn't know why, but he took heart at that, too. "Twenty-five thousand," Cody said.

Callie did a double take. "That's all they asked?" She appeared not to be able to imagine that.

"No," Cody clarified with a disgruntled frown. "They asked a million."

Callie's emerald eyes narrowed thoughtfully. "But you didn't know it was my brother and Pa doing the asking at that time, did you?"

Cody sighed. He figured they might as well discuss this. "Sad to say, I hadn't a clue," he admitted.

Callie's teeth sank into her lower lip. "Weren't you worried that the kidnappers would get angry when they found out how little money you showed up with?"

No, all I worried about was you and your safety, Callie, Cody thought. Unwilling to give that much of his feelings away just yet, he replied in a deliberately careless tone, "That's all I could get on short notice." He looked deep into Callie's eyes and was pleased when she didn't flinch in embarrassment or look away. "Besides, I had it bundled so it would all look authentic."

To Cody's surprise, Callie began to look a little pale. "Did Pa and Buck know how little you were giving over to the alleged kidnappers?"

Cody frowned, remembering how well he had been duped. "No, as far as they were concerned, I had gotten together one million dollars."

"Why did you tell them that?"

At the time, Cody really hadn't been able to say. Now he knew. "Because I didn't trust them, even then," he said gruffly.

Callie started to take a bite of her broccoli, changed her mind, put her fork down and took a sip of wine instead. "What happened when you went to make the exchange?" she asked, a little nervously.

Cody scowled, recalling. "We were supposed to go to this beach around three in the morning. Your brother and father had been instructed not to come. Of course they were there anyway, supposedly to help grab the kidnappers once I had gotten you safely out of the line of fire, but they were out of sight, some distance away."

Callie was completely enthralled by his tale. "Then what happened?" she pressed.

"The kidnappers showed up with a young woman in a long white dress and cloak, a hood over her face. She had her hands tied behind her. They had a gun in her ribs."

Callie paled even more. "And you thought it was me."

Cody felt the blood leave his face. "Yes." Abruptly needing to get up and move around, he stood and poured himself some more wine. "They asked me if I was ready to make a deal. I said yes. But I also told them they weren't getting all the money from me until the deal was complete and I had you safely out of the way." Cody downed his wine in a single gulp. "The next thing I know, I'm surrounded by Mexican police and being hauled off to jail as the prime suspect in a murder-for-hire scheme." Cody regarded Callie contemptuously. "Apparently they'd had a tip—probably from Buck and your pa, I realize now—that

I was really the one responsible for the mysterious disappearance of my bride and was paying to have her killed so I could collect on the insurance. So the police brought a decoy to the beach, as bait, to lure me out into the open. Then arrested me on the basis of the cash and illegally obtained weapon I had."

Callie looked utterly miserable. "Didn't you explain?" she asked, incensed.

Cody poured himself another glass of wine. "For all the good it did me. It took me three weeks and Uncle Max's help to get everything straightened out. By then, your brother and father were long gone, allegedly chasing down a lead they'd gotten on you. The briefcase full of cash had mysteriously disappeared from the evidence room, along with the crooked Mexican cop who had set up the bust. Max and I tried and were unable to turn up anything on you that indicated you were still in Mexico or actually had been kidnapped.

"So we headed back for Montana. Shortly after we arrived, who should turn up again but Buck and your pa. Claiming no luck in finding you, either—their lead had turned out to be a wild-goose chase—they asked me for money. But I had nothing left in my own accounts to give them, and besides—"

Callie regarded Cody gravely. "You were suspicious, weren't you?"

Cody nodded grimly and then explained why. "In Mexico they'd been beside themselves with grief over your alleged kidnapping and disappearance. One month later, they displayed no grief whatsoever and only a sort of vague, nervous curiosity about you. Had you turned up? they wanted to know. Had I heard from you or anyone pretending to be you? They seemed curiously convinced you were still alive and well, despite all other indications to the contrary. So following my gut instinct, I promised to let them know if anything did turn up and I sent them away empty-handed."

Callie sighed and rubbed her eyes. Either she was a very good actress, Cody thought, or she was really distressed.

Finally, she said, "I think you're right in figuring Buck and Pa tried to pull a con on you, but if it makes you feel better, I don't think they ever saw any of the cash. I think the Mexican police—or whoever helped them—got it."

Cody took another sip of wine. "Don't expect me to feel sorry for them for being double-crossed."

Callie's chin jutted out stubbornly. "I'm glad they got double-crossed," she said passionately. "I only wish that they'd ended up in jail instead of you. Maybe it would have taught them something."

"Unfortunately," Cody drawled, not sure whether he should believe her, only knowing that, deep down, somewhere, he did, "it didn't happen that way."

She met his eyes beseechingly. "If only I'd known what was going on at the time, I would have come forward to save you, implicate them and set the record straight."

Wary of being suckered in again—he could feel his defenses slipping away with every moment he spent with Callie—Cody studied her bluntly. "That's what Max said, too," he said tersely as he sat back down at the table. He had gone to enough trouble to cook this meal, he figured he might as well finish it, particularly since Callie did not look as if she had an enormous appetite, either.

"What do you mean?" Callie said, completely stunned. "Are you telling me that Max didn't know about my kidnapping, either?"

Cody nodded reluctantly. He knew how it had been a mistake for him not to go to his uncle from the start; that was one of the reasons he and Max had quarreled and never made up. Cody scowled. He knew that for the rest of his life he was going to regret the fact that Max had died before the two of them could make up.

But his actions had been inevitable, Cody realized with regret. His guardedness, his inability to let others in on what he was thinking and feeling had started when his parents had died.

But to his increasing frustration, dealing with his grief and getting on with his life hadn't been as easy for him, then or now, even though he was made of the same rough-and-tumble McKendrick stock as his brother and sister.

Not wanting to let his Uncle Max and the others down, knowing it was what they all expected of him, Cody had drawn on every ounce of willpower he had and forced himself to toughen up. To his pleasure and surprise, he'd eventually found he could be every bit the sturdy westerner that the rest of them were. Unfortunately, there'd been a downside to all that self-imposed toughness.

Since recovering from his grief, Cody had found it almost impossible to open up, to let himself love anyone except Patience and Trace. Callie had almost changed that once. She was trying to change it again. He just wasn't sure he should let her. He didn't want to go back to feeling like he could take a shot through the heart again. He didn't want to put himself at risk of being hurt, or abandoned, however involuntarily, again.

Aware Callie was still waiting for an explanation and that she wouldn't rest until she got one, he went on reluctantly. "When your pa and Buck showed me the ransom demand, it specifically mentioned Max. It said his phone lines were tapped and if I tried to go to him for help in rescuing you, you'd be dead within minutes. Because I didn't want to take a chance of anything happening to you, I didn't confide in him. I just withdrew all the cash I could get to on my own and tried to bluff my way through the rest."

Callie sighed. She regarded him with compassion. "Max must have been hurt when he found out what had happened."

"Yeah, he was, but he also knew I'd done what I felt I had to do then. Just as I've gotta do what I feel I have to do now."

Callie held her breath. "And that is?"

"Much as we want to, we can't go back and change things, Callie," Cody said tightly, reining in the heartfelt passion he felt for her and replacing it with good old-fashioned horse sense. "We can't pretend the kidnapping and my setup by your con artist family never happened. Because it did."

19:00

MAYBE THEY COULDN'T change the past, Callie thought as she began to clear the table, but she had a chance to influence her and Cody's future, if only she could find a way to get rid of her brother and father. They had ruined her chances with Cody once. She didn't want it happening again. And she knew if Cody saw either one of them hanging around, he would go ballistic.

"I'm going to call down to the bunkhouse and the cattle barns, make sure everything is okay," Cody said gruffly.

Callie knew, after all the intimate talk just now, that he wanted to put some physical distance between them. And maybe that wasn't such a bad idea. She didn't want to feel she was in a marriage or a relationship on her own, with her doing all the giving and getting nothing in return. Yet Cody, with his challenging manner and surprising vulnerability, was tempting her to take the risk and do just that.

"Cisco is supposed to stop by in a few minutes with some papers for me to sign. He usually comes in the back," Cody continued. "In the meantime, I'll be in the study."

Callie set the dirty dishes in the sink. "I'll let you know when he gets here," she promised. In the meantime, maybe she could figure out how to handle him.

Callie wasn't used to charging in where she wasn't wanted. She wasn't sure she liked the sensation. But too much was riding on the outcome of their forty-eight hours for her not to give it at least one last concerted try. And she was no longer too shy to admit it.

She wanted to own a ranch, some place of her own, something strong and solid. She wanted to have a fresh start so she could make something of herself. And she wanted a family, and a good, strong, honest husband who wasn't afraid to stand up for what was right, someone who would not neglect to show his love for her.

Having seen her video, having known her, Max had been aware of all that. He'd felt that because of her love of animals and the outdoors and riding and roping and Montana, the bull's-eye property on the Silver Spur was the perfect place for her to build her nest. And he had known it was the ideal place for her to raise the kids she wanted to have, with Cody.

The problem was the past.

If she had a chance to do it all over again, she would not have leaned on Cody so much or let him try to save her by helping her run away. Instead, she would have saved herself first and then gone to him, but only when her life was in good shape. Instead, she had ended up inadvertently making her problems—Buck and Pa—his problems, and she was very sorry about that, because that experience seemed to have hurt and embittered Cody in a way that might not ever be undone. No matter how much Max, or she, wanted it so, Callie thought as she finished loading the dishwasher.

She had just started on the pots and pans when Cisco Kidd showed up, a sheaf of legal documents in hand. Hat in hand, he entered the kitchen. "Hi, Callie."

"Could I talk to you a minute, privately?" Callie asked, waylaying him before he had a chance to head back to the study.

The germ of an idea was beginning to form. If she was going to get rid of Pa and Buck, she would have to do it on her own. And the sooner the better.

"Sure." Cisco Kidd set down his hat and briefcase genially and pulled up a chair at the kitchen table. He watched her with thinly veiled interest. "Max asked me to be of assistance to all of you in any way I could."

Too nervous to sit with him, Callie paced back and forth. She was taking a risk here, but she had no choice, she reminded herself sternly. "Is there any way you can find out if there are any outstanding warrants on my pa and my brother for me?" she finally blurted out.

Cisco's brows rose. "I can call Sheriff Anderson," he offered.

Callie raked her teeth across her lower lip. "But can you do that without Cody finding out?" she specified worriedly.

"I'm a lawyer, Callie. Of course I can be discreet." Cisco paused to study her bluntly. "Are you sure you should be keeping secrets from him, though? I have a feeling Max wouldn't approve. He reined you two together for forty-eight hours to bring you closer, not the other way around."

Callie's spine stiffened in indignation. She knew Uncle Max's attorney meant well, but she didn't need him making her feel guilty, too. Nevertheless, as she exhaled wearily, she was all too aware she needed Cisco Kidd on her side if she was going to accomplish what she wanted. "Believe me, Cisco, I have no choice."

Besides, whatever secret activities she had to indulge in now would be worth it if she could just get rid of Buck and Pa before the wedding, Callie thought as she picked up a scouring pad and resumed cleaning the broiler pan. Buck and Pa had bilked so many people out of their life savings they deserved to be in jail, even if they were her kin. Not to mention what they had done to Cody and to her in Acapulco, Callie sighed regretfully. If not for the two of them, she and Cody might be happily married now.

Cisco watched Callie resume scrubbing the broiler pan with more than necessary force. Obviously realizing the utmost discretion was called for in this situation, he pushed back his chair and closed the distance between them. He stood looking down at her, his arms folded in front of him and his back to the counter. "What do you want me to do if I find out there are warrants?" he asked very quietly.

Callie swallowed against the knot of fear in her throat. As she looked up into the young and handsome attorney's face, she reminded herself she was only doing what was right. "Let the sheriff know they are in the area."

Cisco did not look surprised at her decision. Rather, he seemed to support it wholeheartedly, even as he, too, tensed in concern. "Are you saying your pa and brother are here?" he asked her point-blank.

Callie nodded, flushing all the more as she marshaled her resolve to see justice done. Would she ever stop feeling embarrassed that Buck and Pa were her kin?

"I thought you were going to tell me when Cisco arrived, Callie," Cody interrupted smoothly from the doorway.

At the sound of Cody's voice, Callie jumped a mile. Though she had done nothing wrong, she felt as if she had been caught red-handed in a secret tête-à-tête. Cisco looked equally uneasy; it was clear he didn't like going behind Cody's back. Well, there was nothing to do but brazen it out. A cordial smile plastered on her face, she turned to face Cody. "Well, as you can see for yourself, he's here," she said politely.

"And I've got the papers you wanted." Cisco picked them up from the tabletop and held them out.

His eyes still on Callie and Cisco, grimly studying them both for any sign of deception, Cody took the papers. His manner even more tense and unapproachable, he perused them carefully. Finally, he sighed. "These look fine." Reaching into his pocket for a pen, he scribbled his name authoritatively at the bottom.

"Well, if that's all..." Cisco took the papers back and slipped them into his briefcase. Anxious to be on his way, he snapped shut the lid. "I'll be going."

Cody nodded, his eyes still on Callie. "Let me know if there's any more problems with the ranch tonight," he told Cisco.

"Will do." Cisco tersely smiled his adieu and slipped out the door.

Cody turned back to Callie. A taut silence stretched between them. She knew at once the gloves were off. "Are you going to tell me?"

Feeling guilty for excluding Cody, for she knew he hated being cut out of the action and relegated to the sidelines more than anything else, Callie picked up the mesh bag of baking potatoes and took it back into the walk-in pantry. *I have no choice but to do this on my own if I want him back,* she told herself firmly. And she was honest enough to admit to herself that she did want him back, had for years and years now. Even if he hadn't exactly welcomed her with open arms.

Slender shoulders squared, her back to Cody, she put the potatoes on the shelf and mentally braced herself for the thorough interrogation she knew was coming. Cody was not the type of man anymore to let anything drop, never mind her tête-à-tête with Cisco Kidd.

Cody followed her inside the small space, his large, muscular frame solidly blocking the only exit from the storage closet. "What was going on here a few minutes ago?" he demanded.

Refusing to let either his size or his strength intimidate her, Callie focused on the suntanned column of his throat. She did not want him to see how much she yearned to tell him everything. "I don't know what you mean," she said stubbornly.

Cody planted his hands on either side of her head and backed her against the wall. He towered over her, his blue eyes intent. She could see the pulse working in his neck, feel the evocative warmth of his body. "I think you do," he said, very softly.

So what? Callie knew that to give Cody an inch in terms of explanations would be to give him a mile. She did not want him to think he could goad her into submission. She was her own person these days. He might as well know and accept that before they took their relationship even one step further. She angled her chin up at him defiantly and said with complete honesty, "In all the time I've known you, Cody, I have given you no reason to distrust *me*."

Cody's lips curved cynically. He leaned closer, so they were touching in one long, electricity-filled line. "Now that," he drawled, "is a matter for debate."

For whom? Callie's temper flared. It was bad enough being kin to Buck and Pa without being blamed for everything lousy that they did. She planted her hand on the solid wall of his chest and pushed with all her might. It was like trying to move a five-hundred-pound boulder. "Look, either you trust me not to hurt you or you don't, Cody." Either he knew her heart and soul—as she felt deep down he did—or he didn't.

"The only thing I really trust," Cody said, ignoring her efforts to disengage herself as he gathered her in his arms with the same careless strength with which he had made love to her earlier, "is the passion we share." The vulnerability fading from his eyes, he dipped his head to hers and began to kiss her.

Savoring his hunger and his impatience, Callie leaned into the sensuous caress. Her heart pounded as his palms slid up her back to her shoulders, then down again to her breasts. She opened her mouth to the probing of his tongue, fitting herself more accurately to him and moaning softly in the back of her throat. She had never imagined she could feel this way, would want to feel this way, but she did, and that brought home the stark reality of the situation like nothing else.

"Uh-huh," Callie told him breathlessly as, hand to his chest, she tore her mouth from his and decisively called a halt. "If we're going to make love again, Cody," she said firmly, her mind made up, "we're going to do it on my terms."

Chapter Ten

"And what terms would those be?" Cody drawled.

Callie would have liked it if she could have demanded love from him, straight out. But she knew that wasn't going to happen, not for a long while. Because of what her family had done to him, Cody still didn't trust her. And without trust, there could be no love. It was as simple as that.

If she wanted to make a life for herself with Cody—and she was increasingly willing to admit to herself that she did—she would have to do it via the back way, so to speak. She would have to take the biggest risk she had ever taken in her life and give herself to him while asking nothing in return. Maybe in that way she could prove to him how much she really cared about him.

"Forget what Max is forcing us into. I want to have an affair with you. Where no promises are made, no emotions are involved."

For a second, Cody seemed startled. He paused, as if anticipating this to be some sort of trick on her part. "Just sex?"

Callie nodded. "Sex—" *and this was important* "—and a truce," she specified bluntly. "I don't want to fight with you anymore, Cody." She only wanted to concentrate on all that was good and positive between them. In an environment like that, Cody would begin to let his guard down, Callie reasoned securely. Their love could grow.

And he did care about her, in his own way, even if he wouldn't admit as much to himself yet. Callie was sure of it. Otherwise, he never would have run away with her years ago, and he would have given his heart to someone else in the seven years since then. But he hadn't, for the same reason she hadn't. Because if the past twenty-seven hours had taught her anything, it was that there was no one else for either of them and never would be. Just as Max had guessed....

Cody stepped back. He stared at her, spellbound. "That's quite a proposition you've made."

And also the most daring thing I've ever done.

"I'll have to think about it," he said laconically, jamming his thumbs through his belt loops and rocking back on his heels. "I'm not promising anything."

Knowing Cody was a man who prided himself on his independence, Callie considered it a start.

His expression abruptly brooding and intent, Cody turned on his heel and left the pantry. Still rocked by the electricity of his kisses, Callie watched him grab his Stetson and denim jacket. "Where are you going?" She had hoped he would stay and take her up on her offer!

He gave her a brief, sidelong glance. "To talk to Patience."

She hurried to catch up with him. "I'll go with you."

"No." He put out a hand to block her way. "I'll be back before my thirty minutes is up." Giving her no time to reply, he slipped out the door without a backward glance.

18:30

CODY FOUND HIS SISTER in her writing studio, working on her syndicated advice column to the lovelorn, which was rife with western homilies and sage practical advice. "Where's Josh?"

Patience typed in "Save" on her computer, so no data would be lost, and pushed away from her desk. "Checking on a mare who's about to foal."

Cody edged closer. He hated to interrupt her work, but he needed to talk. "Heard from Trace?" he asked casually.

Patience vaulted to her feet energetically. "He's got his hands full with Susannah and the kids." Taking his wrist in hand, she tugged him over to the long window seat in front of the windows. As they sat down, she curled her blue-jeaned legs beneath her. "Haven't you spoken with him?"

"Not yet." The truth was, Cody had never felt all that close to Trace. He had always felt himself to be in Trace's shadow, and even now a subtle, if unconscious rivalry remained between them. It was something he fought. As an adult and a successful businessman-rancher in his own right, he knew he didn't have to compete with Trace for anything. But a part of him still did. Just as a part of him needed Patience's compassion. The downside was that she saw too much sometimes and tried to meddle in his life. But right now she had her hands full with her own problems, so that was unlikely, at least until after the wedding.

"What's up?" Patience asked.

Cody stretched his long legs out in front of him. It felt good to finally be able to unburden himself to his big sister. "The will, of course. I'm going nuts trying to carry out Uncle Max's wishes, never mind meet the terms."

Patience reached over to touch his face. "And yet I see you had time to shave your beard," she teased. Her blue eyes, so like his, gentled with understanding. "Callie have something to do with that?"

"You might say she had a hand in it."

Cody recalled how sensual it had been to have Callie shaving him. How much he had enjoyed having her in his bed. Though he no longer wanted an all-out war between them, he was beginning to feel vulnerable again. He didn't like that much, either. He glanced at his watch, wishing he had more time to sort all this out. The question was where to start. He could talk about his feelings for Callie endlessly and never tell them all. "Listen, I've only got about ten minutes."

"Tell me about it," Patience commiserated. "I've never been on such a tight timetable in my life."

"I'm here because I need your advice," he continued hurriedly. "You know a lot about affairs of the heart and—"

"You're falling in love with her again, aren't you, Cody?" Patience interrupted.

Cody grimaced as she knit her fingers together over one crossed knee. "Is it that obvious?" he asked his sister.

Patience shrugged. "Maybe not to everyone else, but I can see it," she replied softly. "Callie has always been the only woman for you."

Cody stood and began to pace. He had never felt so restless. "That being the case, what kind of fool am I?"

"Stubborn. You don't want this to work precisely because Uncle Max did. I know, 'cause I feel the same way about my own situation," Patience confided ruefully, making a face.

"So what are you going to do?" Cody asked, thinking maybe he could follow her example or at least learn from it.

To Cody's dismay, Patience shook her head and refused to tell. "The question is, What are you going to do?"

Cody sighed as the dark clouds rolled in, obscuring his view of the stars. He knew what Max would have wanted. "Marrying her tomorrow is one heck of a risk." And yet, despite everything, part of Cody wanted to do just that.

"Not marrying her could be worse," Patience predicted direly. She rose gracefully and made her way to his side. Comforting hand on his arm, she murmured logically, "When things fell apart before, you didn't give her a second chance." Their eyes meshed and held as Patience continued matter-of-factly, "Don't you think it's time you did?"

AFTER MUCH DELIBERATION, Callie picked up the ice blue satin nightgown with the plunging neckline, spaghetti straps and thigh-high slits on each side. Unlike anything she had ever owned, it was the kind of outfit that drove men wild, and Callie had always wanted to drive a man wild. Correction. She had always wanted to drive Cody wild.

She grinned, wondering what Cody's response would be when he saw her in this. Maybe when he did, he wouldn't find it so easy to walk out on her, she thought. At the very least, he would know what he was missing, she mused as she laid the negligee aside for later, ran a brush through her hair and sprayed on perfume. At the very best, he might end up giving them a second chance to make this relationship of theirs work.

She heard a door open and shut downstairs. Cody was home. Wanting an indicator of his mood after their latest blowup, she swept out of the bedroom and glanced surreptitiously over the stairs. To her horror, instead of Cody, she saw the back of Buck's head. She couldn't believe her low-down, no-good brother was back! Darn it all, Callie thought as she knotted her hands into fists. Why wouldn't he get the message and leave her alone?

"Callie?" Buck called, just as Callie ducked back out of sight. "I want to talk to you."

She heard his footsteps move toward the kitchen, then back toward the stairs to the second floor.

Damn, Callie thought, already breaking out in a sweat as she slipped back into her bedroom. Now what? Cody was due back in just under ten minutes. He couldn't find Buck here! If he did, their romance was over for sure!

Buck's footsteps were heading toward the master bedroom. "Callie, damn it," he called like a kid playing hide-and-seek. "I know you're in here!"

Callie had no choice; she had to confront Buck. Her slender shoulders squared with righteous indignation, she followed him into the master bedroom. "What do you want?" she demanded with a take-no-prisoners look.

"What do you think? Cash!" Buck retorted, flashing her an evil grin.

"Well, well, what have we here?" Buck murmured with disgusting glee as he moved toward Cody's bureau. "The damn fool left his wallet."

No, Callie thought determinedly as she tried to cut her no-account brother off before he could make good the theft. Unfortunately, he was bigger, meaner and stronger than she. Tripping her off-balance, he planted a meaty hand on her back and sent her sprawling against the bed. Her body screaming at the rough treatment, Callie watched Buck empty Cody's wallet and toss it back on the bureau with a thud. Once she would have tolerated this. No more.

She was already simultaneously looking for something to use as a weapon and wondering if Buck—like Pa—now carried a gun, when down below the door opened and shut again.

"Callie?" Cody called, sounding impatient as hell. "Where are you?"

"I seriously doubt he'd like to know the answer to that," Buck muttered gamely. He looked her up and down with a contempt that made her skin crawl. "Too bad we didn't have a chance to talk. But I'll catch up with you again, little sis, just you wait. And then you'll lend me and Pa a hand."

That's what he thought! "And if I don't?" Callie challenged quietly, praying Buck would get out of there before Cody saw him and real trouble erupted on the Silver Spur Ranch.

Buck's glance turned brutal. "Then we'll put Plan Two into action."

"What's that?" Callie whispered, her heart beating like a wild thing in her chest.

"You'll find out soon enough." Buck grabbed her arm and twisted it brutally. "Unless you can get us a damn sight more cash. So I'd work on that if I was you." He released her with a shove and she landed on the bed.

Moving soundlessly to the window, Buck opened the sash, stepped out onto the porch roof and dropped to the ground.

Cody's footsteps were hard on the stairs. But before Callie could compose herself, he stumbled to a halt at the doorway. He couldn't have looked more incredulous. Callie drew a deep breath and hoped he wouldn't suspect Buck had been in the house. Most of all, she wanted to protect Cody from any further heartbreak or disappointment. He had a hard enough time trusting as it was. "You're back!" she said.

"Would appear so." Bracing both hands on the door frame, Cody mocked her with a glance. Once again, he seemed to know intuitively that something was up. "Been waiting long?" he drawled as he let go of the frame and edged toward her.

Aware of the way his eyes had homed in on her, and the way her arm was aching from the way Buck had twisted it, Callie swept to her feet. "Not too long," she allowed a little breathlessly.

Cody stopped just short of the bed, clearly sensing something was amiss. "So what's going on?" he asked, determined to find out.

"Nothing much." Fixing him with the kind of smile she reserved for the most difficult people, she indicated the stairs. "Want to go downstairs and talk awhile? You can tell me all about Patience. And Trace."

"Actually—" Cody hooked his thumbs through the belt loops of his jeans and fixed her with a brooding stare "—I'd be more anxious to know why you're so jumpy all of a sudden." He tracked the incriminating flush in her cheeks with eyes that had narrowed to dark blue slits. "What have you been up to, Callie?"

"Nothing. Nothing at all."

Cody gave her another long, considering look, then crossed to the window. He glanced out. "Hmm."

Callie's heart fluttered in her chest. She should have realized she couldn't hide anything from him; he knew her too well. "What?"

"Unless I'm mistaken..." Cody pivoted and gave Callie another long, thorough perusal.

Without another word, he shouldered by her and headed out the bedroom door and back down the stairs. Knowing an unprecedented delay in Cody's search was her only prayer of salvation, Callie hurried after him. By the time she caught up with him, he was kneeling in the grass beside the porch. "Look what we have here," he said, directing the illuminating yellow beam of his flashlight onto the thick wet grass. "Man-size footprints."

"No surprise about that," Callie breezed, shivering as the cool air hit her breasts. "Uncle Max's attorney probably left them when he was here earlier."

"I don't think so." Cody gave Callie another sharp-eyed glance meant to fill her with unease. "He came and went through the back, remember?"

"Oh."

"So who was it, Callie?" Cody asked. Planting an arm on either side of her, he trapped her against the porch. His lower body molded against hers, he wrapped his arms tightly around her. "Who was here tonight?" he asked, tugging her even closer.

Callie lifted her chin and drew in a bolstering breath. "No one." *Who counts.*

"Mmm-hmm." His gaze meshed with hers, Cody gave her a cynical half smile. "You'll excuse me if I check that out?" He released her as swiftly and unexpectedly as he had hauled her close.

Feeling as if her knees would barely support her, Callie stumbled backward. "Now where are you going?" she asked, hurrying after him.

Cody refused to answer and merely headed for the stairs.

Callie's worst fears were confirmed as he headed straight for his bureau, and then his wallet. Damn, damn, damn, she thought as he examined the empty contents.

He held it up with two fingers and dangled it in front of her. "I'd have thought you would at least wait until after the wedding before you ripped me off."

Callie gulped. She had never seen him in a more dangerous, less forgiving mood. "What exactly is missing?"

He tilted his head. "Like you don't know," he said sarcastically, continuing to survey her in that slow, insolent way.

Callie flushed self-consciously. "I don't." Not really. All she had seen was a flash of plastic and a flash of green. Which reminded her, she really needed to call her own credit cards in and report them stolen the first chance she had....

Cody slammed his empty billfold back onto the bureau. He grabbed her by the shoulders and drew her up short. "Who's in on the scam with you this time, Callie?" He shook her roughly. "Your pa and your brother, or someone else?"

Callie wiggled out of his grasp. Having no defense for her behavior, she concentrated on his. "I am not going to stay here and be accused when I am not guilty of one damn thing." *Except being fool enough to love you!* Chin high, Callie spun away indignantly.

Cody caught her arm and reeled her right back to his side. "I've got news for you, Callie." He laced a staying arm around her middle that felt like an iron band. "You will stay," he informed her as his glance roved her upturned face with barely leashed passion. "And you will answer all my questions."

"The alternative being?" Callie prodded.

"There is no alternative for us," he murmured hoarsely, looking as if he wished he were anywhere but there. "Haven't you figured that out?"

Before she could formulate a reply, Cody's lips found hers. He gripped her waist and kissed her with passion and fury. Her lips softened instantly under his, and her ready acceptance infused them both with a sharp, urgent need.

Groaning, having lost the last of his self-control, Cody dragged his mouth back and forth across hers. He tasted the corners of her lips with his tongue. He drank of her deeply. He cradled her head in his hands and sank his fingers into the lush, wild softness of her hair.

Callie was aware of the need and the yearning in him, but without love it would never be enough.

Desperation filling her soul, Callie yanked herself away from him. A pulse hammering in her throat, she whispered emotionally, "Damn you, Cody McKendrick, I am not going to let you make love to me out of anger or a need for revenge." He had to at the very least need and want her, and perhaps someday soon even love her.

"Haven't you figured it out yet?" Cody whispered, tangling his hands in her hair yet again. He dipped his head and delivered another long, thorough kiss, which weakened her knees and sent her senses into overdrive. "The way things are between us, it's not going to happen any other way."

Callie looked up into his face and knew he'd left her no choice. The depth of her hurt gave her the strength to push him away. "As long as you feel this way, it's not going to happen at all!" she stormed right back.

Cody was quiet for a moment. Then he shook his head as if that would clear it. As the seconds ticked out tensely, the passion faded from his eyes. "You're right," he admitted with hoarse reluctance. "This is nuts. We can't stay here."

Then where could they go where it would be any different? Callie wondered. As much as she would have liked to thank her decorating that afternoon for his most recent display of desire for her, it wasn't the place creating the intimacy between them, it wasn't even the terms of Max's will, it was their feelings. And those, she knew, were only bound to deepen, despite Cody's obvious wish to the contrary.

Wearily, she watched him rummage through his closet and come out with a denim jacket. "What are you doing now?"

He eyed her split skirt and silk blouse impatiently. "Get dressed in some warm clothes," he commanded roughly, already doing the same.

But Callie didn't follow orders unless she agreed with them. "Where are we going?" she demanded irritably.

Cody tossed her a sweater growling, "You'll find out soon enough."

Chapter Eleven

17:00

"You think you want to be a rancher?" Cody asked her as he parked the truck on the top of a rise overlooking a good part of the Silver Spur cattle operation and cut the engine. "Then you ought to be able to spend a night on the range."

Callie didn't mind hard work. She did mind being jerked around. "For no purpose?" Callie challenged.

"Oh, there's a purpose." Cody climbed out of the cab and reached into the bed of the truck for a bedroll.

"I'd like to hear it," Callie said as he climbed back into the cab and settled the bedroll between them on the bench seat.

Cody pulled the brim of his hat lower over his eyebrows and stretched his long legs out in front of him. "Someone's been trespassing on the Silver Spur operation. From where we're going to be, we'll have a clear view of the road. I see any vehicle that doesn't belong, I'm going to take after it like a bat out of hell." Cody pushed the seat back as far as it would go so there was maximum leg room between him and the dash.

Callie hated to see him looking so darn comfortable. "We're going to be out here all night?" *Until dawn?* "Is that the plan?" she asked incredulously.

"Looks like." Cody turned slightly toward her and gave her a taunting smile. "Got a problem with that?"

Callie blew out a frustrated breath and swung around so her back was flush against the passenger door. Just because he planned to play sheriff all night didn't mean she had to stay awake. According to the terms of Max's will, all she had to do was stay near him. She looked hopefully behind the seat at the narrow cargo space on the floor and then at the bed of the truck. She saw no other bedrolls. "I don't suppose you've got a sleeping bag or a blanket I could borrow."

"No. And that's another thing you gotta learn." Cody waggled a lecturing finger her way. "As a rancher, you're responsible for your own gear."

A sharp retort played on the edge of Callie's tongue.

He didn't think she could handle it. Having failed in his efforts to sweet-talk her off the Silver Spur, he was now trying to scare her away. Well, it wasn't going to work. Callie reached for the thermos of steaming coffee she'd brought along. "Fine. I'll be responsible for my own bedroll then." *Now that it was too late for her to bring anything along.* "You're responsible for your own coffee."

Cody slanted her a bad-boy grin. "Darlin', I got my own beverage."

Callie didn't like the way he said that. She watched him reach past her and remove the flask from the glove compartment of his truck. "What's in the flask?"

Cody regarded her unrepentantly as he uncapped it and took a long, thirsty swig. "Guess you'll never know."

Inwardly, Callie fumed, but outwardly she kept her face expressionless as Cody recapped his flask and reached for the rifle.

Her anger with him mounting, she watched as he checked to see if it was loaded. Unfortunately, it was. "You're not planning to use that on anyone, are you?" she asked.

"Humans?" Cody put the safety on, double-checked it, then slid it carefully back in the gun rack behind the seat.

"Not likely. But all nature of beasts are out here this time of night."

Callie knew the wildlife in that area of Montana was plentiful. It included deer, elk, moose, even the occasional bear and coyote. "You can't scare me, Cody, no matter what you say or do."

"Fine. Then you won't mind getting out of the cab so I can catch a little shut-eye."

Callie blinked. He was carrying this a little too far, even for him. "And where, pray tell, am I supposed to go?" she asked.

Cody shrugged as he turned up the collar on his denim jacket. "That, my soon-to-be neighbor and once-and-future bride, is up to you."

16:54

CODY STRETCHED OUT on the bench seat, propping his bedroll behind his head. He watched as Callie lowered the tailgate and climbed into the bed of the pickup truck. He wondered what she would think if she knew that the beverage he was drinking had been plain water. Not that it really mattered. There was no doubt about it. She was royally ticked off. Which made them just about even. He was ticked off, too.

Callie was keeping something from him, Cody thought. Maybe even more than he would ever care to know. She was doing it now. She'd done it when he'd known her before. He could tell by the way she wouldn't look him in the eye, in her deliberate evasions and carefully worded answers to some of his questions.

There were some areas of her heart and life that were open to scrutiny. Other areas were strictly off limits. And that was what bothered Cody most. He wanted to love Callie with all his heart and soul. He admitted it.

But how could he love a woman who continually shut him out? Who told him only part of every story? Who kept things from him even now? Never mind contemplate marrying her, will or no will....

Cody didn't know a lot about marriage, only what he'd witnessed between his parents as a child, but he knew one thing, he thought fiercely. His parents had shared everything with each other, even up to and including their death. There had been no secrets in his parents' marriage. There would be none in his.

Furthermore, did she really think she could entertain another man in his house, right under his nose? Did she think she could go around lying to and deceiving him and he wouldn't notice? An hour later, he still had an ache in his heart that wouldn't quit. Of course it was his fault. Once again, he had ignored all the danger signs and allowed the two of them to get too close, too fast.

He hoped that staying out on the range all night would make her so mad at him it would be no hardship at all for them to stay apart. If she was still seeing red when they got married tomorrow, even better. With her considerable temper flaring, she was bound to walk out on him right away. At the very least she'd avoid him like the plague. And sooner or later, she'd realize she wasn't cut out for this life and she would sell the bull's-eye property back to him. He could build the house he had always dreamed of building. And with her out of his system once and for all, he could marry and settle down and have a family of his own. The fact that every time he envisioned his wife, he envisioned Callie was of no consequence, he told himself sternly. Nor was the fact they were already married and had been since Mexico.

He knew some would call it a sham wedding, but deep down it didn't feel like a sham to him. And that went double since they'd now made love. Not as man and wife, as he'd hoped they would, but as two people who had been, and always would be, passionately in lust—or was it love?—with each other.

His only hope of surviving this situation emotionally was to get Callie out of his life again once and for all, Cody thought as he stared at the ferocious clouds above. And that was what he was determined to do.

CALLIE SAT IN ONE CORNER of the pickup bed, her back against the rear window of the passenger compartment. Cup of coffee in her hands, knees drawn up to her chest, she stared at the black sky overhead. The storm that had been closing in all evening was getting incredibly near. The wind was whipping up and in the distance she could hear the plaintive howl of a coyote. At least she assumed it was a coyote. She knew there was a lot of wildlife in territory this wild, and that it all liked to come out at night. For the moment, however, she was safe enough, since she doubted any wild animal would be ornery or clever enough to jump up over the closed tailgate and into the bed of the pickup with her. And if she was threatened, surely Cody would protect her.

Without warning, it began to rain. Callie swore as big fat drops fell on her head. In the distance, near the horizon, wicked lightning flashed. She turned around. Cody was wide-awake and drinking from that darn flask again. She knew he knew it was raining, yet he made no offer to let her come into the cab of the truck with him.

It began to rain harder. Callie took off her jacket and tented her head and shoulders with it. There was still no response from Cody. The next time lightning illuminated the sky, Callie began to count. When she hit three, an ominous roll of thunder followed. The storm was three miles away, but it was getting closer.

Adrenaline pumping in her veins, Callie looked around. She'd be damned if she would stay in the bed of the pickup like a sitting duck, regardless of what Uncle Max wanted. Will or no will, she was getting out of here.

CODY HEARD THE CREAK of the tailgate opening and knew he had won. Callie was going to come to him and beg to get inside the cab with him. He'd let her, of course, but *only* after she had told him everything she had been keeping from him so far. And the first thing he wanted to know was who she had been entertaining.

Noticing it was taking her an awfully long time to circle around to the front of the truck, Cody glanced in the rearview mirror. He was shocked to see Callie striding away from the truck, toward the woods.

Damn that woman, didn't she know the trees were every bit as dangerous as the open plain?

Pushed into action, Cody vaulted out of the truck. "Callie, come back here!" he ordered grimly.

Pumping her arms and legs all the harder, she yelled back, "Go to hell!"

The pelting rain practically blinding him, Cody dashed around and planted himself directly in her path. Like her, he was getting very wet, very fast. "Where are you going?"

Callie balled her hands into fists at her sides. "Where do you think?"

Cody bit back an oath. His plans hadn't included either of them getting wet, and he was uncomfortably aware of how her wet sweater clung to her breasts. "You may not have noticed," he pointed out smoothly, "but you are headed into the storm, not away from it."

Callie squared her slender shoulders and shrugged off his warning. "Can't be any worse than what I've already suffered," she announced stubbornly as the rain began to pour down on them in earnest.

Cody wanted nothing more than to pick her up and carry her back to the truck if need be, but he did not want to show he cared. She had enough of a hold on him as it was. On the other hand, trying to talk sense into her was something he would do for any of his hired hands under the same circumstances. Tipping the brim of his hat back with one finger, he regarded her patiently. "You'll get struck by lightning," he said calmly.

"Why should you care?" Callie countered thickly.

Cody couldn't be sure but he thought those were tears running down Callie's cheeks.

"You don't care about me," she accused, looking almost more miserable than he felt as lightning flashed overhead. "I don't think you ever did."

Cody swallowed as thunder rumbled in the sky.

She was getting to the heart of the matter, all right, but he saw no reason to do so in the torrential rain. Nor did he have any desire to get struck by lightning, which was getting closer all the time.

"Get in the truck, Callie," Cody ordered grimly. If she wanted to continue discussing this, and he didn't, they could do so somewhere safe.

"You get in the truck," Callie countered, pivoting on her heel. Hands swinging at her sides, she marched away from him. "I've had enough of you for one evening!"

Cody snorted in derision and took off after her. Three paces, another flash of lightning and an almost simultaneous clap of thunder and he was at her side.

She swore. "I told you—I'm walking out of here."

"Not in this storm, you're not." Putting an end to the argument once and for all, Cody scooped her up into his arms and flung her over his shoulder like a sack of potatoes. She was damp, warm and completely resisting.

"What do you think you're doing?" Callie pushed on his waist ineffectually.

His mouth set grimly, Cody headed for the truck. "What I should have done a long time ago. Taking you home."

15:40

"ALL RIGHT, WILD MAN. You have proved your point." Callie faced him in the ranch house kitchen. She was soaked to the skin and so was he.

Cody swept his hat off his head and sent it sailing across the room, where it landed with a crash. "Darlin', I haven't *begun* to prove my point."

She knew that he was furious and he had no reason to be. Unfortunately, Callie couldn't explain without incriminating herself further in his eyes. "I'm getting out of here."

She headed for the back door. Cody moved to bar her way. Every virile inch of him braced for action, he folded his arms in front of him. "I thought we had settled this," he said firmly, inclining his head toward the door behind him. "That storm is vicious."

A warm rush of color suffused her cheeks. "You are not the boss of me, Cody McKendrick."

He watched her closely. "Maybe not, but I still am not going to let anything happen to you. So you're staying here, whether you like it or not, Callie." As he completed his command, his voice dropped another emotional notch.

"Because of Uncle Max? And the will?" Callie challenged, scowling.

"Because of me." Cody tossed off his soaked denim jacket. Wordlessly, he closed the distance between them and took her into his arms. Before she could protest, he lowered his head to hers and kissed her thoroughly, and he did not stop until she was soft against him, her mouth open beneath his. "I couldn't live with myself if anything happened to you," he confessed huskily at last.

Callie realized the impossible had happened. The old innately gallant Cody was back. Without warning, tears of happiness were streaming down her face. Her emotions were in tumult. "Oh, Cody—"

"'Oh, Cody' what?" he asked, baffled, as he smoothed the damp ends of her blond hair away from her face.

"It's too late," she said, crying. "Too late for us to go back and remake the past."

"It's never too late," Cody disagreed softly.

As if to demonstrate that, he drew her into his arms and kissed her even more passionately. And while they were kissing, there was a brilliant flash of lightning, followed by a deafening crack of thunder, loud enough to drive them apart. And then the lights went out.

"THAT SOUNDED awfully close!" Extricating herself from Cody's arms, Callie paused a moment to let her eyes adjust to the sudden blackness in the room, then rushed to the window. All she could see in the darkness of the night was the gusts of wind and the blowing rain. Shivering, she turned to Cody, who was looking out another window toward the same vantage point. "Did you see where it hit?" she asked anxiously.

Cody pointed to the mailbox at the end of his drive. Callie could see that the metal box had been split in two and knocked to the ground, and what was left of the wooden post was flaming. Thankfully, the rain was already putting the fire out.

Callie shivered uncontrollably as she realized that could have been her or Cody who had been struck if he hadn't insisted they get out of the storm when they had. Realizing they were both drenched to the skin, Callie watched as Cody moved to a kitchen drawer and brought out a powerful flashlight. "I'll call the power company," he said. He dialed, then, frowning deeply, put the kitchen phone down. "On second thought, I won't."

"What's wrong?"

"The phone is dead. It happens a lot when we get bad storms. I'm sure it'll be fixed by morning."

"How do you know it's the lines and not just your phone?" Callie asked, shivering again, this time more from fear than cold, although the storm was still raging mightily.

Cody reached into his pocket and picked up his cellular phone. He dialed again, but there was too much static and interference on the line and the call did not go through. "Like I thought," he said after he hung up. He folded the phone and put it on the counter. "You okay? You seem awfully jumpy."

"It's the storm." *And Buck and Pa and not knowing where they are or what they are up to now.* She hoped they weren't foolish enough to come back and try to take shelter here at the ranch house along with her and Cody. But she knew they were arrogant enough to try anything.

"Look. We're dripping everywhere. Let's get a bottle of brandy out of the pantry and get out of these wet clothes." Cody lit the way with the powerful beam of his flashlight. He stopped short as he opened the pantry door. "What the hell—"

Callie came up behind him. She saw what he saw and moaned. "Oh, no..." All their clothes were in a heap in the pantry and they had been doused with maple syrup, butter, catsup, mayonnaise, steak sauce...

Cody stared grimly at the mess. "Someone was here in our absence."

"Apparently," Callie murmured tightly, unable to hide the depth of her bitterness.

Cody laced an arm about her shoulders and gave her a hard, searching look. "You feeling okay?"

"Jim-dandy, under the circumstances," Callie said wearily as even more tears welled in her eyes.

Expecting Cody to lash out at her and blame her for this, too, she stiffened her spine and braced herself for the tirade. Instead, he said gently, "You don't look very good, Callie."

Which wasn't surprising, Callie thought. It looked as if absolutely every item of clothing she possessed, including the new things in her trousseau, were here, covered with sticky, smelly goo. And what if they weren't alone? "Maybe we should check the house out first," Callie suggested. Still shivering with the combined effects of the cold and shock, she edged away from him slightly. "Make sure everything else is okay."

As Cody studied her, his gaze turned cautious. "You want to tell me what you think is happening here?"

Callie brushed by him and ignored the question. "I think we should check the rest of the house out to make sure whoever did this isn't still here. Hopefully, it was just some teenage vandals playing a prank," she concluded desperately.

"We don't have teenage gangs or vandals out here, Callie."

Ignoring his thoughtful gaze, Callie raced to the back door, which was somewhat illuminated by Cody's flashlight. She checked around it, saw nothing and no one suspicious, then locked up. "I think we should check the entire house anyway," she said. If Buck and Pa had done this, she was going to cart them off to the sheriff herself. "It won't take long if we split up."

"All right," Cody said after a long pause. "You do this floor. I'll check everything out upstairs, gather up some towels and blankets and be right back."

As soon as he left, Callie saw movement outside the back door. Headed up the steps was Ray Anderson, the local sheriff. He had a yellow rain slicker on over his khaki uniform. A very honest and blunt-spoken man, he had been one of Max's poker-playing buddies and a regular at Pearl's diner when Callie had worked there during her teenage years.

"Callie?" He lifted the beam of his flashlight until they could see each other clearly. "Everything okay in there?"

Callie closed the door to the kitchen so they would not be overheard. Then she held the back door open and motioned the sheriff out of the storm and into the mudroom. She knew she had to trust someone. She figured it might as well be the law, since she was going to be talking to them eventually anyway. And Sheriff Anderson had had several run-ins with Buck and Pa years ago, when they were attempting to peddle their faulty insurance to senior citizens in the general area. Buck and Pa might never have given

Sheriff Anderson reason enough to arrest them, but they had skated dangerously close to the edge more than once.

"No," she said quietly, watching the rain drip off the brim of his hat. "It's not." Taking a quick breath before she could lose her nerve, she rushed on, "My pa and Buck are back in town. They were both here tonight. I saw Buck empty out Cody's wallet. I'm not sure how much cash he got but I know he stole several credit cards."

Sheriff Anderson focused on the way she was wringing her hands. "You saw this and you didn't try to stop him?"

Callie was silent, ashamed. She lifted her hands in a helpless gesture. "I tried but he tripped me and shoved me away. Then Cody came back and—" Callie couldn't go on.

"Does Cody know?"

"Only that they were stolen. Not who did it."

"He called in to report the theft."

"Yes. Before the storm hit."

Sheriff Anderson studied her in silence. Finally, he said, "Cisco Kidd told me what's going on, that you've asked him to find out about outstanding warrants on your kin. I checked. There are a few."

"Good." Callie drew a deep breath and wiped her eyes. "It's what I figured."

"So if you can tell me where they are, I'll show up and arrest them. Get them out of your hair."

"Thanks."

"Before I do that, there's something I need to know. Are you afraid of your brother, Callie?"

Tears gathering in her eyes, she nodded. She wanted to tell Cody everything about Buck and Pa's sudden reappearance in her life, but she feared he would never understand, not in a million years. And that in turn made her want to leave before Cody ended up hating her, again. She knew she couldn't bear it if they ended up more estranged than before.

"What about your pa? What's he been up to?" Sheriff Anderson continued to press.

Callie gulped. That subject was even more complicated. She studied the rain-soaked toe of her boot. "He wants me to extort money from Cody."

"And you refused?" Sheriff Anderson raised his voice slightly to be heard above the roar of the wind.

"Yes. But I know him. He'll be back to try again. So will Buck. They're even talking about implementing a Plan Two, whatever that is." Callie only knew it sounded evil.

The sheriff frowned as lightning forked across the sky. "You think they're responsible for the mischief on the ranch lately, the theft of the bull, the fire in the fields and so on?"

Callie nodded. "And some petty vandalism that was done inside the house tonight."

Sheriff Anderson frowned. "What does Cody have to say about all this?"

"He doesn't know it's them, not for sure, anyway," Callie said sadly.

"But you think he guesses."

Callie thrust her hands in her pockets and shrugged. "At some of it. At least, he's hinted as much."

Sheriff Anderson was silent a long moment. "This must be pretty hard on you," he said sympathetically at last. "Being caught between Cody and your family."

Emotion tightened her throat as Callie shook her head in silent misery. "I keep thinking about my ma and how she would have expected the family to stay together, no matter what." She would have expected Callie to be able to control Pa and Buck, the way she had. Of course, her ma had never expected that Pa and Buck would become as dangerous, or criminal, as they had.

"Sometimes you have to do what is right, even if it goes against what someone else wants," the sheriff said gently. He looked behind him at the dark and stormy night before turning back to Callie. "You think those two are going to come back tonight?" he asked flat out.

Callie bit her lip. She hated to call out the cops to stand guard over them just yet. She and Cody were starting to get so close. She could feel it in the way he had kissed her. He might not want to want her, but he did. He might not want to protect her, but he couldn't help that, either.

She looked up at Sheriff Anderson. "I don't know. Maybe."

"With the telephone lines down, I've been handing out a few of these." The sheriff reached into his pocket and pulled out a small, square, electronic device. He paused just long enough to punch in a code, then handed her a beeper. "I want you to keep this with you, Callie. If you see them, page me, and one of my deputies or I, whoever's closest, will be out right away to haul them to jail. Meantime, I got other places to check on."

"Thank you."

The problem was, Callie wasn't sure that simply arresting her kin for what were up to this point mostly misdemeanor offenses would do the trick. In fact, she realized miserably, if Pa and Buck spilled their guts about the Mexico debacle to everyone in town and made Cody a laughingstock of the community—or, worse, got off without even being convicted because of lack of concrete evidence against them—it might even make things horrible for Cody.

No, there was only one way to free Cody from Buck and Pa once and for all, now that she had alerted the sheriff to their presence. And that was for her to leave. Without her here, they would never be able to blackmail Cody again. Without her to use as a weapon against Cody, Buck and Pa would have no choice but to be arrested or leave, never to return again. Either way, they would be out of Cody's life forever.

Chapter Twelve

Cody locked every door, every window, checked every closet and under every bed. Gathering up a couple of towels and an armload of blankets and quilts, he went back downstairs to the back parlor.

Callie wasn't there. Frowning, he called her name and was met with only eerie silence. Deciding to search her out, he swept through the rest of the downstairs. She wasn't in the living room, study or kitchen. And neither were the keys to his truck. Instead, there was a hastily scrawled note on the kitchen table.

> I'm sorry, Cody, truly I am, but I can't go through with this. Talk to Cisco Kidd about the inheritance. When you do, you'll find out there is another way for you to keep the ranch. You don't have to lose everything. Just me....

Cody stared at the note. What the heck was she doing now? Did she really think all he cared about was the ranch? Okay, so prior to her showing up again, the Silver Spur cattle operation had been all he cared about. But that was then. This was now. Damn it, she was not running out on him again!

His temper sizzling, he headed out the back door and stopped dead in his tracks. Just as he suspected, his pickup was already heading down the gravel lane, away from the house. To his relief, the thunder and lightning had eased up for the moment, but the rain was coming down so hard visibility had been reduced to a mere hundred yards. Even so, he was able to see the brake lights come on before they disappeared into the misty night.

14:52

CALLIE GOT approximately a half mile away from the house when she realized she couldn't go any farther. She couldn't run out on Cody again. Because that's exactly what she was doing, running away. Just like she'd run away from the jobs that didn't quite work out, and the family she loathed, and her marriage. When her mother had been alive, it had been different. She'd at least tried to face up to her problems. Since then, she either hadn't had the strength or had simply felt, in some instances, that it wasn't worth her time and energy to try to change things, that it would be easier and simpler for all concerned if she just moved on. And maybe it had been, Callie didn't know. She only knew that this was one situation and one man that she could not run from, not anymore. She knew that in her heart, and it was time she started listening to her heart.

She had to muster up all her courage and stay and face up to the future, whatever it held. She had to have faith that it would all work out somehow if she just gave herself, and Cody, a chance. But first she had to help him get and keep his inheritance from Uncle Max. Without the ranch, Cody would never be happy. She couldn't live with herself if he lost all he had worked so hard for because of her.

Thrusting the truck into reverse, she backed it around ninety degrees to the right. Shifting it back into drive, she pressed on the accelerator. Rear wheels spinning, the truck reacted as if it were held in place by a steel hook and chain and stayed right where it was. Callie tried again. The engine roared louder. The wheels spun harder. To no avail. She was still stuck.

Realizing she was only digging herself deeper into the mud on either side of the narrow ranch lane, Callie cut the engine and laid her head on the steering wheel. She had fifteen minutes to get back to the house, fifteen minutes to trudge back through the pouring rain. Or it would all be over anyway, because she and Cody would have been apart more than thirty minutes. His inheritance would be permanently out of their reach. And it would be all her fault.

Callie laughed softly at the irony of the situation and shook her head. It was funny how close she had come to having everything again, only to risk it all by trying to run away, and she couldn't even do that competently because she'd changed her mind again, decided to go back and then gotten herself stuck.

Would Cody believe she had wanted to come back on her own now, given the position of the truck? Or would he think she had been forced back due to bad driving? Heaven knew he hadn't given her much credit up until now.

Figuring she would find out the answer to that soon enough, Callie began to gather up her gear. She had her arms full when the passenger door opened and an equally drenched Cody slid in beside her.

She swiveled to face him, not really surprised to see that he had come after her. Deep inside, she had wanted him to come after her. She always had. Callie regarded him warily. "I presume you got my note?"

Folding his hands behind his head, he stretched his long legs out in front of him. "Why else would I be here? And thanks for getting my truck stuck in the mud. We're going to have to walk back now, you know."

"I know—"

He lifted a hand and ever so gently touched the curve of her cheek. "So what made you stop and try to turn around?"

Callie leaned into his touch. "You saw that?" She kept her eyes locked with his.

"Trust me," he drawled with a half grin as he dropped his hand and sat back against the passenger window, "it would have been hard to miss."

True. Callie curved her left hand on the bottom of the steering wheel. "It occurred to me that I have been running from trouble all my life, and that maybe it was finally time I started facing up to it instead."

Maybe it was time she took those "eight seconds" Max had talked about and used them to the fullest, rather than have a lifetime of regrets ahead of her.

"Well, I'm trouble, all right," Cody murmured, tipping the brim of his hat back and sliding over to take her in his arms. "And maybe I have been pushing you a little too hard." He nuzzled the soft skin of her neck. "But I'm glad you had a change of heart. 'Cause I've had one, too. I don't know how people build successful marriages, Callie. But I know we all have to start somewhere and build from the ground on up. So I'm willing to try a little harder if you are, to see where this passion of ours is leading, to see if we can't make our relationship work after all."

Callie did want to make love with him again, so very much. She wanted a relationship and a satisfying marriage, too. But she was leery of hoping for too much for fear of being disappointed again. "What about the ranch?"

Cody shrugged. "I'd rather worry about the 'us.' I think it's what Max would want." He drew back slightly. "Ready to go home?"

Callie knew here was her chance to tell Cody everything, including the many reasons why she was all wrong for him. But when she opened her mouth, no words came out.

Instead, all she could think about was their dwindling time together. She knew it was precious, as were her growing feelings for Cody and his for her.

They could talk about Buck and Pa anytime.

But they'd only have one evening before their wedding.

Cody framed her face with his large, work-roughened palms. "We'll work it all out, Callie. The ranch, our love affair, this marriage Max got us in, everything. I promise. But not here and not now. We'll do it after we get home."

13:22

MAYBE CODY WAS RIGHT, Callie thought. Maybe she should slow down, stop trying to solve everything at once and work on things one at a time in order of their importance. And first and foremost, now and forever, was her rekindled love affair with Cody. With the wedding Max had scheduled only half a day away, the time to work on that was now. As long as she knew where she stood with him, that was.

"You still want to marry me, even after I ran away again?" Callie asked, as she jumped down from the cab of the pickup truck and into the warmth of Cody's waiting arms.

Cody gave her one of his hellion grins from years past. "And not just because it's the only way I'll inherit," Cody continued gently as he swept off his hat and fitted it over her brow to protect her from the driving rain. "Our little foray onto the range tonight, not to mention the stunt you just pulled, gave me plenty of time to think, Callie. As hard to believe as it is, I think I've come to terms with the fact that I am never going to get you out of my heart, Callie Sheridan," he drawled. "At least not any time in the next fifty or sixty years. That being the case, I think this marriage Max wants for us—this real marriage—is something we definitely ought to pursue. And all that aside, it's also something I want to do," Cody concluded, bending his head to give her a slow, thorough kiss.

Callie wreathed her arms around his neck and returned his searching kiss passionately. Cody might not want to admit it, she thought elatedly, but he was changing, coming back to civilization again. Max would be proud of that. And so was Callie. Realizing at the same time that they were getting drenched, they broke apart laughing. "There are better places for doing this," Cody teased.

Callie clasped her hand tightly in his. "I agree."

Their heads bowed against the blowing wind and rain, Cody tucked her hand in his, and they headed back toward the house, slipping and sliding on the muddy ground as they went.

Even though their progress was slow, the weather abysmal, Callie knew there was no better time to get a few other things straight, as well. "When we get married, Cody, you can run the entire ranch. Even my part of it." In fact, she was going to deed the land over to him so he would own it outright, but she was saving that fact as a surprise, sort of a wedding gift *extraordinaire.*

Cody lifted a brow as the lightning flashed to the south of them. He regarded her speculatively, even as he moved to shield her as best he could from the pelting rain. "What about your own dream of making an independent life for yourself here in Montana?" he asked as he tucked her in close to his side.

Callie knew now that the happiness she had felt here in her teens had all been due to Cody. That had been what she had come here hoping to replicate. "I can still pursue that, in other ways."

Cody slid a hand behind her back as they hurried up the front steps. "Not as easily without working control of your inheritance," he pointed out, pressing a light kiss to her lips.

Reveling in the way he was protecting her again, even at cost to himself, Callie kissed him back briefly. "Nothing worthwhile ever comes easily, Cody," Callie countered breathlessly as she swept off his hat and handed it back to him for drying. "Don't you know that?"

"I'm beginning to." He paused on the front porch as the rain beat the roof overhead in a steady, drumming rhythm.

Callie looked into his eyes and knew she was finally getting her life together, in all the most important ways, at long last. And it had nothing to do with what job she held or what state she lived in. It had to do with Cody and the life and family they would one day build for themselves.

"Is it my imagination or does this all feel a little familiar?" Callie quipped as he took her hand in his and they walked inside.

Cody shut the door and gathered her in his arms, drenched clothing and all. Nothing had ever felt so good to Callie as he did at that moment. "It isn't your imagination," he said softly, feathering kisses across her brow, down her cheek to her lips. He tangled his fingers in her hair and kissed her sweetly. "And it does feel a little familiar, and it should, because the Silver Spur is going to be your home starting tomorrow, thanks to Uncle Max." He paused, his lips curving up in anticipation. "Once we get the legal details settled, I have a feeling you'll be coming in and out of this ranch house a lot. Probably burning pots and rearranging furniture and redecorating as you go." He ducked her laughing swing. "Which is—" he kissed her again, more sensually this time "—exactly—the way—it should be."

He was awfully open to her renewed presence in his life all of a sudden. He also looked as if he wanted very much to take her to his bed and stay there a very long time.

Callie wanted to be with him, too. But aware Buck and Pa could be lurking anywhere in the vicinity, Callie glanced around nervously. "Cody, after all that's happened today, maybe we should—"

"Check out the house before we get too serious? I agree." He stepped back slightly but did not release her. "I also think we should do it together."

Callie looked down at herself. They were surrounded by mini puddles of rainwater. "We're dripping everywhere."

Cody gave a relaxed shrug. "It's all right. It'll dry."

Cody took the flashlight and led her through the house. It was completely untouched. Realizing that Pa and Buck had not been back in their absence, Callie breathed a big sigh of relief. For once, she did not have to worry.

"Okay, we're alone. We're safe. And the house is secured and locked up tight as a drum. Now, you want to tell me what is going on with you and making you so jumpy. And I mean the entire story, Callie," he warned softly, his protective instincts coming to the fore once again, "not just bits and pieces."

She had come back here to confront him, but suddenly it seemed like a very tall order. What if she told him and he decided to spend the night hunting down Buck and Pa? What if he found them, and the resulting melee—and Callie was sure there would be a melee when the three of them met face-to-face again—prevented Cody from making it to the wedding, and then inheriting?

She wanted to tell him, of course. She just wasn't sure this was the time. Perhaps after the wedding...after the honeymoon...would be better?

Needing time to think, Callie moved to the window, then drew the shades, shutting out the outside world and the storm that continued to rage overhead. The house had taken on a definite chill. Without warning, Callie found herself shivering uncontrollably. She crossed her arms tightly beneath her breasts. "It's complicated, Cody. I'm not sure I want to get into it all tonight."

He lifted a brow and continued to watch her steadily. "It's not as if we have anywhere else to go tonight, or anything else to do."

"True." Callie watched while Cody spread out some quilts on the leather sofa in the back parlor. While Callie stood behind him and stripped off her jeans, boots and shirt, he knelt to start a fire in the grate. Clad only in her undies, which were still a little damp, she toweled the layers of her hair and wrapped herself in one of the thick quilts he'd taken off the beds earlier.

The comforter engulfing her from foot to chin, she curled up in one corner of the sofa.

Noting she was still shivering, Cody stood. "I'll be right back." He took the flashlight to the kitchen and returned with a bottle of brandy and two glasses. He opened the bottle and poured a generous amount into a snifter. "This will help you warm up."

Callie shook her head, afraid the fatigue and the alcohol would work to loosen her tongue to disastrous result. "Thanks, but no," she said politely.

Cody pressed it into her hands anyway. His blue eyes were even with hers. "Afraid of letting your guard down, even a little bit?" he queried softly as he continued to watch her in that unsettling way of his.

In so many ways, Callie thought wistfully, wishing she could make him understand everything. "Yes, I guess I am." They had risked so much. To lose it all now would be unbearable.

Curving her fingers around the glass, he guided it to her lips and forced her to take a small sip anyway. He gave her an exasperated smile. "Then you know just how I feel whenever I'm around you."

The brandy forged a burning path to her stomach. Callie coughed and warmth flowed into her cheeks. Another drink and her teeth had almost stopped chattering.

Satisfied, he stepped back and began to unbutton his soaked shirt. "Nevertheless, we can't go on this way, Callie." His shirt hit the floor. Then his boots, socks and drenched jeans and briefs. Unselfconscious in his nakedness, he rubbed a towel briskly over his hair and down his body. Wrapping a blanket loosely around his shoulders, he grabbed his own snifter of brandy and sat down beside her. "We can't keep fighting each other and telling each other only half-truths. I can see you're scared." He inhaled the brandy's aroma, then took a long drink. "But I have to know what's going on. I have to know what made you run away from me tonight. And I have to believe it's more than the fact you and I had a fight tonight or that we made love this morning that has you jumping around like someone who's just seen a ghost of summers past. So what's happening? Is someone blackmailing you? Is that what's been going on?''

Callie put her glass aside and wrapped her own blanket around her all the tighter, obscuring her body from the neck down.

She wanted to tell him everything, but she was afraid if she did he would be out of there like a shot, hunting down Pa and Buck, storm or no storm. And there was no telling what he would do to them if he found out how much they had been pressuring her to join in their criminal activities.

She stared at the leaping flames of the fire with stony resolve. ''I know you're trying to help, and I appreciate it, Cody, really I do, but I don't want you involved.'' *I don't want you hurt again, especially on my account!*

Cody turned to face her. He trailed a hand gently down her face. ''Suppose I've decided I've spent too long on the sidelines already and want to be involved?'' he asked softly. ''What then?''

Callie thought of Pa holding the gun on her before supper. Though she tried to shut them out, his vicious words rang in her ears. *We wanted you to know we mean business.... Cody McKendrick owes us.... And your brother Buck and I are going to finish it.... You find a way to get us a big cash settlement as dowry, gal, or else....''*

Trembling at the memory, Callie vaulted to her feet and stalked closer to the fire. ''You were hurt by your association with me once.'' In fact, it was clear to see from his hermitlike existence that what had happened in Mexico had almost destroyed him. She twisted her fingers in the comforter and told him miserably, ''I couldn't bear it if it happened again.'' *I couldn't bear it if this time it were all my fault.*

''Which is why you were going to leave me tonight?'' Cody guessed.

She stared into the fire a long moment. Then, gathering all her courage, she pivoted to face him. "And why I am still going to leave tomorrow, immediately after the wedding, just for a few days," Callie confirmed calmly as she made up her mind, telling herself it was best that way for both of them.

She would lure Buck and Pa away on her own, away from Cody, call the sheriff and have them arrested, and then she would come back to Cody, free and clear, and tell him everything, thereby saving him all the grief. After all he had done to protect her in the past, she owed him that much and more.

"I just need time to get some personal matters straightened out." She bit her lip, knowing this time she wasn't running away from Cody but making it possible for her to go to him. Able to see he didn't view it that way, however, she persuaded softly, "It'll be better that way, you'll see."

Cody got up. He lowered the blanket to his waist and knotted it there, then stalked wordlessly to her side. His hands on her shoulders, he pulled her against him. She was nestled against his hard, solid body, her head on his bare chest, with only the comforters they had wrapped around their bodies between them. He pushed back the edge of the blanket and kissed the curve of her shoulder. "Without a wedding night?"

"We can have our wedding night now, if you want." Callie splayed her hands across his shoulders and leaned into him with sensual abandon.

"And you think that'll make up for it?" His eyes glittering with anticipation, Cody sank down into an armchair and pulled her between his thighs.

Comfortably ensconced on his lap, Callie eased her arms about his neck and looked up at him earnestly. Cody was a strong man. Strong enough for this. "I know what I am asking of you is unusual, but I'm asking you to trust me," she said softly. *I'm asking you to think the worst of me and love me anyway.* Because if he could do that, then she

would know he really loved her. And then she would be able
to tell him everything and know he would understand.

Cody's shoulders tensed. His expression altered swiftly.
"How can I do that, Callie? How can I trust you when
you're still shutting me out this way?"

Reminded of the way his own family had shut him out
from the trauma surrounding his parents' tragic accident,
the long wait, their death, Callie fell silent. She knew what
he was saying. She didn't think telling him about Pa and
Buck would make things any better for him. Not tonight,
not tomorrow. And certainly not if that knowledge kept
him from inheriting the Silver Spur cattle operation—or
worse, sent him back into the emotional wilderness from
which he had just begun to emerge.

Besides, she thought wearily, Sheriff Anderson already
knew. He had encouraged her to do the right thing. And
Callie was. If Buck and Pa returned, she was going to turn
them in to the authorities. Meantime, Cody needed to be
distracted. If that meant a silly argument with her, so be it.

"Fine. You want to be difficult, then be difficult," she
stormed. Aware he was angry, upset again, she pushed away
from his lap and started to step by him.

Cody sprang to his feet and caught her arm. As he tugged
her back around to face him, his blanket fell to the floor,
revealing six feet of naked, muscular male. "You think
walking out on me again, even for a few days, won't hurt
me?" Cody demanded gruffly. His eyes were as dark and
turbulent as the storm outside.

Callie tried not to notice how splendid his naked body
looked in the gleaming firelight, or how much she wanted
to touch every inch of him. "I—we—need some time to
sort through things on our own. Until that happens, you're
better off without me, Cody." It was her turn to protect
him, she thought anxiously, just as he had tried to protect
her by taking her away to Mexico. If only she could make
him see that.

"No." His gaze slid down her body, taking in the supple curves and still-damp skin. "I was never better off without you, Callie," he said hoarsely. He tunneled his hands through her hair, tilted her head back and kissed her with surprising tenderness. Lifting his lips from hers, he said in a low voice that seemed wrenched from his very soul, "I will never be better off. Don't you get it? I need you, Callie." His hands glided down her spine to her waist. "I've needed you in my life from the first moment we met and I'll need you with me the rest of my life."

Callie had longed to hear him say that. "Oh, Cody, I need you, too," she whispered joyfully. She let the blanket fall to the floor and stood on tiptoe to kiss him full on the lips. "So very, very much."

Cody smoothed the hair from her face. "Then let me look at you," he said in a choked, emotional voice.

Feeling gloriously beautiful and very much a desirable woman, Callie stepped back. Her heart pounding, she lifted her eyes to his.

WANTING TO REMEMBER everything about this moment, this night, Cody let his glance sift slowly over her. Callie was beautiful, dressed or undressed, but she had never looked more radiant than she did at that moment. Her hair tumbled in damp disarray to her shoulders. Her transparent ivory-lace bra and bikini were damp and clinging, outlining clearly the shadowy vee and the pale pink nipples. Her long, silky legs and slender thighs filled him with a longing that was almost painful in its intensity.

Wanting her to know how much he desired her, he cupped her bottom with both hands and pressed her against his erection. With a soft sigh, she rocked against him. Linking her arms about his neck, she stood on tiptoe and initiated a sweet, evocative kiss. Cody knew they were far from solving all their problems, but he did not care. He had to have her. He deepened the kiss, letting his tongue sweep into her mouth. Her lips softened on his, inviting him farther into her sweet, urgent heat.

Groaning at the waves of pleasure soaring through him, followed swiftly by an even more urgent need, Cody sank down onto the sofa. She followed, straddling his lap. Her hands braced on his shoulders, she sat back slightly as he unclasped her bra and freed her breasts. Her nipples were ripe, pink berries begging for his caress. She trembled as he bent and kissed them, one by one. She twined her hands around his shoulders as his mouth moved urgently, demandingly on her breasts.

Then they were kissing again. Moving to the floor. Stretching out alongside each other. Needing to know she was his and his alone, Cody ran a hand up and down the insides of her thighs. "Now," she whispered.

Cody smiled and directed his hand higher to the soft inner folds. "Not yet."

"Cody—" she whispered as his tongue found her depths. "That's it, say my name."

And she did, while she bucked and writhed and finally came apart in his arms. And she was still saying it as he swept up her body and took her again, completely this time. Surging deep, surging slow, he sheathed himself completely in her, filling her to the core, until the fever of their lovemaking simmered within her, and him, into a white-hot blaze of release.

For long moments neither of them was capable of doing anything. They couldn't move, could barely breathe. Finally, afraid he would crush her if he didn't change position, Cody shifted to his side. Callie went with him but stayed cuddled close. "If only it had been like this before," she sighed regretfully as he kissed the soft, vulnerable curve of her throat.

"I wanted it to be," Cody confessed as he kissed her fingertips and then the palms of her hands, her wrists. "I wanted you so much I thought I would die from the wanting. I *still* feel that way.'' *And always will.*

Abruptly, Callie looked as if an enormous burden had been lifted from her shoulders. Smiling, she reached for him again. Fitting her lips to his, she drawled provocatively, ''It'll pleasure you to know, Cody McKendrick, that I feel that way, too.''

Chapter Thirteen

04:13

Cody woke to find the sun streaming in through the windows. Being careful not to wake Callie, he glanced at his watch. Damn. It was nearly noon. He couldn't recall the last time he had slept so late. 'Course, he couldn't recall when he spent the whole night making love, the last session being just before dawn....

Not wanting to wake Callie just yet, he eased out from under her and slipped from his bed. As he grabbed for the clothes he'd been wearing in the rainstorm, which were still a little damp, his eyes fell on his empty wallet.

He frowned. He never had gotten a straight answer out of Callie about that. Whether he wanted to admit it or not, someone had been here last night. And that someone, who was likely a man, judging from his boot size, had left here with the contents of his wallet and Callie's protection.

Cody wanted to believe there was a good reason for Callie's silence. But she was going to have to start leveling with him—about everything—if they were ever going to have a future.

Deciding his jeans were still too damp to put on, Cody wrapped a sheet around his waist and headed downstairs to see about drying their clothes and putting some coffee on. To his surprise, there was still no electricity, either. He was standing there, contemplating what to do, when a knock sounded on the back door. Cody strode over to let in Cisco Kidd, who had a garment bag in each hand.

"The clothes are for the wedding," Cisco reported, handing them over. "Max felt you might be needing them."

"You can say that again."

Cody caught Cisco looking at his bed sheet. "Don't ask," Cody warned.

Cisco merely grinned and shrugged. "Never would have occurred to me," he drawled right back.

Cody peered outside. Under normal circumstances, he would have been out checking damage at first light. Today he was more concerned about what was going on with him and Callie.

To be able to go back and change history, to somehow be able to "do over" his entire relationship with Callie had been an unacknowledged dream of his for as long as he could recall. Max had given him the chance to have the life with Callie that he had wanted before things went wrong in Mexico.

Of course, Cody thought ruefully, had he only known Buck and Pa were following them, he would not have run away with Callie to Mexico at all. He would have found another solution. He would have gotten her to tell him the truth about her pa and Buck and what was going on there that was making her want to flee. He would have waited to marry her until she was older.

But since none of that had happened, all he could do was try his best to make things work out now, Cody thought.

Aware Cisco was watching him, Cody cleared his throat and asked, "How are things out on the ranch?"

Cisco helped himself to some water from the tap. "From the looks of what I've seen this morning, and it's not much since your place was my first stop, there was a lot of storm damage. Branches blown down, fences tangled up. I ran into Shorty on the way over and he said a couple trees got hit by lightning.''

''What did Shorty say about any major damage to the cattle operation?'' Cody asked anxiously, aware for the first time in seven years that he had completely turned his back on his business and concentrated on his personal life to the exclusion of all else. He wondered what Max would've thought of that.

''All the cattle barns and so on are still intact, but the cattle were mighty spooked. And you've got a couple calves tangled up in some barbed wire fence.''

Cody knew his hired hands would have their hands full getting everything straightened out and back to business. He also knew he had trained them well and that they could handle the situation without him for a couple of days, especially with Shorty running herd on everyone.

''What about the lumber mill and the horse business?'' Cody asked.

''Haven't heard yet. I expect they've got some damage, too, though.''

''You haven't talked to anyone personally?''

''Only on the shortwave radio or cellular phone, since all the regular phone lines are still down. Patience was a little harried. She said she'd have to call me back when things weren't in a state of emergency, whatever that meant. I had no chance to ask 'cause she hung up on me,'' Cisco continued, looking a little irritated. ''I couldn't get in touch with Trace at all and that worried me a little, though I imagine that's to be expected since he probably has his hands full with Susannah and all the kids. At any rate, I'm headed over there next.''

''When will the regular phone lines be fixed?'' Cody knew out in the country it could take a while.

''The phone company is hoping service will be restored by nightfall tonight—at the earliest.''

Cody frowned. This was not good.

Cisco Kidd continued, "They haven't found where the line was hit yet. Not to worry, though. I was able to use my cellular phone to call into my office in town and notify everyone that the wedding is still on. In fact, catering crews are cleaning up debris and setting up tents on the bull's-eye property as we speak." Cisco paused. "The ceremony starts at 4:00 p.m. sharp. Max had special tents erected, so you all can dress there and emerge in your wedding finery to surprise the guests."

"Callie and I will be there," Cody promised. "Meantime, if you need me, I'll be here." He was not letting Callie out of his sight.

Cisco grinned. "When Max cooked up this plan a few days before he went off on his journey to the great beyond, I told him he was nuts. Seems like he knew what he was doing after all."

"You knew in advance everything that's been going on the past few days?" Cody asked.

"Everything Max arranged to happen after the reading of the will," Cisco confirmed.

"Did you have anything to do with all our clothes being taken?"

"Max had me replace Callie's own clothes with a trousseau. Pearl helped with the size and style."

Cody shook his head. That wasn't what he was talking about. "No. I mean last night."

Cisco looked at Cody blankly.

"Did you send anyone over here last night?"

"No." Cisco began to look concerned. "Why?"

"What about Zeus? And the crops being burned? None of that was meant to be symbolic, was it?" Cody knew he was clinging to straws; he couldn't help it.

"Not by me, or Max, 'cause we had nothing to do with it." Cisco paused. "You got any idea who might be behind all of this?"

Cody shook his head and got a glass of water himself. If Max and Cisco had had no part in it, then who had?

3:02

"RISE AND SHINE, DARLIN'." Cody walked into the bedroom carrying a tray. He set it down on the nightstand beside his bed and perched on the edge of the mattress.

At the movement of the bed, Callie—who'd been sleeping on her stomach—lifted her head from the pillow. Her hair was tousled. Her eyes shone with a sleepy glow. Her lips curved into a sexy smile as recognition dawned. "Hi," she said softly, flipping gracefully over onto her back and reaching for him with both hands.

Cody clasped her to him, aware she was naked beneath the sheet draped artlessly across her middle.

"What time is it?" Callie pressed her lips against his shoulder.

Cody wrapped his arms around her and gathered her close. He wished they could stay this way forever and never let the outside world interfere again. "Almost one."

Callie cuddled against him. "In the afternoon?"

"Mmm-hmm."

Callie stretched against him sinuously. "I can't believe I slept so late."

"You were tired." Cody held her gently. "We both were."

Callie smiled. With her fingertip, she traced the curve of his mouth. "It has been a hellacious couple of days," she agreed on a sultry whisper.

"Which are about to come to an end," Cody agreed. He let go of her long enough to pour her a cup of coffee from the tin pot he'd put on the fire. "Breakfast was made in the fireplace this morning."

Callie propped herself up on some pillows, the sheet across her breasts dipping dangerously low before she managed to right it. She blinked in surprise and began to look a little worried. "Is the electricity still off?"

"Afraid so. Not to worry. We can still get showers before the wedding," Cody reassured her. He pointed above them. "I have a solar water heater on the roof."

Callie shuddered. "Thank heaven," she murmured in relief. "I never was one for cold showers."

Unable to help it, Cody grinned. "You've caused me to take more than one in my time," he teased.

Callie put her coffee cup aside. She pushed to a sitting position and propped herself up on several pillows. "No more."

"No," Cody agreed softly as he fitted the tray across her lap. "No more." Callie was in his bed, and in his life, to stay. At least if he had anything to say about it. . . .

Callie took the plate he offered her. "This looks great, Cody." She munched on a strip of crisp bacon and forked up the fluffy eggs. "I hate to say it, but you cook better on a campfire than I do on a stove."

Cody shrugged. "Practice makes perfect."

"Mmm. I can think of some things I'd like to work on," she teased with a lascivious wink.

"Insatiable, are you?" he teased back.

"For you," Callie admitted in a deep, sultry voice, "yes." They kissed sweetly, lingeringly. Before Cody knew it, they were making love again and it was one-thirty.

"We better get a move on if we want to get to the wedding on time," he said lazily.

Callie nodded, and Cody was pleased to see she was beginning to want to get married again as much as he did. "What are we going to wear?" she asked.

"Almost forgot." Cody got up from the bed and came back with the two garment bags of wedding clothes.

"Oh, Cody," Callie breathed when he showed her the dress Max had had made up specially for her. "White satin and alençon lace, a veil, leg-of-mutton sleeves and a full skirt! It is exactly what I've always wanted."

And exactly what she should have had the first time around, Cody thought. Bless Uncle Max for giving it to her now.

02:00

"DAMN, BUT YOU LOOK beautiful, Callie," Cody said as she came down the stairs after her shower, wearing jeans and one of his shirts. They had both showered, and the June sunshine had dried their clothes. Though Cody had wanted to go ahead and dress in their wedding finery, Callie was too superstitious to let him see her in her wedding dress before the ceremony, especially since a place to change had been arranged for them at the wedding site. She didn't want to take any chances that something would go wrong again.

As they stood in the front hall, Callie put her hands on his shoulders and stood on tiptoe to deliver a soft, fleeting kiss to his lips. "I feel beautiful when I am with you." She stepped back, sighing her contentment. "And for the record, you look very handsome, too." Her gaze swept their casually clad forms. "Even if we both look more like we're going to a hoedown than a wedding," she finished ruefully.

"Not for long." Cody hauled her close and delivered a slow, soul-searching kiss that had Callie tingling from head to toe.

"It's funny," Callie said, when he had lifted his head from hers. She gazed rapturously up into his eyes, marveling at the happiness they'd found. "So much time has gone by when we've been apart. But in the last two days, it's like nothing important has really changed after all." She paused shyly, smoothing her fingers across his chest as she admitted, "It's almost like we've gone back in time to the days before we eloped." To a time when she felt that anything was possible, if only they were together.

Cody slipped an arm about her waist and hauled her close. "I feel that way, too," he said gruffly.

"I loved you then, Cody, with all my heart," Callie told him seriously, knowing that part of him trusted her despite all the damning evidence to the contrary. "Just as I love you now."

Cody grew very still and searched her eyes.

Callie swallowed. She had no qualms about doing her best to shelter Cody from further hurt, no matter how difficult it made things in the meantime. "Which is why I have to do everything I can now to protect you—because I know now that is what true love is about," she explained tremulously.

Cody released his breath slowly. He eyed her with a trace of wariness. "It sounds like you're leading up to a swan song," he said cautiously. One he did not want to hear.

Callie shook her head, her eyes misting with tears that were part happiness—for the time she'd had with Cody—and part fear—for what lay ahead of her.

To be party to anything less than honest was eating at her inside, and she knew she was going to have to face up to her responsibility as a decent human being, kin or no kin, or lose all respect for herself and become just as much a victim as her mother had been. Callie didn't want to feel ashamed anymore. She didn't want to spend her life in deep denial, covering and making excuses for Pa and Buck, or worse, trying to keep them from succeeding in their criminal activities and out of jail. And she didn't want to kid herself about the way things really were, or be afraid to admit that she had made a mistake—as her mother had in marrying Pa—in enabling them to do the criminal things they did. Because she saw by her mother's example that refusing to face up to the cold, hard reality of a situation could only lead to heartache and disaster. Cody did not deserve any more heartache and disaster. He had already been through far too much.

"I just want you to know how much last night and this morning meant to me. I want you to know I will always, always remember it," Callie assured him sincerely as her eyes locked with his. "And that's going to be true no matter how crazy things get at the wedding, or after." She just prayed she could handle it, with the sheriff's help.

"You're not going anywhere, Callie," Cody said fiercely, drawing her back into his arms. "Two hours from now you're going to be my wife. We're going to have a lifetime to spend together."

"I was afraid of that." A low voice sounded behind them.

Callie and Cody turned to see Buck and Pa coming toward them. They'd obviously come in through the back, as Cody habitually left the kitchen door unlocked.

Callie took one look at their faces and knew they were out for blood this time.

"I was wondering when you two would show up again," Callie sighed as she reached inside her purse and surreptitiously punched the code into the beeper the sheriff had left with her. *Hurry,* she thought. *Please, hurry.*

Beside her, Cody had gone completely still. Beneath his shock, a quiet fury was beginning to build.

"Callie, we got to hand it to you," Pa crowed. "Your talent knows no bounds. You still know how to lead this young fella around by the nose." His eyes glittering greedily, Pa turned to Cody and offered up a smug smile. "Buck and I are gonna enjoy living next door to you."

Callie had the impression it took every ounce of willpower Cody had not to deck her father. "What are they talking about?" Cody hauled in a deep breath and turned to look at Callie.

Callie knew she was at a place where she could lose everything again. Panic swelled within her as she regarded Pa and Buck with undisguised contempt. "They're trying to get rich off you again," she said, making no bones about how she felt about that.

"And Callie here's been in on it all along," Pa said.

Buck nodded smoothly and added to the bald-faced lie. "Who do you think helped distract you while we stole Zeus and burned your crops? Why, your little wife-to-be even let us help ourselves to a little cash and credit cards from your wallet."

"Not that Callie here isn't experienced in cons," Pa continued, beaming with false pride. "Why, she's been helping me and her brother out for a long time."

Callie's face first turned white, then pink. She knew there was enough truth in everything they claimed to make their story sound plausible. She could only hope Cody knew her well enough to realize it wasn't true. "They're lying," she countered angrily, moving closer to Cody even as she wondered if Pa had brought that gun he'd been brandishing about. Putting her body slightly in front of Cody to block the path of a possible bullet, she said, "I never wanted any part of anything they've done."

"Oh, really? Then why didn't you tell Cody we were around again that first night when I met you out behind his cabin?" Buck asked complacently. He pulled a pack of cigarettes out of his pocket and lit one.

Cody moved so he could see Callie's face and shot her a quick glance. It was obvious to Callie that he was recalling the cigarette butt he had found outside the cabin that first night and the excuses she'd made.

Flushing with embarrassment, Callie splayed a hand across her chest. "I didn't know they would be here," she said desperately. "I haven't been in touch with them for years!"

For Cody, that was a moot point. "Why did you lie to me?" he demanded gruffly.

Callie held his eyes and worked to slow the pounding of her pulse. "Because I was afraid."

Pa and Buck erupted into ugly laughter. "Believe that and I've got a silver mine to sell you, too," Pa chided rudely.

"I'm going to have you arrested." Cody brushed by Callie and headed for the cellular phone he'd left in the kitchen.

As they all followed, Buck drew on his cigarette. "You can try," he told Cody as they gathered round again in the sunny ranch house kitchen. "There isn't enough proof to make any charges that you might level at us stick. All your going to the sheriff now will accomplish is that everyone will know what went down in Acapulco years ago."

Callie had only to look at his face to know that Cody still felt humiliated by that.

"They're going to know that Callie helped us dupe you," Buck continued, cruelly rubbing it in. "They're going to know how she played you—and Max—for a fool, then and now."

Pa grinned wickedly. "Bet you wish you didn't have to marry her, don't you, Cody?" he taunted with an evil leer. "Not that you really have any choice in the matter." Pa threw up his hands. Spying the bottle of brandy from the night before, he uncorked it. "You don't marry her, you don't inherit the ranch. Once you do, of course, you'll still have to be nice to us." Pa chugged the liquor deeply, straight from the bottle. "Otherwise, everyone in the county will have to know how we've duped you. And the McKendricks will be the laughingstock of all Montana."

"Or in other words," Cody surmised grimly, watching Pa wipe his mouth with the back of his hand, "whether I marry your daughter or not, I can look forward to a life of endless blackmail."

"That's about it," Pa affirmed as he took another long, careless drink, then passed the bottle to Buck. "But not to worry. Once you've seen the light and cooperated with us, Buck and I don't plan to be around much. With the cash that you and the Silver Spur cattle operation can supply us, we envision many years of living the high life, far away from Montana."

"In the meantime," Buck added, "we want the pleasure of seeing you privately and thoroughly humiliated, as you will be when we're standing beside you, watching you speak your vows with Callie here. Who knows? With half of Montana invited to the big do, Pa and I might even be moved to speak up when the minister asks if anyone knows any reason why the two of you should not be joined in holy matrimony."

Callie sucked in a horrified breath and glared at her kin. She knew they were just mean enough to do it. "You wouldn't—"

Buck shrugged carelessly. "Might be kind of fun," he allowed cruelly. "'Course, we might be persuaded not to cause a scene at the weddin' if your sweet hubby-to-be will just sign some property over to us now. For instance, he could start by giving us the papers to Zeus, free and clear. One hundred thousand from the sale of that bull ought to hold us for a few days, right, Pa?"

Callie felt sick as her pa nodded.

"Then of course we'd be back for more," Buck promised.

Callie had seen and heard enough, and so had Cody. She turned to Cody and gripped his arm. "I don't want you to lose anything on account of me, Cody," she told him fiercely. "Marry me so you can inherit the ranch, and I'll leave right after."

Pa studied Cody. Instinctively seeming to know that Cody was having doubts because of all she hadn't yet confided in Cody, Pa said, "Of course, if you don't marry Callie, all Callie has to do is say yes to marrying you in front of all those witnesses, and she gets it all."

"I don't want your land or your money, Cody. I never did. If you want me to prove it, I'll go to the wedding and refuse to marry you. Then I'll have no claim to anything here, and neither will Buck or Pa," Callie pleaded.

"And Cody will still lose his ranch, 'cause he can't inherit anything without you."

Callie's chin lifted defiantly as she rounded on her kin. Tears in her eyes, she stormed, "Cody can make his fortune in ranching all over again if he has to. He could even live happily enough without it. What he can't live with is the likes of you, and neither can I. I've had it with the both of you! I am not going to take any more! Do you hear me?"

"What a regular little actress you have turned into," Pa drawled with a great degree of surprise and pleasure.

Buck shook his head in agreement and placed a mocking hand over his heart. "If I didn't know you better, I'd be taken in myself."

Silence fell between them. Callie turned to look at Cody and knew she was once again on the verge of losing everything. Only this time she was not going to run. This time she was going to stand and fight and put everything on the line. "You either believe I love you or believe I don't," she said firmly, choking back a wealth of hot, bitter tears. "This isn't the way I would have chosen for either of us to find out. But one way or another, Cody, you have to decide now."

01:30

CODY WATCHED her lower lip tremble. He saw the hurt pride mingled with the fear in her eyes and knew it was the moment of truth. Callie wanted to know if he lumped her in with her no-account relatives. She wanted to know if he believed their ridiculous lies. The truth was he could have cared less what Callie's no-good family thought or did. So what if they wanted to humiliate him in front of half the state of Montana? Callie was what mattered now. Callie was all that mattered. He was not going to let Pa or Buck hurt her anymore.

His mind made up, Cody held out a hand to her. "Let's go," he said gruffly. "The wedding starts in less than an hour and the minister's waiting."

Buck and Pa exchanged a look then shook their heads in mutual derision.

"As touching as this scene is, I'm afraid we can't let it continue," Pa said in a wheedling tone, stepping to bar their way to the door.

"Yep. Looks like we're going to have to go with Plan Two," Buck said.

Callie and Cody drew apart slightly. Callie gasped as they noticed Buck was holding a small revolver.

"There is no way anyone but Callie is going to inherit the Silver Spur cattle operation," Pa continued, fury kindling in his eyes. "Even if it means we have to kill Cody and let Callie collect as his widow." He pulled out their missing marriage certificate.

"So you had it," Cody said grimly.

"Yep," Pa admitted. "Took it from y'all's hotel room in Acapulco same time we lifted Callie's goodbye letter. Of course it wasn't much good to us without Callie. But we figured it might come in handy again, in case she ever showed up. And sure enough, it has."

"I will not be a part of this con or any other," Callie vowed passionately.

Though she was still held loosely in Cody's arms, Pa grabbed her by the elbow. "You are going to be a part of this con, little lady, or Cody dies."

One hand clutching the belt at Cody's waist, Callie turned. Still holding tight to Cody, she squared off with her pa. "You've never been violent before," she countered coolly.

She had a point, Cody thought. Callie's brother Buck and her pa were unconscionable thieves, yes, and liars *extraordinaire*, but they were not cold-blooded murderers. If they had been murderers, they would have killed him in Acapulco rather than let him live and possibly talk....

"There's never been so much cash at stake before," Buck said. His eyes were full of greed. Watching him, Cody wondered if Callie's family was about to turn the corner from con artists to murderers.

"You value his life, you will come with me and come with me now, Callie," Pa ordered.

Callie sighed her regret. Like Cody, she seemed very much aware that both Buck and Pa were watching her carefully.

Callie turned back to Cody. "I guess this is it," Callie said sadly. The soulful look only he could see told him that she planned to do just the opposite.

Gearing up for battle, Cody nodded. "Just like when Zeus was in the cabin," he replied meaningfully, catching Callie's intent. "You start out thinking everything's going to be fine, and then you find out it's not."

"So you have to do what you have to do," Callie added without missing a beat. "What worked then *has* to work now."

Just that quickly, they broke apart. Cody went for Buck's gun, Callie elbowed her pa in the stomach, hard. There was a tussle, and then both Buck and Pa were down on the floor. Cody came up holding the gun.

"Get on the shortwave radio and call the sheriff," Cody said.

00:57

CALLIE WAS AS ANXIOUS to see if her call for help had been received, via beeper, as she was to get Pa and Buck out of their lives. Her whole body sagging with relief, she said, "Gladly."

"Wait a minute," Cody said, glancing out the window. "Talk about timing. There's Sheriff Anderson now."

"I'm glad you called me," Sheriff Anderson told Callie minutes later as Buck and Pa were handcuffed, read their rights and loaded into two squad cars by the two deputies assisting him in the arrest.

"You don't seem surprised I did," Callie murmured softly as she walked with him back to the front porch. She had expected to feel guilty for turning in her own kin. Instead, all she felt was relief. Cody was safe from harm, his legacy from Max still intact. Now all they had to work on was their future together. Compared to what they'd already been through, that wouldn't be hard at all.

Sheriff Anderson gave Callie a fatherly smile. He patted her on the shoulder. "I had an inkling you'd do the right thing when it came right down to it."

"Wait a minute," Cody said to Sheriff Anderson as he came up to join them. He looked from one to the other, stunned, then narrowed his eyes at Callie. "Are you saying that you and Callie talked about this situation before this afternoon?"

Too late, Callie realized she should have confided in Cody about that visit sooner. But she hadn't, because she hadn't wanted to spoil the mood.

In answer to Cody's question, the sheriff nodded. "I stopped by last night shortly after the lights went out. Callie told me she suspected her pa and Buck were up to no good again. Since the phone lines were down, I gave her a beeper and preset it with the code to notify me if they came back to bother her."

"I see."

"Callie must've hit the alarm button on it the moment they showed up," Sheriff Anderson continued.

"I did," Callie admitted.

"Well, I've got a lot to do if I want to make it to that wedding on time. I'll see the two of you later?"

Cody extended his hand to the sheriff. He shook hands stiffly. "Yes," he said, sounding unusually vague. "We'll talk later."

The sheriff got back in his squad car and drove off.

Callie turned to Cody. The brooding look was back in his ocean blue eyes. She reached out to take his hands. His fingers did not close over hers as she hoped they would. A chill of foreboding slid down her spine. "What's wrong?" she asked.

Withdrawing even further into himself, Cody shouldered by her and headed back into the house. "Like you even have to ask?"

Callie dashed after him. She grabbed his arm to stop his flight. "I thought you'd be happy that the truth was out in the open."

His disappointment in her evident, Cody stared down at her grimly. "I'd have been a lot happier if I'd known what was going on a lot earlier. Say, while it was all happening," he finished.

The lack of understanding in his eyes was as chilling as the thought of a life without him. Callie drew in a deep breath. "I didn't want to upset you," she explained.

Cody's biceps flexed beneath her fingers. A mixture of hurt and disappointment glimmered in his eyes. "Sure that's all it was?" he taunted.

In a panic, she edged closer. The rigidity of his arm, the fact he clearly did not want her touching him made her drop her grip and step back a pace. "What else could it have been?"

Cody regarded her furiously. "Suppose you tell me." Silence fell between them.

Cody's lips curved up in a cynical smile. "You know," he drawled pointedly, "I thought my days of being left on the sidelines were over. Guess not," he finished, his voice heavy with irony. Brushing past her, he slammed into the house, tore through the hall and back to the kitchen.

In a panic, Callie hurried to catch up with him. "This isn't the same as what happened when you were younger, with Patience and Trace," she said breathlessly, watching as Cody snatched up the keys to his pickup truck and shoved them in the pocket of his jeans.

"You're right," he retorted, whirling around to confront her. "It's worse. *A hell of a lot worse.* You had every opportunity to confide in me last night, but you still shut me out. The first time we were together, I made allowances because you were so young. But for you not to confide in me now, after all we've shared—" His voice broke. He was so angry he couldn't go on.

"I'm sorry, Cody."

"We both are. It doesn't change a damn thing."

Silence fell between them, more painful than before.

Cody caged her against the counter. "You want to know what really gets me?" His voice dropped another devastating notch. "The fact you could tell Sheriff Anderson what was going on, but you couldn't tell me. Was anything ever going to change between us? Or is this the way it will always be? You with your secrets. Me with barely a clue as to what's going on."

Too late, Callie saw she had made a tremendous mistake in not confiding in him sooner. "I was trying to protect you."

Cody shook his head and pushed away from her. His lips thinned in disgust. "That, I have heard before."

Callie watched as Cody stalked into the mudroom and snatched up a pair of heavy work gloves. "Where are you going?"

His expression was fierce as he whirled on her. "Where does it look like? Out to work on the ranch."

Callie couldn't believe he was resorting to that again. She'd thought his loner days were over. "Cody. For heaven's sake. The wedding is supposed to start in less than an hour! Can't we talk this out?"

He snorted in derision. "You don't really think I'd marry you now?" he queried in raging disbelief.

Callie struggled to keep a handle on her own skyrocketing emotions. "I had hoped," she said with as much tranquility as she could manage.

"So had I," Cody retorted bitterly. He grabbed her arms and brought her up short against him. "I had hoped things were different. I had hoped by now that you loved me enough to bare your soul to me, the way I bared mine to you."

"I did!" Callie shouted back. She had told him practically everything.

"No, Callie, you didn't," Cody disagreed with a deliberate iciness that cut straight to her soul. Releasing his grip on her abruptly, he towered over her. "Because if you had, you would have told me everything. If not before we made love last night, then certainly after. Or even this morning."

Callie gulped, aware he had a point there. "I wanted to," she said tearfully after a moment.

"But—" Cody prodded mercilessly.

What could she say to that? Callie wondered miserably. That she hadn't expected him to believe her when she told him she was not part of Pa and Buck's heinous scheme? That she hadn't wanted to risk losing him all over again? Callie swallowed. "I wanted to wait until the time was right."

Cody's jaw tightened. His eyes never left her face. "The road to hell is paved with good intentions," he said in a low, deadly voice. "Face it, Callie. As painful as it is, I have. The time never would have been right for you to confide in me about this or anything else. And if we had been fool enough to marry, as Uncle Max wanted us to, I would have been signing on for a lifetime of half-truths and hurt. And that I just can't do. Not for you," he told her grimly. "Not for anyone."

Chapter Fourteen

00:45

Shorty hopped down from his truck and ambled over to Cody. Pushing his hat back on his head, he shook his head at the mess and lamented, "If today isn't a day for disaster, I don't know what is. One crisis after another. Trouble everywhere you look."

Cody paused in the act of shoveling the mud from beneath the rear wheels of his pickup. He was not enjoying digging his truck out of the muck Callie had left it in, and he didn't like the ominous way Shorty had spoken.

Swearing silently at the prospect of more trouble, he stuck his shovel in the mud and pushed himself upright. "Is everyone all right?" Cody asked gruffly. He'd been so caught up in his own problems he hadn't thought to ask, and they had suffered one hell of a storm the night before.

Shorty rested his gloved hands on his waist. "I expect they will be by the time we get everything straightened out," he said sagely. "But don't you worry none about Patience or Trace or their loved ones, Cody. You worry about you and that young beauty you're letting slip away."

Cody felt a lecture coming on that he did not want to receive. "Better be careful, Shorty," he warned grimly as he went back to digging out his truck. "When your hand is in a bobcat's mouth, you don't go pulling on his tail."

"Nor do you keep silent when it's obvious things are going to hell in a handbasket for someone you damn near raised," Shorty shot right back as he grabbed another shovel out of his own truck and lent a hand. "And Max and I both put in a lot of time on you, Cody. What the heck are you doing out here anyway?"

"What does it look like I'm doing?" Cody dug into the mud more viciously. "I'm trying to get my pickup truck out of the mud Callie stuck it in last night."

"In case you've forgotten, buckaroo, this is your wedding day. The blasted ceremony's in less than half an hour," Shorty stressed, pointing to his watch.

Cody scowled at the clear blue sky overhead. It looked like he was never going to have the kind of marriage his parents had after all. "Well, the hoopla's happening without me."

"You get struck by lightning last night? 'Cause somethin' sure happened to set you off. You look mad as a hungry bear."

Cody could see he was never going to get any peace unless he came out with it. Even though it went against his grain to reveal anything of what he was thinking or feeling when he didn't have a mind to do so, he told his ranch foreman curtly, "It's over, Shorty. With me and Callie. It's time to put out the fire and call in the dogs." Time to admit their love just wasn't strong or pure enough.

Finished with one rear wheel, Shorty went over and started working on the other. "I see. Does she know that?"

"I would certainly hope so." Cody gritted his teeth as he joined in the shoveling and thought about the easy way Callie had betrayed him again. "I made it plain enough."

Shorty sent a shovelful of muck flying. It barely missed Cody. "If a duck had your brain, it would fly north for the winter."

Cody sent another shovelful of muck back at Shorty. It missed him, too, but just barely. "Anyone ever tell you that your advice is about as welcome as a skunk at a lawn party? 'Cause they should.''

Shorty helped clear the second wheel. Finished, he grabbed the two empty grain bags Cody had brought along and put them under the wheels for traction. "I'm tellin' you, trying to talk to you this afternoon is like being in a battle of wits with an unarmed man.''

Cody picked up the shovels and emphatically tossed them both into the bed of his truck. He'd meant what he said about feeling as dangerous as a bobcat this morning. He couldn't recall ever being in a fouler mood. He felt as if it were Christmas morning. He'd got up and discovered absolutely nothing under the tree. "You got something to say to me, Shorty? Just spit it out. And be quick about it.''

"All right,'' Shorty generously agreed, making no effort to spare the sarcasm as he inched off one mud-covered glove. "Since you went to all that trouble to invite me so nicely, I will. What in tarnation are you doing out here when you've got a wedding to go to?''

"I told you,'' Cody repeated, unable to recall when he'd felt so disillusioned. "It's over between Callie and me. So I am not—I repeat—I am not marrying her.'' *Not even if hell freezes over.*

Shorty bristled at him, then paused and shoved the brim of his hat off his brow. "Even if it means you lose the ranch?''

Cody shrugged, very much aware that while it was Max who had showed him how to build an empire, it had been Shorty who had taught him all there was to know about the day-in, day-out routine of punching cattle. It had taken fourteen long years to make the Silver Spur what it was today. "I built this one up. I can always build up another one,'' he announced confidently.

Shorty humphed, but did not dispute Cody's claim. "I thought the Silver Spur meant more to you than that.''

It did. But Callie, damn her conniving soul, meant even more. "Uncle Max never should have tied my owning it to marrying Callie," Cody countered.

Shorty gave him a pitying look. "In my opinion, that is the first sensible thing your Uncle Max ever did as far as you were concerned. I loved him, too, God rest his soul, but Max overindulged you to a fault. He never should have let you shut out the whole goldurned world. Or hide out there in the outpost for days at a time. But he did, and now the rest of us poor souls are having to deal with the fallout."

"Which is what?" Cody spit out, more wrought up than he could ever recall being.

Shorty threw up a hand. "Your determination to end up alone and penniless while that bride of yours is set to inherit everything."

Cody blinked, sure he'd heard wrong. "What are you talking about?"

"Callie's going to the wedding anyway," Shorty related. "I saw her a few minutes ago, driving off with Pearl. She had her hair all in curlers and a wedding dress slung over her shoulder, but knowing that gal the way I do, I have every confidence she'll look as purty as a picture by the time that ceremony gets started over at the bull's-eye."

"Hold it. Callie's showing up at the wedding anyway?"

Cody tried but could not contain his shock. He couldn't believe she would go there without him, especially knowing that he would rather be dragged buck naked through the streets rather than show up to participate in that dog-and-pony show!

Shorty got in the truck, drove it out of the mud, then shut off the engine and got back out again. "Yeah. What were the terms of the will again? She shows up, willing to marry you...and you're not there...and she gets everything. Yep. Sounds like that is one smart cookie you're turning down, Cody. Gotta hand it to her. She fixed it just fine. The way things are going, she is set to inherit everything."

"Not everything," Cody interrupted irritably. "I still get the bull's-eye property . . . as long as she shows up."

"I'm sure that'll really satisfy you," Shorty drawled sarcastically. "Especially since the two of you will be living right next door to each other. You on your little tiny spread with enough room for maybe ten to twenty head of cattle if you're real careful and manage your property carefully, and Callie with her gazillions of acres and hundred thousand head of cattle. Yeah, you ought to be right happy, the way it sounds to me."

"I can't believe she would actually do that." Cody threw down his heavy work gloves and kicked the bed of the truck. Then kicked it again for good measure. "She said she wasn't interested in any of the money! Or the land! She said all she wanted was to make me happy!"

Shorty shrugged and headed back to his own battered pickup. He called over his shoulder, "Guess you were wrong about that, too."

00:23

"HE'S NOT COMING. I just know it," Callie told Pearl miserably as she carried the garment bag holding her wedding dress into the changing tent. Outside, the guests were beginning to arrive. Five hundred chairs had been lined up in neat rows, three separate altars arranged. And they only had twenty minutes to go.

"Now you just hold your horses, gal. And don't give up on that man of yours yet."

"I only wish he were my man," Callie murmured as she set down her makeup case with a disgruntled thud. "But Cody is so damnably self-reliant, I don't think he will ever be anyone's man." *She had to accept it; he would always have that wall around his heart.*

Oblivious to Callie's depression, Pearl poked her head outside the changing tent. "Unless I am mistaken, that is his truck coming toward us now."

Callie's hopes rose, then fell, then rose again. "I don't think I want to talk to him before the ceremony," she said querulously.

"I don't think you have any choice. But I'll try to head him off."

Pearl stepped outside the tent, closing the flaps behind her.

"Cody, stop right there! The groom cannot see the bride before her wedding," Callie heard Pearl say.

"Who says I'm the groom?" Cody growled.

Before Callie could do more than draw a breath, Cody charged inside.

They faced each other breathlessly. To her dismay, the tux he should have been wearing was nowhere in sight. Worse, Callie noted, Cody's jeans, shirt and boots were covered with mud. "I don't know what you've been doing," she remarked, "but you look like you lost."

"Cute."

"Pearl's right," Callie said stiffly. "You shouldn't be in here."

"Tough," Cody countered in a low, tense voice. "We have to talk."

Callie did not want to be hurt any more and he had already hurt her plenty. Her head held high, she sashayed away. "I think we already did that."

"Callie—" He reached for her arm.

With some deft footwork, she evaded his grip. "Look, Cody, if you're here to talk me out of agreeing to marry you today, forget it. Unlike you, I am perfectly willing to go through with the ceremony. And then, as per your explicit wishes, I am walking away." *My heart intact.*

He regarded her with a stone-faced expression that indicated to her that he hadn't changed his mind about her one whit. "So you're selling the Silver Spur cattle operation?"

"No," Callie replied archly, "I'm giving it away." She held up a hand before he could interrupt. "And don't try and talk me out of it, because Cisco has already drawn up the papers and they are all signed." This was the first thing Callie had done upon arriving at the wedding site.

"I see," Cody said heavily, as if he had suspected she would betray him all along. "To whom are you turning this ranch over, may I ask?" he said tersely, as if braced for the worst.

Callie tilted her chin at him defiantly as she finished taking the curlers out of her hair. "Why do you care?" she challenged.

"I care."

"About the land," Callie asserted, swallowing hard to hide her hurt as she brushed her hair into soft, flowing waves. "Not about me."

"I never said that," Cody countered. He left the tent briefly and returned with the garment bag containing his tux.

"You didn't have to say it," Callie told him wearily as she sat down before the mirror Pearl had brought in for her and began to apply her makeup. "I saw it in your eyes."

Cody routinely shucked off his muddy boots, shirt and jeans. He scrubbed his face and hands with the wet washcloth he had brought in. If Callie had thought he was there to marry her because he loved her, she would have been overjoyed. As it was, she knew he was just doing it to collect on his inheritance.

"I cared about you more than you'll ever know," Cody asserted, hastily pulling on his black tuxedo pants and starched white shirt.

Ha! Callie thought as she shrugged out of her own shirt and jeans and into her petticoat, camisole and dress. "Then why are you running away from what you and I could have, Cody?" She lifted her skirt and pulled on first one thigh-high stocking, then the other. "And don't deny it," she said, drawing the flower garter over her slender ankle to just above her knee before slipping on her white satin pumps. "You are running. Take it from an expert. I know."

Cody stood with his shirt unbuttoned, his tie dangling on either side of his collar. "Because you've spent your life running," he guessed.

"Yes," Callie said softly as she fitted her veil and head-piece over her hair. Unable to do up her buttons on her own, she gave up and turned her back to Cody.

He did them up deftly, the warmth of his fingers ghosting over her skin.

"First, from the sordid truth about my pa and brother Buck. Then from the possibility of anyone—especially you—finding out I was from a family of criminals. Then from our brief, failed attempt at marriage. And a series of jobs. And even the second chance at a marriage with you and the opportunity to build myself something strong and solid and enduring here in Montana."

When he had finished helping her with her dress, Cody put both hands on her shoulders and turned her to face him. "You say that as if the two things are one and the same."

"They aren't," Callie countered, meaning it. "Because in the final analysis the land Max left me, by itself, doesn't matter a plugged nickel to me." The only thing she had ever really wanted was to marry Cody.

Cody shook his head. "And yet you're willing to be here and stand up in front of everyone who's anyone in this entire state and say 'I do' while I say 'I don't.'"

Callie buttoned up the front of his shirt and began working on correctly knotting his bow tie. "Yes. I am willing to do that. And you want to know why I am willing to do that?" Callie poked a finger at his chest. "I am willing to do that because I love you more than life itself and I don't give a hoot and a holler who knows it. Do you hear me, Cody?" she said as her pent-up feelings came tumbling out, surprising them both with their ferocity. "I love you," she said thickly, as happy, frustrated tears misted her eyes. "I always have and I always will and—"

A stunned look on his face, Cody pressed a finger to her lips. "What did you say?" he interrupted, coming a little closer.

Callie's heart took a little leap, then settled into a strong, steady rhythm. "I love you," she repeated in soft defiance.

Silence of a different sort fell between them. Cody rubbed his jaw thoughtfully.

And Callie thought, but couldn't be entirely sure, that she saw the beginning of the sparkle come back into Cody's eyes.

Cody continued, more seriously. "Although, Callie, if you'd just told me sooner about your pa and Buck bothering you, we wouldn't *be* in this mess."

"I was afraid what you'd do to them if you found out."

Cody hooked a foot under the chair that had been set up at her vanity table and dragged her onto his lap. "You may have a point there. I wanted to kill 'em both seven years ago, and that is nothing to the emotion I feel toward them now."

Callie rested her head on his shoulder. "And I was also afraid you wouldn't believe me when I said that I hadn't known they followed me here, and that I had not ever wanted anything to do with any of their schemes to get rich off you or anyone else, for that matter."

"Forty-eight hours ago, I probably wouldn't have believed that," Cody admitted, stroking her back.

"But you do now?" Callie persisted, looking deep into his eyes. She was aware she was wearing her heart on her sleeve again; she couldn't help it.

Cody nodded.

Callie swallowed, almost afraid to hope. Yet she wanted a lifetime of love and laughter with Cody so much. "What changed your mind?" she asked softly.

"A lot of things. Max's admonition not to mess things up again. I wanted our eight seconds. A blistering lecture from Shorty, who by the way was right on every count. The knowledge in my heart of what I should and should not do. And last but not least, the fact that you didn't pack up and leave, but instead charged on out here and changed into your wedding dress. I know how you hate people thinking poorly of you or making fun of you, and you set yourself up for some powerful ridicule just showing up here today, especially since you're not even planning on keeping the ranch."

"If we didn't marry for real, it didn't seem right for me to do so," Callie said demurely. "No matter what Uncle Max's will said."

Cody paused. "Did you mean it when you said you loved me with all your heart and soul?" he asked hoarsely.

Callie nodded. She laced both arms about his shoulders as she promised softly, "Now and forever."

00:09

THEN THERE'S SOMETHING I have to tell you," Cody said.

Callie tilted her face up to his and looked earnestly into his eyes.

"I love you, too." His breath was expelled in a long, hot rush and his voice dropped another husky notch as he pulled her closer still. "Always have and always will."

"Oh, Cody," Callie whispered as her heart filled with boundless joy. Though she'd known it in her heart since he'd made love to her last night, she had about given up on ever hearing him speak the words. Now that he had, tears of happiness streamed down her face.

"Now, Callie..." Cody slanted her a teasing grin and made a great show of mopping up her tears with the pads of his thumbs. "Don't cry. You're not supposed to cry on your wedding day."

"I can't help it," Callie said thickly. In coming back to Montana, she had hoped only for a better life and instead had found paradise. "I am so happy."

"So am I." Cody hugged her to him fiercely. They kissed again, this time with tenderness. When they finally drew apart again, both of them filled with the most delicious sense of well-being, Cody said huskily, "Max was right. You are the woman for me, the only woman for me."

Callie smiled as she smoothed her thumb across the ruggedly shaped lines of his clean-shaven jaw. "And you're the man for me."

His eyes darkened. His hold became less sensual, more protective, and he released a long, slow breath. "Even so, there are some things we should discuss," he said seriously.

Callie had an idea where all this was headed. "Like our future," she said.

"Right." Cody paused, then grasped both her hands in one of his and continued gruffly, "About the ranch. I admit I haven't thought about it long, but I think you were right in wanting to give it away, because all this inheritance stuff has done is complicate the relationship between us. So as far as I'm concerned, you can give it to whoever you want. Because when it comes right down to it, there's only one thing I want from you."

He looked so serious. Callie drew a quick breath. "And that is . . . ?" She wanted so much not to disappoint him again.

Cody pressed his lips together firmly as he decreed, "For starters, no more of this marrying each other only to rescue each other from some terrible fate, like you running from your family, or me trying to get back the cattle operation I worked so hard at building up. If we marry, I want it to be because we love each other and always will. And I want it to be a real marriage in every respect. I want us to be as committed to each other, and to our relationship, as my parents were."

These were terms she could meet. Happy tears flooded her eyes and streamed down her face. "I think I can do that," Callie said thickly. "In fact, I know I can."

"Good," he confirmed huskily, holding her close. Gently, he stroked a hand through her hair. "'Cause I'm counting on us building something real and lasting this time."

"Although I think there is something you should know, too, Cody," Callie said passionately, looking deep into his eyes. "You are the one I planned to give the ranch to if you didn't show up here to marry me and I had inherited. I never would have let you walk away empty-handed. And I don't want you to walk away empty-handed now. I know how much you love this place. I know how much of your heart and soul you've put into it. I would never ask you to give it up."

"So we can stay?"

Callie smiled and wreathed her arms around his neck as she admitted softly, "I wouldn't want us to raise our family anywhere else."

As they smiled at each other, there was more noise outside the tent, then Pearl coughing loudly in a way meant to garner their attention. "Hurry up, you two," she called impatiently as the music began. "The ceremony's going to be starting any minute."

Cody poked his head out the tent. "Hold your horses, Pearl. We're coming."

00:00:17

"DO YOU SEE TRACE and Patience?" Callie asked as she searched around for her bouquet.

"No, not yet." Cody frowned. "And I don't see their respective mates, either."

"Do you think they're coming, that they'll get here in time, too?" Callie asked worriedly.

Cody looked at her and grinned, his optimism for the future as contagious as his smile. "I hope so," he murmured softly, taking her into his arms yet again. "I'd hate for us to be the only ones who are this happy. Wouldn't you?"

Callie nodded. "It's just too bad Uncle Max couldn't be here for this."

Cody smiled and shot a glance heavenward. "I have the feeling he knows."

Weddings by De Wilde

Since the turn of the century the elegant and fashionable DeWilde stores have helped brides around the world turn the fantasy of their "Special Day" into reality. But now the store and three generations of family are torn apart by the divorce of Grace and Jeffrey DeWilde. As family members face new challenges and loves—and a long-secret mystery—the lives of Grace and Jeffrey intermingle with store employees, friends and relatives in this fast-paced, glamorous, internationally set series. For weddings and romance, glamour and fun-filled entertainment, enter the world of DeWilde...

Twelve remarkable books, coming to you once a month, beginning in April 1996

Weddings by DeWilde begins with
Shattered Vows
by Jasmine Cresswell

Here's a preview!

"SPEND THE NIGHT with me, Lianne."

No softening lies, no beguiling promises, just the curt offer of a night of sex. She closed her eyes, shutting out temptation. She had never expected to feel this sort of relentless drive for sexual fulfillment, so she had no mechanisms in place for coping with it. "No." The one-word denial was all she could manage to articulate.

His grip on her arms tightened as if he might refuse to accept her answer. Shockingly, she wished for a split second that he would ignore her rejection and simply bundle her into the car and drive her straight to his flat, refusing to take no for an answer. All the pleasures of mindless sex, with none of the responsibility. For a couple of seconds he neither moved nor spoke. Then he released her, turning abruptly to open the door on the passenger side of his Jaguar. "I'll drive you home," he said, his voice hard and flat. "Get in."

The traffic was heavy, and the rain started again as an annoying drizzle that distorted depth perception made driving difficult, but Lianne didn't fool herself that the silence inside the car was caused by the driving conditions. The air around them crackled and sparked with their thwarted desire. Her body was still on fire. Why didn't Gabe say something? she thought, feeling aggrieved.

Perhaps because he was finding it as difficult as she was to think of something appropriate to say. He was thirty years old, long past the stage of needing to bed a woman just so he could record another sexual conquest in his little black book. He'd spent five months dating Julia, which suggested he was a man who valued friendship as an element in his relationships with women. Since he didn't seem to like her very much, he was probably as embarrassed as she was by the stupid, inexplicable intensity of their physical response to each other.

"Maybe we should just set aside a weekend to have wild, uninterrupted sex," she said, thinking aloud. "Maybe that way we'd get whatever it is we feel for each other out of our systems and be able to move on with the rest of our lives."

His mouth quirked into a rueful smile. "Isn't that supposed to be my line?"

"Why? Because you're the man? Are you sexist enough to believe that women don't have sexual urges? I'm just as aware of what's going on between us as you are, Gabe. Am I supposed to pretend I haven't noticed that we practically ignite whenever we touch? And that we have nothing much in common except mutual lust—and a good friend we betrayed?"

BRIDE'S
BAY RESORT

UNLOCK THE DOOR TO GREAT ROMANCE
AT BRIDE'S BAY RESORT

Join Harlequin's new across-the-lines series, set in an exclusive hotel on an island off the coast of South Carolina.

Seven of your favorite authors will bring you exciting stories about fascinating heroes and heroines discovering love at Bride's Bay Resort.

Look for these fabulous stories coming to a store near you beginning in January 1996.

Harlequin American Romance #613 in January
Matchmaking Baby by Cathy Gillen Thacker

Harlequin Presents #1794 in February
Indiscretions by Robyn Donald

Harlequin Intrigue #362 in March
Love and Lies by Dawn Stewardson

Harlequin Romance #3404 in April
Make Believe Engagement by Day Leclaire

Harlequin Temptation #588 in May
Stranger in the Night by Roseanne Williams

Harlequin Superromance #695 in June
Married to a Stranger by Connie Bennett

Harlequin Historicals #324 in July
Dulcie's Gift by Ruth Langan

Visit Bride's Bay Resort each month wherever Harlequin books are sold.

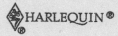

HARLEQUIN ®

BBAYG

Fall in love all over again with

In this collection of original short stories, three brides get a unique chance for a return engagement!

- Being kidnapped from your bridal shower by a one-time love can really put a crimp in your wedding plans! *The Borrowed Bride*— by **Susan Wiggs**, *Romantic Times* Career Achievement Award-winning author.

- After fifteen years a couple reunites for the sake of their child—this time will it end in marriage? *The Forgotten Bride*—by **Janice Kaiser**.

- It's tough to make a good divorce stick—especially when you're thrown together with your ex in a magazine wedding shoot! *The Bygone Bride*— by **Muriel Jensen**.

Don't miss THIS TIME...MARRIAGE, available in April wherever Harlequin books are sold.

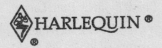

The Magic Wedding Dress

Imagine a wedding dress that costs a million dollars.
Imagine a wedding dress that allows the wearer to
find her one true love—not always the man she
thinks it is. And then imagine a wedding dress that
brings out all the best attributes in its bride, so that
every man who glimpses her is sure to fall in love.
Karen Toller Whittenburg imagined just such a dress
and allowed it to take on a life of its own in her new
American Romance trilogy, *The Magic Wedding Dress*.
Be sure to catch all three:

March
#621—THE MILLION-DOLLAR BRIDE

May
#630—THE FIFTY-CENT GROOM

August
#643—THE TWO-PENNY WEDDING

Come along and dream with Karen Toller
Whittenburg!

WDRESS1

If you are looking for more titles by

CATHY GILLEN THACKER

Don't miss these fabulous stories by one of
Harlequin's most renowned authors:

Harlequin American Romance®

#16494	FIANCÉ FOR SALE	$3.50	☐
#16506	KIDNAPPING NICK	$3.50	☐
#16521	BABY ON THE DOORSTEP	$3.50	☐
#16526	DADDY TO THE RESCUE	$3.50	☐
#16568	MISS CHARLOTTE SURRENDERS	$3.50 U.S.	☐
		$3.99 CAN.	☐
#16607	DADDY CHRISTMAS	$3.50 U.S.	☐
		$3.99 CAN.	☐

(limited quantities available on certain titles)

TOTAL AMOUNT	$
POSTAGE & HANDLING	$
($1.00 for one book, 50¢ for each additional)	
APPLICABLE TAXES*	$_____
TOTAL PAYABLE	$_____
(check or money order—please do not send cash)	

To order, complete this form and send it, along with a check or money order
for the total above, payable to Harlequin Books, to: **In the U.S.:** 3010 Walden
Avenue, P.O. Box 9047, Buffalo, NY 14269-9047; **In Canada:** P.O. Box 613,
Fort Erie, Ontario, L2A 5X3.

Name: _____

Address: _____ City: _____

State/Prov.: _____ Zip/Postal Code: _____

*New York residents remit applicable sales taxes.
 Canadian residents remit applicable GST and provincial taxes.   HCGTBACK6

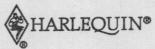

HARLEQUIN

AMERICAN ◆ ROMANCE®

®

*With only forty-eight hours to lasso their mates—
it's a stampede...to the altar!*

WILD WEST
Weddings

by Cathy Gillen Thacker

Looking down from above, Montana maven
Max McKendrick wants to make sure his heirs get
something money can't buy—true love! And if his two
nephews and niece want to inherit their piece of his
sprawling Silver Spur ranch then they'll have to wed the
spouse of *his* choice—within forty-eight hours!

Don't miss any of the Wild West Weddings titles!

Once in a while, there's a story so special, a story so unusual,
that your pulse races, your blood rushes. We call this

LOVER'S LEAP is one such story.

As if pushed, a near-naked man jumped into Maggie Macintyre's canoe, toppling
them into the churning river. But her anger at the wild man with the long raven
hair and the hard bronze body disappeared when she saw the intensity of a lover's
longing in the depths of his black eyes...as if he'd loved her for a century or
more. But who was this stranger who'd told her she was the woman of his dreams?

#632 LOVER'S LEAP
by
Pamela Browning
May 1996